A NOVEL

by

ALLAN WINNEKER

FIC
WINNEKER
10/13

authorHOUSE®

AuthorHouse™ LLC
1663 Liberty Drive
Bloomington, IN 47403
www.authorhouse.com
Phone: 1-800-839-8640

Published by AuthorHouse   07/03/2013

ISBN: 978-1-4817-4688-5 (sc)
ISBN: 978-1-4817-4687-8 (hc)
ISBN: 978-1-4817-4686-1 (e)

Library of Congress Control Number: 2013907584

This is a work of fiction. All of the characters, names, incidents, organizations, and dialogue
in this novel are either the products of the author's imagination or are used fictitiously.

DEDICATED

*To the Courageous Men & Women of
the United States Border Patrol*

TABLE OF CONTENTS

PREFACE

I HAVE WRITTEN this novel to dramatize, albeit in a fictional manner, the outstanding dedication and commitment of the courageous men and women serving the country as members of the United States Border Patrol.

The dangers they face in protecting and securing our borders from those who fail to respect the laws of the land are considerable. It looks, to this author, to be a thankless and unappreciated job. Difficulties, politically motivated and otherwise, tend to get in the way of our recognition of the efforts they expend on our behalf.

The story behind *Border Line* will provide the reader with a glimpse of some of the aspects of the war being waged every day between the Border Patrol, along with other law enforcement agencies, and the dangerous, ruthless drug cartels that move their illegal products across the border. Whether the trafficking is in marijuana, cocaine, or methamphetamines, the financial stakes are very high. The violence that regularly accompanies these transactions is often deadly.

The travails of Randall Powell, the Agent central to this story, although seemingly unique, suggest that the dangers inherent in the task of patrolling our borders can never be overstated.

This book only scratches the surface in that regard.

Part I

A Routine Patrol

CHAPTER 1

DAY 1

THE INEXORABLY RISING, early August sun, already intense and firing up the Tucson landscape at seven in the morning, broke through the bedroom blinds as Rusty Powell finished his shower and was shaving in the bathroom before heading down to the kitchen for breakfast. Another 100-plus degree day was in the offing.

An early riser, Melinda Powell was up at six, had already made a pot of coffee and was finishing up a couple of scrambled eggs when her husband walked into the kitchen and from behind, gently planted a couple of kisses on her neck.

"Ouch, you stabbed me with your badge again, mister!" All Melinda had on was a thin, black, lacy negligee, with little protection from Rusty's Border Patrol ID badge hardware. "Sit yourself down. Juice is on the table. The eggs are just about ready to go on the plate. How many slices of toast, sir?"

"Two's fine. I have to get going. There's a meeting at eight. Everybody with second shift duty has to be there. What's your day look like?"

"I'm meeting Cindy for lunch. We're going to decide on the date for her garage sale. She has a boatload of stuff to get rid of before the move. The rest they are going to donate to their church and some to Goodwill. Scott just learned that he has to start the new job in San Diego on September 1."

"That's pretty quick", Rusty said, as he climbed aboard the bar stool at the island in the kitchen and swallowed a gulp of hot coffee. "I'll give him a call to touch base. Let's try to get together with them for dinner Saturday night."

"I'll ask Cindy, but they're obviously up to their eyeballs trying to get everything done before the move."

Scott and Cindy Kendall were the Powells' closest friends. Leaving Tucson, where Scott was a district sales manager for Kraft Foods was going to be an emotional experience for the two couples. Melinda was already anticipating the loss of her best buddy. As gregarious and popular as Melinda was, it was invariably Cindy that she leaned on for emotional support.

Rusty inhaled his eggs and toast, gulped down what remained in his coffee mug, and kissed Melinda goodbye. "Have a great day, honey. Say hi to Cindy." He grabbed the holster that housed the Berretta 96D "Brigadier" pistol, assigned to all Agents, clipped it to his belt and headed for the garage to get aboard the heavily traveled 2010 Honda Civic and hit the road.

The drive to Nogales from the Powells' ranch-style home in West Tucson, a little over 60 miles, was less than an hour drive, mostly along Interstate 19, a barren, boring run of highway, and the only direct way to get from Tucson to Nogales. The majority of Border Patrol agents assigned to Nogales made the drive every day. Tucson was far and away the more desirable place to hang their hats.

Randall Powell, known as Rusty to everyone but his mother, Rose, and a few aunts and uncles, was a 29-year old U.S. Border Patrol Agent, assigned to the Nogales, Arizona station, one of most active, heavily staffed, and notoriously dangerous border crossings in the country.

Rusty and Melinda made the move to Tucson in 2010, when Rusty accepted the Border Patrol position after a five-year tour of duty in the Marine Corps. His career choice had always been law enforcement since the age of twelve. A hair over six feet, solidly built, with buzzed auburn hair and brooding soft green eyes, Powell was a handsome, but rugged looking native of Joplin, Missouri. His dry sense of humor and gregarious personality endeared him to men and women alike.

Melinda met him at a University of Missouri football game in Columbia, where they were both juniors at the time and dating other classmates. That first meeting did it. They were inseparable from that day on.

Rusty's father, Lloyd, was a career Marine officer, retiring after twenty years of service. Thanks to his dad, the Corps was in Rusty's blood. Marriage waited until he finished officers training at Quantico, Virginia three years later. The couple was married in a small church in Melinda's hometown of Poplar Bluff, Missouri.

After two long tours of duty in Afghanistan, Powell easily concluded that he was not going to follow in his father's footsteps and make the Corps a career. A few months after his discharge, he applied and was accepted to attend the Border Patrol Academy in Artesia, New Mexico. The 58-day course was grueling, both physically and mentally. Having just left the Marine Corps, he was in excellent shape. Nevertheless, the Border Patrol training was a true test. And Rusty, not even close to being fluent in Spanish, was required to learn the language, managing to struggle through the Academy's additional 40-day task based program.

During the three months of Rusty's training, Melinda waited at her parent's home until Rusty could be assigned to a Customs & Border Patrol station, immediately after graduating from the Academy in late April 2010.

CHAPTER 2

GARY CHILDERS WAS assigned to work with Rusty that day. For obvious reasons, agents rarely worked alone. Childers was a six-year Border Patrol veteran, a California native, serving his first three years at a station in El Paso. He and Rusty functioned well together. When out in the field as a team on patrol, which was frequently the case, Powell did the tracking, while Childers provided security when on the move. He was an excellent marksman and comfortable with a variety of firearms.

That morning, there were 45 Agents on duty. The Patrol Agent in Charge, Carroll Page, entered the Nogales station meeting room following muster call. Page, a ten year Border Patrol veteran, had pretty much seen it all. Prior to the major buildup in the size of the force, implemented during the George W. Bush administration, the organization was grossly understaffed and stretched to the breaking point. Agents were often forced into making dangerous, risky decisions, often working alone. Carroll Page was a seasoned, tough customer, and knew the drill. A native of Fresno, California, he served as a staff sergeant in the Army and was decorated for his service in the first Gulf War. Tall and wiry, his closely cropped blonde hair was receding at the forehead. He sported a wide, graying moustache that completed the tough guy image. He was rarely seen without his aviator-style sunglasses.

That morning Page looked even more serious than usual. "This is shaping up to be one hell of a day", he said, scanning the room full of Agents.

"We brought in 122 undocumented last night. Seems like the boys in Altar were particularly busy yesterday, shipping folks up here by the bushel via the Highway." Page was referring to the rugged road known as Devil's Highway that winds through the Sonoran desert and mountains, eventually reaching Nogales, Mexico, where the illegals, Mexicans eager for work, could often find their way across the border.

Page continued. "If we apprehended that many last night, I would expect you to see tracks on a bunch of other ones trying to get north today. With the heat, a few may be unequipped with enough water to stay alive. So be heads up. Don't take unnecessary chances, and stay hydrated yourselves. We could hit 110 this afternoon. That's' all."

The second shift personnel scattered; some went to the office to check emails. A handful of agents moved to take up their post at the border crossing station; several teams that had field assignments got to their vehicles after getting their still-open cases from the shift handoff. Rusty and Gary Childers took a handoff from two other agents who ended their shift. The assignment was to pursue what was believed to be a group of at least four illegals that managed to escape capture in the wee hours of the morning. The agents were issued a Jeep J8, a vehicle rigged for rough terrain, for the day's work. After loading the Jeep with food, water, ammunition and additional communication gear, they took off. Rusty drove. They headed west-northwest toward the Pena Blanca Reservoir. It was 9:30 in the morning. The red-orange desert sun was already punctuating its ominous presence.

A Predator B unmanned drone aircraft, based in Sierra Vista, Arizona, about 75 miles to the east, was provided with a radio message from the Border Station that specified the direction the Mexicans had taken once crossing the border, just west of Nogales. The drone, which had sophisticated tracking gear and infrared cameras, began the search a few hours earlier. Powell and Childers were able to communicate with the drone specialists in Sierra Vista who controlled the aircraft's movements. Both agents were confident that the Predator would eventually spot the suspects and pinpoint their numbers and location. That would make it far easier for the agents on the ground to catch up with them later in the day.

Childers was already bathed in sweat. His sunglasses were incessantly covered with sand, making it difficult to keep his focus on the terrain ahead. Rusty was driving, but Gary, although used to the drill, was responsible for their security, and was fighting the harsh conditions.

"On this heading we'll see more snakes than illegals for the next few hours".

"No doubt,", Rusty said. "Let's hope the Predator spots these guys before noon. I wouldn't bet on it, though. Brennan and Gonzales said they had about a three hour head start."

"Yeah, but in this heat they're going to have to make beaucoup stops. There isn't a hell of a lot of heavy brush in this direction to give them cover. What did you bring for lunch?"

Rusty laughed, as he negotiated the Jeep around some rough, rocky ground. "The menu is bologna and Swiss on stale rye. The chips are stale too. What can I say old buddy; things are tough?"

Childers didn't respond right away, as he was cleaning off his sunglasses and making a concerted effort to keep from falling out of the vehicle, as they drove over a large, somewhat hidden sinkhole in the sand. "That'll do. And to supplement our tasty water supply I brought some Gatorade to wash it down."

CHAPTER 3

CINDY DROVE HER Ford Explorer, loaded with items she was donating to their church, to the Powells' place to pick up Melinda. Their plans had changed. Originally, Melinda was going to drive. Cindy pulled into the Powells' driveway, beeped the horn and Melinda appeared, darting out the front door, dressed for the hot day in powder blue shorts, snowy white blouse and a pair of silver flats from 9 West. Her long blonde hair was pulled back in a ponytail. About 5'9" in her bare feet, Melinda towered over most of her girl friends, with the exception of Cindy, who was about the same height.

What separated Melinda from Cindy, and her other friends as well, was a near perfect figure, with long, slinky legs, a nothing waist and beautifully shaped full breasts. High cheekbones, pronounced dimples when she smiled, and full, soft lips completed the picture. She could easily have had a career in modeling intimate apparel, or swimsuits, but loved to write. Her degree in journalism from Missouri gave her more than adequate credentials for a career with a news organization, but she chose writing children's books instead and was about to finish her third effort in that regard. The first two sold reasonably well, through bookstores and via the website she created, virtually on her own.

Cindy, on the other hand, dropped out of the University of Tennessee in her sophomore year and attended a cooking school in Nashville, where she eventually found a job as a sous chef at a French restaurant. When Scott accepted a position in Tucson, Cindy found it somewhat difficult to land a reasonably well-paying job. The birth of their first child, a boy they named Wilson, nicknamed Will, put an end to her job-hunting efforts. With Scott's new position in San Diego, the Kendalls would be able to manage quite well with one wage earner in the family.

A phenomenal cook and pastry baker, Cindy tried, without success, to get Melinda to work with her on a cookbook. Now they would have to resort to emails and phone calls to stay in touch.

The love of cooking and baking presented a formidable challenge in managing Cindy's waistline, as well as that of her husband Scott. Both struggled with the battle of the bulge. They belonged to a health club and usually worked out two or three times a week, but of late, given Scott's impending job change and the relocation task, the workouts were put on hold.

They motored on to the Kendall's church and dropped off a number of bags of clothing and an assortment of table lamps that were going to be donated to one of the church's local charities. From there they stopped for gasoline and then headed to a nearby Olive Garden for lunch. The restaurant was not one of Melinda's favorites, but the soup and salad option was fine. The conversation was focused on the garage sale planning. The date for the sale was set. It would be held the second Saturday in September. Scott will have started his new job in San Diego by then. But Rusty would be there to help and Melinda agreed to help with all facets of the event. She even volunteered to write the ad for the *Arizona Daily Star*.

The girls talked their way through lunch, paid the check and headed back to Melinda's to finish the garage sale planning. Around 3PM, Cindy drove home, stopping off at a neighbor's home to retrieve little Wilson, a month away from his third birthday.

CHAPTER 4

BEN ROSETTI, THE lead man on Predator drone control in Sierra Vista, gazed intently at one of the computer screens with real-time views from the aircraft. Nothing that would have matched up with the description provided by the Nogales CBP Station was visible at the moment. The search specs related to a group of maybe four or five men on foot, that in all likelihood crossed the border on the western side of Nogales around 4AM in the morning. Given the amount of ground that a group that size, staying together, could cover in six hours, the drone was scanning an area about 20 to 25 miles north-northwest of the Nogales border station.

Rosetti then spotted the Jeep carrying Powell and Childers in that direction. He was able to reach the team by phone. "Hey, it's Predator Control at Sierra Vista. My name is Rosetti. The drone has you in its sights. Any further information on the target group's travel? Over."

The voice quality was weak, but Rusty could decipher what Rosetti was saying. "We have you five by five. Thanks for checking in, Rosetti. Nothing yet. We're looking for footprints, and signs of any temporary campsite, but it's a needle in the Sonoran haystack. If we don't get anything by around 1600 hours we will head back to base. So keep looking ahead of us. And thanks. I know you've got other fish to fry. Over."

"No problem. I'm on the controls with this magical flying bird until 1800 hours, so we're in this together. Be safe." Rosetti, a 50-year old veteran of Customs and Border Protection, moved over to Sierra Vista in early 2011. He had often been in Agents Powell and Childers' shoes and knew the drill.

It was high noon and as yet there were no foot tracks or other signs of people movement. So the Agents remained in the Jeep and kept moving in a north-northwest direction, unless and until there were any visible signs that would suggest that they should change course. The ambient temperature, according to the instruments in the vehicle, was 107.

A few minutes later, reacting to a buzzing signal, Childers picked up the headset of their radio receiver. "Powell and Childers here. Over."

"Hey, it's Rosetti. No signs of anybody on foot, but we've cited a beat-up white Chevy Van, no markings visible, and it's heading due north now about five miles from your present location. How it got here is the sixty-four dollar question. It's moving kind of slow, maybe doing 35mph, no doubt because of the rough terrain. It's obviously the all-wheel drive version, and by the looks of it, at least five or six years old. You could probably catch up with it within the hour. I'm getting a closer look now; it's got New Mexico plates – RPK-292. Be careful, guys. I don't like the looks of that thing. Want me to send help? Over."

Rusty looked at Gary. Childers stared back. He spoke first. "What say you, partner? They would have to send a chopper to get to the location quick enough. Is that a good idea?"

"Hey, we've been in this situation before and handled it without any help. Odds are we can deal with it okay. I'm inclined to take our chances. But Rosetti asks a very good question. How the hell did a van get out here?"

"Any decision, sports fans?" Rosetti wanted some kind of response. "Over."

"We're cool", Childers said. "If we run into trouble, we'll ask you to send the Predator over to give us some cover. Over."

"Nice idea, but not an option, short term", Rosetti said, as he checked the flight log for the aircraft. "I have to move her to another area that needs surveillance. It can get back over to you guys in a couple of hours. But you'll probably need help sooner than that. And since the Predator isn't armed, I'm not sure we can do you much good. Over."

"No problem", Gary said. "We'll be fine. Thanks for the heads-up. Over and out."

Rosetti had already given them the coordinates of the van's current location. Rusty adjusted their GPS to a long-range setting and Childers kept the Jeep moving on a straight trajectory in line with the van's reported movement.

Rusty opened an insulated plastic container with ice inside, along with four bologna and cheese sandwiches, a bag of Doritos and two bottles of Grape flavored Gatorade. Their ample supply of water was held in reserve. Given the heat, they had already taken some, but drank it sparingly.

Rusty was still puzzled. "If the van didn't go through the Nogales border crossing, how did it get out here?" Where the high fence ends, there are crosshatched steel vehicle barriers that stretch for miles. "And if it did go through the crossing, wasn't it searched before it was cleared? I guess the New Mexico plates could have provided some cover. But it doesn't make sense."

Childers finished a final gulp of Gatorade. "It doesn't matter at this point. We just have to go check it out."

Rusty added, "And what happened to the four guys on foot that brought us out here in the first place? Looks like they just disappeared."

The terrain got rougher. Rusty kept moving ahead, but he slowed down, primarily to avoid equipment falling out of the Jeep. Childers began double-checking the firearms, making sure that they were loaded and all the safeties were on. There were two Remington Model 870 pump action shotguns on board; one issued to each agent. Their Beretta 96D handguns had 11-round magazines and held one additional round in the chamber. Childers asked Powell to check his sidearm. All weapons were secured.

The agents switched from sunglasses to goggles, as the blowing dust and sand intensified. They quickly ate their sandwiches and washed them down with the Gatorade, as the Jeep trundled forward in the desert. Closing in somewhat, they were now within about three miles of the Chevy van.

CHAPTER 5

"THOSE GUYS MUST be nuts, traveling across this terrain in a van." Childers had a hard time digesting the scenario of illegals chancing the trip under such conditions. It was more typical for vehicles coming up from Mexico to stay on traveled roads.

"Gary, you should know better. These characters will take any kind of risk to get loose over here. I wouldn't be surprised if this was a marijuana or cocaine smuggling mission. They probably figure that once they get far enough across the border they could get over to I-19 and go the rest of the way without any problems. If they came over Devils Highway from Altar, they may think that they're already in the clear."

"Maybe Rusty. And if you're right, and they've got grass in the van, we're going to have our hands full. Especially if there are more than a couple of guys sitting back in the rear."

"No question. I guess in a few minutes we'll find out."

Childers added, "We'd better radio the station and let them know what's going down."

Without responding, Powell grabbed his handset and made the call. He connected with an agent on duty at the crossing station and reported their GPS position and the fact that they were now in pursuit of the van.

The terrain was increasingly rough and hilly. Large quantities of blowing sand and dust filled the bone dry, blistering hot landscape. The agents' goggles were now an indispensible piece of equipment as they forged ahead.

Childers sprang into alert mode, as he heard the faint sounds of another vehicle traipsing across the desert. Its tire tracks were now visible as well. "Rusty, they're just ahead. Hear that noise coming from ten o'clock?"

"Roger that. I'm ready to approach. Get set. I'm speeding up to overtake them."

Childers grabbed one of the shotguns. Powell accelerated and in a few seconds they spotted the van, kicking up dust and sand, about three hundred yards ahead. The Jeep neared the van from the starboard side, away from the driver's line of sight. Rusty knew that he would have to maneuver alongside and then quickly cross in front of the van to get it to stop. It was a somewhat dangerous move, given the unknown passengers and possible cargo in the vehicle. It might not stop, but instead swerve out of the way, or smash into the Jeep straight on.

The driver then caught sight of the Jeep and accelerated, kicking up huge billows of sand, stones and dust. The van started an array of zigzagging movements. Rusty then made *his* move, stepping on the gas pedal and weaving his way toward the front of the van. Suddenly, from the passenger-side front seat, a rifle appeared. The Jeep was now slightly ahead of the van, as Rusty continued his efforts to get in front of the van. Two shots were fired before Childers could raise his pistol to defend himself and his partner. But neither shot hit its intended target.

Rusty succeeded in getting the Jeep in front of the van, which was beginning to slow down. He put his hand on the Beretta and yelled. "U.S. Border Patrol; bring your vehicle to a stop! Two more shots rang out, one a glancing blow across the driver-side door. The other shot missed its mark entirely.

Again, Rusty yelled out, "Border Patrol; stop your vehicle immediately!" He then quickly switched to Spanish and repeated the warning. Two more rifle shots ensued, while the van continued to move, albeit slowly.

Both shots somehow missed Rusty, who was directly in the shooter's line of fire. "I'm hit!" Childers yelled in pain, as he lifted his left arm to his chest. Blood began spurting out of the entry wound. Rusty accelerated and moved the Jeep away from the front of the van. It's driver then pulled the vehicle to a complete stop. Childers slumped down, still clutching his chest, just above the heart.

Rusty knew his own life was on the line, and that the life of his wounded partner hung in the balance. He drew his Beretta and took aim at the individual shooting at them, firing three rounds in succession. The first two shots slammed into the passenger side door of the van, just below the window. Then, a man's low-pitched, shrieking sound signaled to Rusty that the third shot must have done some physical damage.

In a sudden move, the van driver exited the vehicle and began to run. Rusty jumped out of the Jeep in pursuit. Another rifle shot was fired from inside the van. This one hit Rusty in the calf muscle of his left leg and cracked the tibia bone. He fell hard to the ground, but managed to hang on to his pistol and fired at the man still sitting in the van, who was obviously not hurt badly enough to put him out of commission. This time, the passenger fell silent. His head could no longer be seen.

Rusty wanted to get to his partner and give him some help. Hobbling back to the Jeep, he found Childers unconscious. Blood covered the front of this uniform. He showed no signs of life. Still uncertain if he had killed the van passenger, or if more gunshots would follow, Powell moved slowly toward the van, pistol cocked and ready to fire it if someone moved. He peered into the passenger side window. The body was doubled over and unresponsive. Rusty yelled in through the window. "Hombre, speak to me man!" No response.

The van driver disappeared into the desert brush. He would no doubt hide until he thought it was safe to return the vehicle. Without water, there was no way he would last very long himself. Rusty feared that Childers was dead. He knew what to do to make sure, one way or the other. Checking his pulse, there was a very faint sound of a heartbeat. He would have to pull Childers out of the Jeep and lay him on the ground to start CPR. Beginning to do so, Rusty heard a noise from the rear of the van. The Chevy's back door clicked open. Turning around, Powell faced an armed man standing with a sawed-off shotgun pointed in his direction.

"Manos arriba, gringo!" The diminutive, pudgy Latino, dressed in a sweat-stained white tee shirt, baggy jeans, and grease-encrusted Red Sox baseball cap, strongly suggested that Powell raise his hands. Rusty needed to get back to Childers and continue the CPR. "Mi pareja es herido", letting the man know that his partner was hurt, did little to release Powell from obeying the order to give up. There was almost a zero chance of saving Childers at this point. He would need emergency medical assistance to stop the bleeding, which obviously was not in the cards.

Rusty raised his arms after throwing the Beretta to the ground. His leg was bleeding and the pain from the fractured bone resonated throughout his body. Keeping a clear head was first and foremost in his conscious thought. He was distraught about his dying partner, but he could do very little about it. Staying alive himself was a big enough challenge.

The Latino motioned to Powell to come closer to the back of the van. Fearing that resistance was a sure ticket to a desert grave, he limped forward until he was standing no more than six feet from his adversary. Then Rusty collapsed.

"Manuel, amigo, tu puede regresar ahora!" Mister Red Sox fan yelled to his partner-driver to return. "No hay problema!" He then switched, quite smoothly, to English. "It's okay, Manuel! One is dead; the other is on the ground. When he wakes up he will be looking at the end of my gun!

Speaking to Rusty, in case he could hear him, he said, "You see, gringo, I can speak your language good." He had an almost comical smile on his face. His personality seemed to mimic that of the leader of the bandoleros intending to rob Humphrey Bogart and his partners in "The Treasure of the Sierra Madre". It was one of Powell's favorite Bogart films. He was still on the ground, but starting to regain consciousness.

Reaching out and poking Rusty in the belly with the shotgun, the man made a gesture with it to direct Powell to get up and climb into the back of the van. Rusty had little option but to obey his captor. He stood, but put no pressure on the injured leg. As he initiated the effort to get the leg, as well as the other one, up over the rear bumper and into the van, Manuel, the driver, returned, opting to go directly to the driver's seat and re-start the engine. The man with the shotgun tied Rusty's arms and legs together with some rope, and shoved an oily rag into his mouth.

As soon as the rear gate was closed and Manuel's partner was back up front in the passenger seat, they were ready to get underway.

Powell immediately began to scan the visible contents of the vehicle. Under a canvas tarpaulin there was no less than twenty tightly wrapped packages of what looked like marijuana that came into view. He then realized he was sitting on six more of the same size illicit parcels. As he fully regained his senses, he was convinced, by the odor permeating the cargo space, that his initial assumption was valid. It was pot. An ounce of marijuana on the street in Arizona could fetch as much $200 or more. Rusty's rough estimate of the quantity sitting in the back of this van was somewhere around 250 pounds. It would have a total street value of over $800,000.

Also sitting back there was another Latino, situated to the front of the piles of contraband. He looked somewhat perplexed with the goings on, but held a Smith & Wesson revolver aimed at Rusty's head.

The situation at hand was quickly convincing Powell that in short order he might very well join Childers, who was almost certainly deceased. By the looks of things, an almost certain scenario was that these guys were anxious to get the cargo to a stateside drug merchant, collect payment and quickly return to Mexico. One more dead Border Agent was not going to make much difference.

CHAPTER 6

THE VAN'S ENGINE was being revved up, as Manuel the driver would no doubt be anxious to get underway. Rusty's leg needed to be attended to fairly soon, but the prospects of that happening were not particularly good. He discerned a heavy thump emanating from the side of the vehicle, and was correct in his assumption that it represented the body of the presumably dead passenger being dumped out to rot in the desert sun.

He guessed that Childers' body remained in the Jeep. Just as his mind conjured up that notion, Rusty heard the Jeep's engine roar to life. His heart rate accelerated with optimism that perhaps Gary was still alive and was making a valiant effort to head off or follow the van. In reality, Powell's adversary with the shotgun was preparing to move the Jeep into some deep cover, with the obvious purpose of hiding it from any aerial surveillance.

Less than a minute later, the Jeep's engine either stopped completely or was no longer within earshot of the cast of characters in the van. Soon thereafter, the passenger side door of the van opened and quickly closed, suggesting that Mr. Shotgun was now back inside the vehicle, allowing it to move ahead.

The going was slow, given the extremely rough terrain. The van's subpar suspension was evident. Passengers, along with the illicit cargo, wobbled and shook incessantly as they motored on. With every such movement Rusty winced with pain. It was now 2:55 in the afternoon. The desert temperature inched up to 112 degrees and the van's climate control system seemed to be less than optimal. Rusty was covered in perspiration. The smell of the marijuana permeated the vehicle's interior space.

He remained perplexed as to what possible reason these drug haulers had for letting him stay alive. Then the thought struck him; they might be keeping their option open to hold him as a hostage for future use. So far, there was virtually no conversation going on among the three men. He had no idea what they might have in store for him down the road. Finding that Rusty was fluent in their language may have contributed to the relative silence.

Border Patrol Agent shift commander, Carroll Page, was advised that Powell and Childers had called in from the field, and reported that the Predator drone had located them, as well as the Chevy van. Given no further word for more than two hours, Page decided to make contact with the Agents for an update report. After three failed attempts he decided to call Sierra Vista and request a Predator fly-over. He was concerned. Chasing after an unidentified van making its way across the Sonoran desert was high risk business.

The call was transferred to the Predator operations center. Ben Rosetti was still at the controls of the drone. "Agent Page, what's the good word? Any feedback from your guys chasing the van?"

"I was hoping you could tell me something good Rosetti. Where's the drone? I'd sure like to get a reading on their location. It's been a couple of hours since they called in."

"The aircraft is tracking about 80 miles west of them at the moment. I hadn't planned to bring it back to their location for a while. Want me to change things around?"

"Might be a good idea. If your boss has a problem, have him give me a call."

"I told your guys I thought they should call in for backup, but it sounds like they didn't do it. Don't worry about any approvals. I'll send the drone. It won't take too long to get to where the guys will likely be within half an hour. When it's in the area I will call you with a report on what's happening on the ground. You might want to give them a call in the meantime."

"Tried that. No dice. That's why you and I are talking to each other. Got it?" Page ended the call and tried again to make contact with Powell and Childers. No success. In his gut, Page was deeply concerned for the team's well being. Hopefully a drone report within the hour would lessen the concern.

Rosetti reached over to the control keyboard and set the wheels in motion to move the Predator on a line back to the location where he estimated the Jeep would likely be at that time. A few keystrokes later and the aircraft began to adjust its heading. At the programmed speed, it would reach the Jeep's approximated location by 3:50PM.

CHAPTER 7

THE HOLDER OF the outstretched Smith & Wesson made a move toward Rusty, who was at the opposite end of the inside of the van. Not saying a word, he pulled a piece of white rag from his pocket and reached toward Rusty's leg. He smiled and motioned to the leg, which continued to bleed, though not as profusely at the moment. The man's intention was clear; he wanted to hand the rag to his abductee to wrap around the wound.

Rusty reached for the reasonably clean piece of cloth, acknowledged the offer of assistance, and tied the rag tightly around his calf. "Gracias amigo", he said. "De nada", was the man's brief reply. He nodded and crawled back to his end of the van. Rusty made an effort to position his body more comfortably atop the bags of marijuana, but to no avail. While the rag was helpful in slowing the blood flow, it was a compound fracture. He needed surgery to support the broken bone.

The van stopped. The guy in the passenger seat got out. He tried to make a cell phone call, but there was no tower within twenty miles, meaning no signal strength was possible. After a couple of unsuccessful tries, he gave up and got back in the van. After delivering a few expletives to the driver, they once again got underway. Rusty had heard the commentary many times before. It seemed likely to him that the man in the passenger seat was the ranking member of the crew. This would become more apparent as the journey wore on.

About ten minutes later, the ride suddenly became much smoother. Rusty's guess was that they had finally gotten to what felt like a dirt road. While it clearly was not a paved highway, the difference was significant. Rusty, lying face-up on the rear floor of the van, was unable to look out the back window. The busted leg reacted positively to the change.

But it still hurt like hell. Powell was hopeful that the crew would reach their drop-off destination in short order. The typical scenario would be that the pot would be exchanged, on the spot, for cash. Following that transaction, his future was speculative at best.

The crew leader, once again proudly exhibiting his command of English, addressed his adversary. "Hey, gringo, do you want something to eat? I have some very good bananas. If you want one, you can have it."

"I'm not hungry. I just need to have a doctor look at this leg."

"Oh sure. When we get home I will take you myself. Okay?"

Rusty's brain struggled to make sense out of that declaration. Not quite dismissing its validity out of hand, he decided not to respond. No sense stirring the pot at this point. The drama would have to play itself out a little further before Powell was taking any more chances. Rusty glanced at his watch. It was 3:45.

CHAPTER 8

"Bueno amigos! Estamos aqui!" The driver was ecstatic, as the van lumbered into the town of Ajo. From Nogales to Ajo by paved roads and highways, it was more than a 3-hour drive. This wild goose chase through the desert and mountains took the better part of the day. They had no doubt hooked on to a dirt road at some point and followed it to Route 86 - the W. Tucson-Ajo Highway. The drug runners were scheduled to meet their pickup contacts at 4PM. The pickup point was the parking lot behind the 100 Estrella restaurant.

Although not very far from Nogales as the crow flies, the Border Patrol maintained a station a few miles outside the town environs, and regularly checked the dusty desert town of less than four thousand residents. Illegals were often found there, in Sells, or in Arivaca, a town of less than a thousand people, and even closer to Nogales. Powell recognized some familiar Ajo landmarks through the back window. The driver made a few turns and brought the van to a stop at the restaurant. Rusty was convinced that he would never leave the town alive.

The man in the front passenger seat got out first. The wind was blowing and the clouds darkened, signaling to Rusty that a rare rainstorm was about to come through. It was Arizona Monsoon season. Heavy downpours of six inches or more in a short period of time were not uncommon in July and August. The streets of these towns, not having any storm drains in this area, would flood in a matter of minutes. Rusty guessed that this would be one of those storms.

Powell's fellow passenger in the back of the van, took out a cigarette, most likely a joint, and lit it, again flashing a smile that exposed a mouth full of several gold inlays and broken, yellow-brown teeth. Within a few minutes, the back door of the restaurant swung open and two men appeared; both visible to Rusty from the back window. They walked up to the rear door. The man from the front passenger seat, whose name, Rusty learned, was Rico Morales, joined them and they began to converse, in English, to begin consummating the drop-off transaction. Rusty could hear every word.

"You have the money, amigo?" Rico asked. "It is all here; about a hundred kilos." He reached for the rear door handle, as Powell squirmed to avoid any direct contact with his injured leg. It began to rain, slowly at first, but soon coming down in buckets. The back door swung open. Both pickup men were startled to see Rusty, in his bloodstained Border Patrol uniform, staring up from his fetal position on the floor. The larger of the two, both in height and weight, turned to Morales. "What the hell is this? Are you crazy, driving around with this federal agent. Why didn't you just leave him in the desert?

"That's my business. Let's get this thing done. We are headed back to Hermosillo tonight. Comprende?"

The two pickup characters, both seemingly Americans, moved away from the van and spoke in a whisper. Rusty had extraordinarily good hearing, but couldn't make out what they were saying. He was certain that if there was no exchange of pot and cash within the next few minutes, trouble would ensue. That would clearly not be good for all parties concerned.

In short order, the larger man went back to the truck, checked the area for any onlookers, removed a cardboard box and returned to the van. "Okay, let me look at the stuff." Rico pulled one of the bundles of cannabis out of the vehicle and handed it to the man, who poked a hole in the plastic wrapping with a penknife and reached in to grab a handful of the pot. He rolled it around in his fingers and brought it to his nose. "Not bad. Now I want to open another bag; one that I choose." He did so, as the Rico looked on with a look of disdain. The pickup man went through the same process with another handful of the merchandise.

Seemingly satisfied with test number two, he handed the box to Rico, who opened it and examined its contents – stacks of U.S. bills in various denominations. Most were thousand dollar notes. The other pickup man joined them at the van door, as they began to unload the bundles and shift them to another vehicle; a black Dodge pickup truck, with a metal cover on the cargo box. They opened the tailgate and stacked the bundles, covering the payload with a heavy plastic tarp and closing the metal cover. The second man climbed back into the driver seat and closed the door. Ten seconds after the pickup's engine turned over, they were gone.

CHAPTER 9

BEN ROSETTI PROGRAMMED the Predator to return to Powell and Childers' last known location. Just before 4PM, the drone's powerful zoom cameras were overhead and pointed directly at that spot. The barren scene showed two sets of vehicle tire tracks; one set looked to be that of the Jeep. The other set was not recognizable. The afternoon shadows didn't help. Rosetti called the Border Station and asked for Carroll Page.

"Not much to report, Agent Page. The Predator is over the area and she's taking a pretty close look. I would guess that your guys hooked up with whoever was in the van, judging by the tire tracks at that spot. What happened then is anybody's guess. Other than that, I don't know what to recommend as a next step. The drone will continue on a north-northwest heading until I turn her back to Sierra Vista around 10PM. If I get anything that looks worth reporting, I'll let you know. Later, my friend."

"Thanks Ben. If we can't raise the guys by radio in another hour or so, I'm sending a chopper with some Agents. If they see anything from the air, we can send them down to check it out. Let's hope our two boys are out of harm's way. Let us know if your predator hits the jackpot." Page motioned to an agent sitting at a nearby computer keyboard to join him in the squad room.

"Farley, I need you to take the bird out to Pena Blanca and comb that area and north of it for Childers and Powell. We haven't had any word from them for several hours. It looks like they intercepted a white Chevy van just north of there and then both vehicles disappeared. Give me report while you're out there. Okay?"

Shane Farley was an agent with a helicopter's license. A no-nonsense former University of Alabama linebacker, he was six-two, built like a stone wall, but had an easy-going, friendly personality. "Will do, Agent Page. I need to fuel up the bird, but should have her in the air in less than twenty minutes. Can I take Agent McBride along? I could use him for taking some photos and backing me up on the ground."

"Yeah, take him with you. Tell him it's okay with me. Just make sure and keep me posted. Something tells me the guys may be in tough spot."

Farley nodded and left the station office to head out to the chopper pad. It was a minute before 4:30PM. The skies were darkening and the Arizona Monsoon was moving quickly toward Nogales. In no way could the chopper leave the ground. The Predator would also be useless over the heavy cloud cover that was spreading across the area. In less than five minutes, Farley returned to the station office. "No go, Agent Page. Just got a storm warning from the NOAA radar station in Nogales. It looks like the weather will keep us out of commission for a while."

"Crap! These summer storms can hang around. Let's hope that I'm wrong on this one. We've got to find those guys and get them home." Page was not having a good day. His shift ended at 4, but he was hanging around. He looked at the duty schedule. Fred Cooley was on tap to replace him as Agent in Charge, but it was not unusual for the guys to overlap when there were unresolved problems during a shift change.

Back at his computer console, Farley checked radar on the NOAA website. The heavy rain was moving east and would soon cover all of south central Arizona. From Tucson, south to the border, there was a severe storm warning until 11PM.

CHAPTER 10

RUSTY'S LEG, ALTHOUGH continuing to hurt like hell, was no longer bleeding. The cloth provided by his good-natured companion in the back of the van, was securely tied and effective in stopping the flow, but fortunately wasn't constrictive enough to cut off circulation. Bottom line, however, Powell would need surgery to stabilize the broken bone.

Departing the Ajo environs, the van continued on reasonably smooth roads, which made the ride tolerable for the present. He anticipated that this would change soon enough, and Powell rightly assumed that the worst part of the trip would lie ahead. Unfortunately, the horrendous quality of the roads they would travel would pale in comparison to other factors he would be forced to contend with along the way.

Manuel and Rico were in a subdued, but relieved state of mind, riding along with a box containing about $350,000 in cash keeping them company in the front seat. Given the presence of a wounded Border Patrol Agent and the smell of the van's cargo space, the likelihood of this entourage attempting to cross the border back into Mexico via the Nogales frontier was not a consideration. They were compelled to make the trip via a similar route that provided them earlier entry into the U.S. That would entail traveling across the same rough, almost impassable terrain. And this time, it would be at night, although the August evening would normally provide daylight until close to 9PM. But not tonight.

Rico, who seemed the likely commanding officer of the crew, was no doubt compelled to return to Hermosillo and deliver the cash to his superiors. It was a long drive, probably 6 hours through the desert and secondary roads for a sizable leg of the trip, not including any stops in Mexico along the way. Until they reached the main highway, federal road, Mexico 15, a reasonably good road that would take them directly into Hermosillo, the going would be slow. If they got too tired, the plan was to find a place to stay in the vicinity of Santa Ana, where highway 43, heading east from Altar, meets Route 15. The heavy rain was making the trip even slower and more treacherous than they thought possible.

Morales did not anticipate any problems with Rusty. He was tied securely and not very mobile with the busted leg. If he did become an annoyance, he would be shot dead without hesitation, and left to rot in the Sonoran wilderness. But Rico's intentions were clear. Agent Powell would make an excellent hostage. The American government would no doubt be willing to pay a sizable sum to get him back alive. Recent murders of Border Patrol Agents, killed in gunfights with Mexican drug traffickers along the border, made the headlines. They would soon find another dead Agent in the Jeep left behind. Another would be difficult to swallow.

Leaving the Ajo environs, they followed Route 85 on the way into Mexico, before breaking out into open desert close to the border. This was somewhat west of where they crossed into the U.S. early that morning. They would require some good fortune to find an opening large enough to get past the metal barricades and into Mexico. Since there were numerous points along the border away from Nogales where the man-made barriers were either purposely or otherwise moved, Morales was confident that they would get across without incident. Increasing the odds of success was the low ceiling and heavy rains that would make the Predator drones and other border tracking devices a non-issue.

Manuel, clearly tired and hungry from the long day of driving and sundry encounters, clutched the van's steering wheel tightly and motored on.

PART II

Agent Unaccounted For

CHAPTER II

MELINDA POWELL TYPICALLY received a call from her husband sometime in mid-afternoon, once Rusty had a reasonably good idea if he would manage to end his shift on schedule and estimate what time he might get home. Now, as evidenced by the kitchen wall clock, 6PM was a handful of minutes away, , Melinda grew concerned. She was tempted to try his cell number, but a split second before beginning to dial, her iPhone rang. It was her next-door neighbor Tracy O'Neill.

"Hi Melinda. It's Tracy. I hope I haven't caught you in the middle of dinner."

"Not at all, Tracy. Rusty's not home yet. In fact, I was just about to give him a call. He's hasn't checked in at all this afternoon. What's up?"

"Nothing too ominous. Brandon and I just thought you might like to join us for dinner tomorrow night. We're headed over to the Cantina for a few margaritas and an early meal."

"Sounds great. We don't have anything planned. It should be fine. I'll give you call after Rusty shows up. And thanks for the invite." Just then, call waiting let Melinda know that someone was waiting on the line. "I've got another call Tracy. Talk with you later." She pushed the Call button. "This is Melinda."

"Hi Melinda, it's Tanya Childers. It's been a while. How are you?"

"I'm good Tanya; I hope. How are you? Is anything wrong?" Melinda knew that her husband often partnered with Rusty.

"Well, I'm a little concerned. Gary hasn't called in this afternoon. He assured me that he would, because his mom is having surgery today and he wanted to check in to see how she was doing It's not like him to lose track of the time and not check in. Have you heard from Rusty?"

Melinda's heart felt like it missed a beat. This was not good news. Border Patrol duty was risky business. "Haven't heard from him Tanya. He usually checks in way before this. Have you tried Gary's cell phone?"

"I just did. It never even rang. Can you try Rusty's and let me know if you get through?"

Melinda said she would and after ending the call, immediately dialed Rusty's number. Nothing. No ring. No voicemail. She called Tanya and shared the disheartening news.

Rico had taken both Rusty's and Gary's cell phones, yanked the batteries and dropped them in the desert before they took off. He also smashed the two-way radio in the Jeep.

Gathering her senses, Melinda placed a call to the Nogales Border station.

"Customs and Border Protection, Agent Marino. Can I help you?"

"This is Melinda Powell. I'm calling to find out about my husband, Rusty. Is he there at the station, or do you know where he is, Agent Marino?"

Marino had no information on Powell's whereabouts. When Agents' spouses called, whoever took the call was instructed to transfer it to the senior Agent on duty. In this case, due to the missing team and a lack of any information on their status, Agent Page had remained at the station to assist Fred Cooley, his replacement, who was already briefed on the situation.

"Mrs. Powell, please hold". Marino quickly briefed Cooley as to who was calling and why. Cooley came on the line. "Mrs. Powell, this is Patrol Agent in Charge Fred Cooley, the station duty officer. We're doing whatever we can to locate Rusty and Gary Childers, his partner today."

Melinda interrupted him. "I just spoke to Tanya Childers. She's as worried as I am. What can you tell me? Why can't you get in touch with them?"

"Mrs. Powell, for some reason their communications gear is inoperative. They were on patrol northwest of Nogales and have been in the field since 9:25 this morning. I understand their cell phones are not responding, but that can be a function of their remote location. In any case, their radio should have raised them by now. Because of the rotten weather down here, we can't get a chopper up for awhile, and the Predator drone is grounded as well. As soon as we can make contact we will be in touch with you and Mrs. Childers."

Melinda's heart sank. She feared that sooner or later, this day would come. Sitting down at the kitchen table and dropping her head into her hands, she prayed that the storm was the only reason for her husband and his partner falling off the grid. She thanked Fred Cooley and immediately placed a return call to Tanya Childers to give her an update.

CHAPTER 12

RICO MORALES HAD an apprehensive look on his face, as the van approached the border crossing, about 10 miles north and east of Sonoyta, Mexico. Manuel slowed the vehicle to about 20 miles an hour, as they cruised along the rows of corrugated steel barriers lining the terrain on the U.S. side. They were forced to find an opening to avoid crossing at the U.S. border station at the end of Route 85. This was the Sonoyta station, just south of Lukeville, the last U.S. town before reaching the border.

Less than 10 miles down the line of barriers from the border station was an opening. A section of corrugated steel wall had been previously broken through by some kind of heavy-duty vehicle. It was barely wide enough to allow the van to squeeze through, and as they moved through the crossing, the right side of the vehicle made contact with a steel beam and dented the panel on the passenger side, just past the front door. Rico managed a few Spanish expletives as they continued to drive along and finally on to Mexican terrain. The three-man smuggling crew was well aware that the Border Patrol cruised along the U.S. side all the way to Nogales. Given the heavy rain and poor visibility, however, there was no patrolling, either from the air or on the ground.

Mexico Federal Highway 2, a half-decent feeder route to Mexico 15, was slow going. The heavy rain, now blanketing both southern Arizona and north-central Mexico, demanded that Manuel keep his eyes glued to the road. It was a necessity to avoid hydroplaning on the waterlogged, relatively thin layer of macadam. Traffic was moderate; the highway was a major west-to-east link from Tijuana to Ciudad Juarez.

"I am getting very hungry", Manuel said, turning quickly to Rico, who was dozing, off and on, in the passenger seat.

36

"What about you Jose?" Rico spun around and addressed his compatriot in the rear of the van.

"Something to eat would be nice", he said. Now Rusty had the names of the three drug smugglers, but the throbbing in his calf limited his desire to participate in the verbal exchange.

Rico glanced down at his wristwatch. "I want to get to Santa Ana before we stop to pee and eat. Maybe the rains will ease up by that time. In fact, Morales had no delusions regarding the prospects of the weather clearing anytime soon. It was just idle chatter. The monsoons often stayed around for several days.

"Hey gringo, how are you doing back there?" Rico was inviting his hostage to join in the conversation.

Rusty was in no mood to participate. He hesitated, but decided to issue an "I'm okay. Just get me to some place where I can get help for the leg. You busted it up pretty good."

"You will have to wait until we get to Hermosillo, amigo. There is a doctor there who can fix your leg." He turned around and looked at Rusty, laying in an awkward position across the floor of the van. "Right now, I want you to take off your uniform and put on this shirt and these pants. Rico threw the wrinkled khakis and yellow cotton shirt to the rear. Jose, give him a hand."

Rusty had no idea how he might physically negotiate the task. Simply removing his uniform trousers was going to be hell. Jose moved to the back of the van and began removing Rusty's shirt. Then the belt and Beretta holster were dealt with. Rusty took a stab at loosening the trousers, followed by Jose's valiant attempt at pulling the legs down. That elicited a holler from the young man being stripped. "Wait!", Rusty yelled. "Shit, that's not going to work."

Being somewhat of a creative sort, Jose reached into his pocket and pulled out a penknife. With one swift move of the cutlery, he tore the left trouser leg wide open, making it much easier to remove the pants from that point on. "There you go, amigo", Jose said, with a discernible note of accomplishment in his voice. He then helped Rusty with the loose fitting, wrinkled khakis and cheesecloth cotton shirt. The uniform, as well his field boots, wallet, and other agent-issued gear, were thrown under a tarpaulin and would be disposed when they reached Santa Ana.

The difficult driving conditions persisted, exacerbated by a healthy, 35-mile an hour west wind. Manuel was on his second pack of Marlboros since crossing the border into the U.S. nine hours earlier in the day. The combination of pot odor and Marlboro smoke was getting to Rusty. He was on the verge of vomiting, but held it down, accepting the fact that if he did barf, he would no doubt have to sit in it for an indefinite length of time.

Now several miles into Mexico, where the Border Patrol had zero jurisdiction, the prognosis for Rusty Powell was anything but good, and getting worse by the hour. Why he was not already dead was the 64-dollar question.

CHAPTER 13

AGENTS PAGE AND Cooley were frustrated by their inability to release the chopper. NOAA continued to forecast heavy winds and rain for at least the next 24 hours. There was little question that Powell and Childers were in some sort of trouble. Not knowing their situation was the worst aspect of the wait.

The two senior agents were reluctant to send out a search party by ground vehicle, given the foul conditions. And the Predator drone would not be airborne again until the weather at least partially cleared. Cindy Rodrigues, the station's third shift radio operator, continued, as directed by Page and Cooley, to try making contact with the overdue agents. It was highly unlikely that the Jeep's two-way radio, as well as both of their handsets would not be functional. But there were no sounds at all, indicating that the radio in the Jeep was either dead or somehow destroyed.

****

At exactly 8:40PM, a beat-up white Chevy van approached the Nogales border station from the U.S. side. The driver appeared to be Caucasian. He was alone in the front of the vehicle. The three agents on duty were briefed on the description of the vehicle that Powell and Childers had supposedly intercepted earlier in the day. There was also a note to that effect posted on the window of the crossing gate. The vehicle had Arizona license plates, but could have been changed en route.

As the van came closer to the gate, two of the agents walked to it and one of them, Brad Mosley, addressed the driver, who handed them his passport. "Sir, we are going to search this vehicle. We ask that you remain inside. Is the back gate locked?"

"I can't remember if I locked it or not", the driver said. He was a heavyset middle-aged man, appeared to be sober and was dressed in some sort of work uniform. "You're welcome to look back there. I'm delivering a washing machine and dryer to a family in Caborca."

The other agent, Luis de Silva, moved to the rear of the van, quietly placing his right hand on his Beretta. The other agent stayed by the driver side door. "Sir, do you have some paperwork on the appliances?"

"As your partner will be able to see, they are used. A relative in Tucson is sending them down. I am a handyman and a friend of the relative. They asked me to deliver it for them." Agent de Silva opened the rear door and looked inside. The laundry machines clearly were used, but appeared to be in good condition. He opened both the washer and dryer. Both were empty. The only other item in the cargo area was a toolbox, which the agent opened, finding nothing but tools inside. "Looks okay back here", de Silva said, while closing the gate door.

"Thank you sir", Mosley said to the driver. "You're free to pass." He waived the driver on. The van continued through the border-crossing gate and motored on in the pelting rain.

The two agents shared their curiosity regarding the driver, the van, and its contents. Mosley spoke first. "Why the hell would a guy drive that stuff down from Tucson on a night like this? You'd think he might wait at least till morning or for better weather."

Agent de Silva agreed. "Yeah, it's a little weird. Maybe the relatives in Caborca ran out of clean clothes."

CHAPTER 14

AT APPROXIMATELY 9:30PM, Morales and his two compatriots, along with Rusty Powell, who was doubled over in the rear of the van, pulled into Santa Ana, Mexico. A rural community of about 10,000 people, many of Pima Indian lineage, the town was a little over a hundred miles from Hermosillo. While the decision to drive all the way to Hermosillo that night was not yet made, the passengers needed a pit stop and something to eat.

Morales had stopped there many times and often ate at Fernando's Restaurant & Bar. Surprisingly, they had excellent Sushi and that enticed him to make that their peeing and dining destination. No doubt owing to the foul weather, there were no cars in the lot next to establishment, giving Hernandez come concern that it might be closed. But there were lights on above the bar, and the sign out front was also illuminated. Manuel pulled the van into the small lot and turned off the ignition.

This time, Rico's attempt to use his smartphone was successful. Rusty could make out most of what he was saying, although it was difficult, given the speed of the conversation. It seemed evident that Morales must have been checking in with his superiors in Hermosillo. He kept referring to the person on the other end of the call as Domingo. They were debating such issues as their expected arrival time in Hermosillo, the amount of funds in the cardboard box, and the options available in dealing with their hostage.

"He is hurt pretty bad in the leg", Morales said to Domingo. "But he will be worth a lot of money, so we should keep him alive." Rusty could more or less make out what was said and although the future was certainly not a pretty picture, it might well be that he could stay alive; if not indefinitely, at least for a while.

The phone conversation lasted a few more minutes. Finally, Rico addressed the entourage. Manuel and I will go in and do what we need to do. Jose, you stay with our guest for few minutes. Manuel will come back and eat in the van. "Gringo, you will stay in the van. We will bring you some food and a beer. Sorry, but if you need to pee, do it in your pants. We will not be long. Manuel and Rico left the vehicle and entered the restaurant.

It was at least 15 minutes before Manuel returned, holding a large brown paper bag and two bottles of Modelo beer. He climbed into the drivers seat, turned around and handed Jose some of the food and a bottle of the beer. Then Jose moved to the rear of the van and assisted Powell in handling a cheese sandwich and downing the Modelo. Jose then exited the vehicle to use the facilities and grab his own refreshments.

Rusty had peed in his uniform pants some time before he was required to change clothes. So his bladder was not an issue, even after finishing off the Modelo. His hands were tied, but he was able to negotiate both the sandwich and beer with Jose's willing and amiable assistance.

Another 20 minutes later and the van, along with its full complement of passengers, were underway. The restaurant was only one short block away from Mexico 15. Once they were on the road, they headed south. The pelting rain and persistent wind continued to make driving difficult and quite a bit slower than Rico hoped for. Under those conditions it would be another two hours before they reached Hermosillo.

CHAPTER 15

A FEW MINUTES before midnight, the white Chevy van, replete with its complement of four passengers, pulled into a residential neighborhood and drove up to the garage door of a two-story stucco residence. The rain had tapered off somewhat, but the wind continued to howl. Rico, picking up the cardboard box, exited the vehicle, walked up to the front door of the house and knocked three times. After waiting half a minute or so, he rapped on the door another three times. This time, it opened a crack and a tall, slender woman peeked out to verify the person's identity. Then the door opened wide.

The attractive woman stepped away and Morales, signaling Manuel to join him, walked in. Seated on a large, floral-printed sofa were two men. The older and heavier of the two stood upon Rico's entrance, and gave him a hug. "My friend, you have had a very long day."

"We are very tired, Domingo, but we brought you some money, and also an extra gift. He should prove to be very valuable indeed."

Domingo acknowledged Manuel's presence, nodding an invitation to come in and sit down. Taking the box of money he asked Rico, "Where is your Border Patrol companion; in the van?"

"My friend Jose is with him", Rico said. "We had to disable him somewhat, and his left leg will need medical attention. Should we bring him in?"

Domingo turned to address the other man, quite a bit younger and muscular, still seated on the sofa. "Ramon, why don't you call your doctor friend and ask him to meet us here in the morning? In the meantime, Rico, have Jose bring him in. I don't want to keep him here, but for tonight it will be okay. Tomorrow, after we have the doctor treat his leg, we will take him to a safer, more secure location."

Ramon rose from the sofa, stretching his powerful 6'6" frame, and walked to the door, waiting for Domingo's directive to proceed. Rico waived to Jose, who opened the back door of the van and helped Powell climb out. Jose and Rusty were joined by another man, who escorted them into the house.

First addressing Ramon, Domingo then delivered his next set of orders. "Take him to the first bedroom at the head of the stairs, lay him down and tie him to the bed. Then lock the door from the outside with this key. When you come back down, give your doctor friend a call and ask him to be here around ten in the morning. Rico, you and Manuel go get some sleep. Come back at 9AM and we will decide what to do with your Border Patrol friend. Jose can leave or stay. It's up to him. There is another bedroom upstairs where, if he likes, he can get some sleep. I too am tired and want to go to bed."

All parties concerned went about their appointed rounds. Rico and Manuel left in the van. Both men lived in Hermosillo. Jose lived on a farm about twenty miles away. Ramon had one, and only one, responsibility; keeping Rusty under wraps.

Domingo Fuentes was a major player in Calimar, the largest drug trafficking cartel in the state of Sonora. The only individual above him on the mob's power ladder was Sancho Lopez. Cocaine was the principal export and moneymaker for the cartel. Marijuana and methamphetamine ran a close second and third in volume and revenue. As U.S. production of meth was being somewhat curtailed, the Mexican cartels were filling the void.

Fuentes was known throughout the Sonoran region of the country as a smart businessman, and a ruthless enforcer. If other cartels made the tactical misstep of encroaching on Calimar's geography, manpower or customer base, he would take whatever steps he deemed necessary to shut the door. In effect, Domingo was Sancho Lopez's enforcer and second in command. Lopez, a senior citizen of 83, although recognized as a financial genius, became more or less a figurehead in the business.

Rico doubted that Fuentes appreciated bringing a Border Patrol Agent to Hermosillo as a hostage. Kidnapping was generally not considered a desirable offshoot of the cartel's principal business; drug manufacturing and exportation. But Hernandez was hopeful that Fuentes would view the hostage as a quick and easy method of generating extra income for the organization.

Manuel dropped Rico at his home and drove the van to his apartment on the east side of the city.

CHAPTER 16

Day 2

THE RAIN AND wind subsided overnight throughout most of the region. Sunrise over West Tucson, Arizona was greeted by clear blue skies. It had been a sleepless night for Melinda. She repeatedly called the Nogales border station, speaking on most occasions with Agent Fred Cooley, who apologetically reported no progress in locating Powell and Childers since they disappeared almost 14 hours ago. It was now 8:30AM.

Cooley turned over his duty officer responsibilities when his shift ended at 6AM. Carroll Page left the station around midnight. There was very little he could do in support of Cooley, given the continuing foul weather and the inability to get a chopper in the air to conduct an effective search.

The clearing weather conditions enabled Chet Gorsky, the current agent in charge, to release the MD 660-N helicopter at 8:10AM. Airborne a few minutes later, the chopper headed north-northwest on the heading provided by Predator drone controller Ben Rosetti the previous afternoon. The break in the weather was somewhat unanticipated. NOAA's forecast was much more pessimistic, but the strong winds were helpful in moving the front more quickly through the area. Current reports indicated that additional squalls could pass through southern Arizona sometime that evening.

Agent Garrett Hayes, accompanied by Agent Rita Menendez, was the chopper pilot. Hayes was a former Navy helicopter rescue pilot, having served two tours in the Persian Gulf during the Iraq and Afghanistan wars. Assigned to the Enterprise Carrier Strike Group,

46

flying an SH-60F helicopter on sea rescue missions, Hayes was an excellent choice for this job.

Hayes headed for the Pena Blanca Lake area as a starting point. His instructions were to stay on the aforementioned flight path and report back to the station in half an hour. The sky was cloudless for the time being.

In addition to the chopper search, Sierra Vista released the Predator drone about the same time, and it was programmed to fly its normal east to west pattern just north of the border. Simon Booth was at the controls of the drone.

Agent Gorsky maintained ongoing contact with Booth, so that any sightings would be immediately relayed to Hayes in the chopper.

****

Melinda called Tanya Childers, who had also stayed in touch with the Nogales station throughout the night. "Come on over, Tanya; we need each other to get through this. I'm not doing too well. Didn't sleep a wink last night."

"Me neither", Tanya said. "But at least they finally got the chopper in the air. Let's pray they find our guys, or at least find a good trail that they can follow."

"Praying is an understatement", Melinda said. She added that Gorsky reported the drone being deployed as well. "They also agreed to send out a ground team if necessary. I don't think there's anything else we can ask them to do. Do you?"

"Not really. I think the helicopter is the best bet, because the crew can land and check the scene out if they see anything suspicious. The drone can just fly around up there and report back to its base. Then somebody has to go out there and that takes time. Maybe Randy and Gary took cover in some shelter to get out of the storm."

"True, but the weather's cleared. If they did take cover they should be back in the Jeep by now, and on their way back to the station."

Melinda needed to voice her thoughts in such a way as to help maintain a modicum of control over her emotions. With a wrinkled forehead and reddened eyelids, she offered a hopeful perspective on the immediate future. "We can sit here all day and let our minds conjure up all sorts of scenarios. Let's just keep in contact with Agent Gorsky. I'm confident that if the drone or the chopper has a positive sighting he'll let us know. That's really all we can do."

CHAPTER 16

PABLO SANTOS DEL RIO, a rather portly, but dignified man in his late fifties, was a licensed physician, attending to his many friends and their families in Hermosillo. Del Rio was Ramon's second cousin. More or less a general practitioner, he frequently reached beyond the limits of his formal medical training and rose to whatever challenges the situation might call for.

"This man's leg is broken, in fact, shattered, and needs to be surgically mended. If this is not attended to in short order, he will have permanent damage, and could lose the leg. I want to call an ambulance and have him taken to Hospital CIMA Hermosillo. It is an American-owned facility; they will be able to treat him more effectively than at Hospital San Jose."

Morales and Domingo Fuentes stood next to the bed where Powell was restrained, intently considering the advice of Dr. Del Rio, Ramon's family friend. Fuentes responded. "We cannot do this, Doctor. Too many questions would be asked of our detainee. We must find another solution."

"There is no other acceptable solution, señor. He either goes to a first rate hospital for the surgery, or he will be crippled and limping severely for the rest of his life. Is that the outcome you wish for this young man?"

Fuentes was not used to, nor fond of anyone giving him such an ultimatum. "Frankly, Dr. Del Rio, I do not give a damn what his outcome might be. It is of no consequence to me if he limps or wins a marathon. Do what you can for him today. We will worry about what happens with him tomorrow."

"Very well, Señor Fuentes. I have advised you of the consequences. Leave us please. I will do what I can for him, and that will be that."

Rusty was awake, but was given a sedative and was groggy at best. Del Rio first cleaned the wound thoroughly, stitched the entry and exit areas and secured a piece of bare wood to the back of the calf to stabilize the splintered tibia. He then injected morphine to help subdue the pain, but this would only be a short-term solution for the intense pain that lied ahead. After another injection, an antibiotic called doxycycline, was administered, to stave off infection, Del Rio left the room.

"Thank you, doctor, for coming this morning", Fuentes said, as he ushered Del Rio to the front door. If we can find the time to take our guest somewhere for further treatment, we will do so."

Shaking Fuentes' hand, Del Rio executed a slight nod of his head, intended to show his host some degree of respect. "Dear sir, if the bone is not repaired fairly soon, it will be too late. I have made him comfortable for the next few hours. Later today, he will be in severe pain. I have given Ramon some pills to administer when the patient clearly needs relief. Good day."

Rico joined his boss in the front sitting room, immediately following the physician's departure. "What now, Domingo? Do you agree that we notify the Border Patrol authorities, and let them know that the gringo is alive and in our hands?

"And what, my dear friend, do you suggest we demand for his eventual return?"

"This is clearly your decision. I am only suggesting that a substantial payment by the Americans for his return could be forthcoming. If, after we make our demands, they refuse to act accordingly within a reasonable amount of time, we dispose of this Agent Powell and that is that."

CHAPTER 17

THE PREDATOR DRONE cruised the area north and west of Nogales, in the same general direction as the CBP helicopter, piloted by Garrett Hayes. The weather, continuing to cooperate with the search efforts, was mostly sunny, with slightly cooler temperatures and less windy surface and airborne conditions. It was 9:50 in the morning.

Hayes and Menendez kept their eyes pealed on the Sonoran desert terrain, mixed with mountainous areas just south of the city of Sells, Arizona. The drone was on a more southern heading, closer and parallel to the border. Agent Menendez checked the map lying on her lap. Arizona route 86 was visible from the chopper and just north of their current location. Looking back down at the ground, a reflection off of some metal object immediately garnered her attention.

"Hey Garrett, check out the glare at 2 o'clock. See what I see?"

"Looks like there's something under that brush. Let's go down a little closer and take a look."

Hayes dropped the aircraft from 1,000 feet to just over 200 feet and slowed its speed to get a better view of the suspicious, seemingly metallic reflection. Menendez again broke her silence. "It's a vehicle! Might even be the Jeep. Let's go down."

Hayes wasted no time. In less than a minute the chopper touched down, about 100 yards east of the sighting and shut off the engine. Menendez called in to the border station and reported the information, including their map coordinates. The two agents then walked toward the shiny object.

"It's the jeep!" Hayes yelled. They ran to check it out. Moving some of the brush away to take a close look, Menendez turned to her partner with a look of horror on her face. Childers' body was curled up in the front passenger seat of the Jeep. Hayes lifted the last piece of sagebrush and got an eyeful of the corpse, covered in clotted brown blood. There were literally hundreds of pockmarks on his face and hands; an obvious sign of recent vulture activity. The noise of the approaching chopper had no doubt chased them away.

"God, it's Childers", Hayes said, finding it difficult to handle the sight of his fellow agent rotting in the desert sun. "Radio the station and give them the lousy news. Any sign of Powell?"

Menendez scanned the general vicinity of the Jeep. The rain and wind of the previous day and night completely wiped out any signs of vehicle or foot traffic in the area. "Nothing visible Garrett. I'll call in." She ran back to the chopper and used the radio to reach the Nogales Station. Hayes moved in for a closer look. Childers' weapon was obviously confiscated. The chest wound appeared to be all that was needed to put him down.

"Agent Menendez reporting in. We located the Jeep. Agent Childers is dead. Looks like a gunshot wound to the chest was the cause of death. No sign of Agent Powell. Over."

"Cruise the area for another half hour to see if there are any signs of Powell." It was Chet Gorsky, who took the call. "Then get your butts back here. We'll decide on next steps when you bring the chopper in. Be sure and mark your location down to the anthill. We'll come right back with a heavy-duty vehicle to bring in Childers and the Jeep. Hope you haven't contaminated the scene. Over."

"Copy; no sir, other than a few pieces of sagebrush, we haven't touched a thing. See you in a bit. Menendez over and out."

CHAPTER 18

AFTER A QUICK circular trip around a few miles of adjacent desert, Hayes brought the chopper back to the station. He and Menendez reported in to Gorsky, who was already finalizing the order to dispatch a tow truck to pick up the dead agent and the Jeep. Hayes handed him the vehicle's coordinates. "It's about a three hour drive with a heavy vehicle."

Gorsky had second thoughts. Another option was to radio the Tucson Sector station and request a Sikorsky UH-60 Black Hawk helicopter, capable of hauling the jeep on a sling. If it was immediately available, that would be the better choice. He phoned Tucson. Fortunately, it was already fueled and on the pad, ready for deployment. Gorsky needed senior level approval for its release to Nogales. He got it without hesitation from the Section Operations Officer (OPS) in charge.

After relaying the location coordinates of the Jeep and its deceased passenger, Gorsky signed off. The Black Hawk was released and lifted off at 11:10AM. The Customs and Border Protection station chief in Tucson ordered the vehicle and its cargo back to Tucson, where it was to be held for criminal investigation by the FBI.

"Tell me what you think about what you saw", Gorsky asked Hayes and Menendez, who sat with him in the Nogales station duty officer's cubicle.

Menendez was first to respond. "Well, the Jeep was intact; no apparent damage to the chassis, wheels, passenger compartment, or anything else. Agent Childers was sort of curled up in the front passenger seat; shot in the left chest. There were no weapons in the vehicle. That's about it."

"What she said", Hayes added. "It looked to me like the Jeep was purposely covered up with desert brush, branches and the like to avoid it being spotted from the air. My guess is that Rusty Powell was taken alive by the bad guys, or he too would have been killed and left behind."

"Looks like this thing is out of our hands for now", Gorsky said. "Tucson will take over, once the Black Hawk gets back with the cargo. Garrett, you need to file a written report on this thing. The FBI and ICE will debrief you guys in any case, but let's get it on the record. Okay?"

"No problem", Hayes said. "Agent Menendez is a better writer than me, so if it's okay with you, she'll be the scribe. What do we say or do about Rusty Powell?"

"In your report, just say what you told me. There was no sign of him, right? The FBI no doubt will take it from there. That's all, guys. Good job. Go get something to eat, if your stomachs can handle it. It sure couldn't have been a pleasant scene."

Both Hayes and Menendez nodded their affirmation and departed to get cleaned up and take a needed break.

Gorsky called Sierra Vista and reported to the Predator operator on duty that the Jeep was found.

He also phoned his immediate superior, Division Chief Roland Escobar, based at the Tucson CBP office, for guidance on the proper way to notify Tanya Childers of her husband's death. Almost as difficult would be calling Melinda Powell to report Rusty's disappearance, with not a single clue for further investigation. Escobar was out for lunch, and expected to return within the hour. Gorsky decided to break for lunch as well. Leaving a voicemail for Escobar to return the call, he headed for the nearest Subway, close by on Mariposa Road.

Walking through the door of the restaurant, Gorsky noticed Hayes and Menendez at one of the tables having their lunch. He smiled and nodded, walking directly to the sandwich preparation line to order his sub. His cell phone signaled an incoming call. It was an admin assistant at Tucson headquarters, letting him know that the Blackhawk was in the air and within a few minutes of the Jeep's location.

"Let me know when the bird gets back to your station.

The caller acknowledged his request.

CHAPTER 19

"WE NEED TO find another place for our friend the Border Patrol Agent", Domingo said, as he and Ramon looked in on Rusty, partially awake, but heavily medicated. "Do you have any ideas?" Ramon, although one of the Calimar cartel's most feared strongmen, was also a clever and resourceful member of Domingo's inner circle.

They left the bedroom and walked to the other end of the hallway.

"I have a small apartment on Pasco de la Cascada. My girlfriend Alicia often stays there when she comes to Hermosillo. It is quiet and the only entrance is very secure. I could take him there, but he will need to be guarded; no?"

"Excellent idea. Call Diego Molina and tell him that he will be staying there with our guest. Hopefully, it will only be for a few days. Does the place have two bedrooms, or will Molina have to sleep on the couch?"

"It has two bedrooms", Ramon said. "But I am not sure if Diego is around. I will call him to make sure. If he isn't, I can go and stay there, if it is only a couple of days. Mariana won't care." Mariana, Ramon's wife of twenty years, was aware, as many Mexican spouses were, that her husband had a younger female companion on the side.

"Very well", Domingo said. "I am leaving this matter in your hands. And please keep Rico informed on our guest's whereabouts and condition. He will have to deliver him back to the Border Patrol if things go as planned. So get going. I would like this matter attended to sometime this afternoon."

"No problem, Domingo. Consider it done. I will have the gringo out of here before dinnertime. If necessary, I would like to have your permission to allow Del Rio to attend to his injured leg if it becomes a bigger problem."

"You have my permission, but under no circumstances can he be taken to the hospital. It is much too risky. If the man becomes too unruly, we will have to deal with him in a different manner."

Ramon considered this to be his marching orders. If Rusty became difficult to handle, he would be eliminated, with no further discussion. The two men returned to the parlor, as Hernandez walked in and met them for a late lunch. Rico was looking for a decision from Ramon on the matter of Powell's future. He was aware, however, that his boss would need tacit, but explicit, approval from Sancho Lopez, to finalize the matter.

"I am thinking that $10 million would be a reasonable sum for the U.S. to pay for the return of their federal agent. It is a small price to pay, and they would avoid having to report to their people that another border patrol agent was killed in the line of duty." Morales had given the subject a fair amount of thought during a sleepless night at home. This seemed to be a number that both Fuentes and Lopez would accept.

Domingo wasn't so sure. "I am okay with this number, but Sancho is a very cautious man. To him, this man's life is less important than keeping our affairs away from Mexican public scrutiny and under the American FBI's radar. But I will present the case to him tonight. If he agrees, we will need to decide who makes the contact with the feds and what conditions we propose for the exchange. In the meantime, Ramon is removing the man from my home and taking him to his apartment. He will have Diego Molina guard him until we decide on his disposition."

CHAPTER 20

ROLAND ESCOBAR HAD Richard Martinez on the line, with the speakerphone turned on.

"Richard, we've got DHS approval to get your people involved in a missing Border Patrol Agent situation. His partner was shot and killed while the guys were on a patrol, chasing some bad guys. It's only a day-old situation, but we're almost certain this is drug related, so we might even need some DEA involvement."

"Kind of early to bring in all the horses, Roland", Martinez said. "Don't you think we should wait another couple of days.? If it's an abduction, you might hear from the bad guys for some ransom money."

Richard Martinez, the Special Agent In Charge of the FBI's Phoenix Region, inclusive of Tucson and surrounding areas, had recently been assigned to head up the operation after five years in the FBI's Columbia, South Carolina office. It was there that Martinez gained Bureau fame, heading up a multi-discipline federal team in a much publicized terror attack. The commanding general at the Parris Island Marine Recruit Training Depot was kidnapped by radical Islamists and several high-profile murders were connected to the case. Martinez's dogged pursuit of the three terrorists ended up with their deaths on a vessel bound for the Middle East. The general survived the ordeal. Martinez garnered substantial recognition in the process.

The son of a native Mexican father and U.S.-born mother, Richard, 47, was born in Monterrey, but relocated to Gallop, New Mexico with his parents at age ten, where his father became a police officer. A graduate of the University of Texas El Paso, Martinez earned his law degree at Tulane after a stint in the Marine Corps. He joined the FBI two years later. A ten-year marriage ended when his wife died of breast cancer. There were no children.

A large and muscular man, at 6'4" and 230 pounds, he was known for his bulldog-like tenacity and contrasting easy-going mild personality. He made friends easily; once he made one, it was for life.

Escobar was determined to get the wheels turning to find his missing agent. "Fair enough, Richard. But DHS concurs that the wheels should start turning, or we will likely lose another fine young Border Patrol Agent. The cartel that works out of Hermosillo has been active as hell of late. It's a gut feeling, but we think they might be involved."

"In that case", Martinez said, "your agent is probably either dead already or will soon be eliminated. Isn't that the way they usually work?"

"Yeah, usually. But I repeat the gut feel on this one. If they were going to kill Powell, why didn't they do it on the spot? His partner, Childers, was shot in the chest and left to rot in the desert. Looks like they might see Powell as a potential source of U.S. ransom funds."

Martinez was skeptical. "But that's not the cartels' MOS, Roland. You know that. Their money is in the powder and pot. Anyway, if your guys at DHS headquarters want to move on this, we're in. You know Sally Henkel?"

"Sure do. But I wanted to clear this with you before moving ahead down here. How do you want to handle this?"

"Sit tight Roland. I'll give Sally a call, give her a quick rundown and I definitely will ask her to give you a call. I think she's just back from vacation, so she can very likely jump on this as quick as you like. Okay?"

"Sounds good Richard. But I sure would like you to stay on top of this one."

"I will do that, my friend. But don't sell Sally short. She's got a great nose for sniffing out the bad guys, as well as an excellent team of agents. And you might like to know that she went through law school with Bennett Frost. He's still in Mexico City and might be an excellent resource for us, once we get a better handle on the situation. And I can assure you that the Bureau will put as many resources on the case as we need."

CHAPTER 21

THE NEXT ITEM on Escobar's to-do list was the toughest assignment he would face that day, or any day in the foreseeable future. Wrapping up his conversation with Martinez, he departed his office and headed for Tanya Childers' home. It was a few minutes before 6PM, when he parked his vehicle in front of the Childers residence.

Hearing the engine sound coming from the driveway, Tanya peaked out of the living room window. Her heart sank. The sight of a Border Patrol Agent she didn't recognize shot bolts of fear through her already worn out physical being. She walked on shapely, but shaking legs to the front door. Before Escobar could ring the bell or knock, Tanya opened it and stared lifelessly at her visitor's tanned and weather worn face. She quickly noticed Escobar's nametag. He spoke first.

"Mrs. Childers, I am Agent Roland Escobar, Division Chief in Charge of Tucson Sector. May I come in?"

Tanya, without saying a word, nodded approval and stepped aside as Escobar entered the foyer of the home, removing his cap. She closed the front door.

"Please sit down, Mr. Escobar", she said, pointing to a pair of casual chairs in the nearby living room."

"Yes, thank you." He walked over to one of the chairs and sat down. "Mrs. Childers, you may want to be seated as well." After Tanya took her seat in the matching chair, Escobar continued. "May I call you Tanya, Mrs. Childers?"

She nodded her approval. Escobar went on. "I am so very sorry to bring you this news, Tanya. Gary was found dead early this morning, in the desert near Arivaca, sitting in the Jeep he was sharing with Agent

Powell. It appeared that he died from a gunshot wound in his chest. Agent Powell was not present."

Tanya was unable to lift her head from her trembling hands, or look up in Escobar's direction, as he finished delivering the horrid message. "Thank you for coming. I hope that Rusty Powell has somehow escaped unharmed. She lifted her head. Would you be so kind as to leave now? I need to be alone to think about what I have to do next." She then broke into tears, and found it difficult to stand without losing her balance.

"Certainly. I fully understand. I also want you to know two things. First; we will find and bring to justice the creeps that committed this crime. Secondly, all of us in the U.S. Border Patrol will do whatever we can for you in the days and weeks ahead." He extended his card to Tanya as they walked to the front door.

Tanya was unable to speak. She nodded her thanks for the offer to help and watched Escobar exit the house and walk to his car. She then squatted down on the floor where she stood, looked up at the ceiling, let out a scream, and wept.

Escobar checked in with his office for messages. There were none. Starting his Border Patrol sport utility, Escobar headed in the direction of West Tucson, a short, less than ten-minute drive. The next stop was a visit to Melinda Powell. He decided not to call in advance, counting on Melinda being at home. Up to now, Melinda had received no additional information on the whereabouts of her husband since he failed to return from the tracking mission with Gary Childers.

Finishing the leftover half of a Domino's pizza, Melinda picked up her cellphone as it signaled an incoming call. The caller's voice was familiar, although she was sobbing and incoherent. "Tanya, is that you? What's wrong? Tanya?"

As Melinda labored to get Tanya to control her crying and regain a modicum of control, the doorbell rang. Walking to the door while staying on the line with Tanya, she looked through the peephole. She didn't recognize the visitor, but the Border Patrol vehicle in the driveway gave the identity away. "Tanya, there's someone here from the Border Patrol. I will call you back in a few minutes."

"His name is Escobar", Tanya said, trying to regain some composure.

"Gary is dead. Rusty is gone. They don't know where he is." She began to lose control again.

Opening the door for Escobar, she was reluctant to end the call, but didn't have much choice. "Tanya, I will call you back as soon as he leaves. Okay?" There was no answer. Tanya disconnected. The dial tone returned.

Escobar spoke first. "Mrs. Powell, sorry to barge in on you. My name is Roland Escobar, Chief Patrol Agent for the Tucson Sector."

"I know, Mr. Escobar. I was on the phone with Tanya Childers when you came to the door. Please come in."

Melinda let her guest into the dining room, where she asked him to sit down and offered him a cup of coffee. He thanked her but passed on the coffee. "I won't take much of your time, Mrs. Powell. But…."

"I know what you're going to say. Tanya just told me. I just want to know what the government plans to do about Rusty." Tears began streaming down her cheeks as she continued. "Who's looking for him? He will die out there in the desert if you don't find him very soon."

"Mrs. Powell, is it okay to call you Melinda?" She nodded. "I assure you that every resource at our disposal will be deployed to find your husband. We have access to every branch of the Department of Homeland Security, as well as the FBI. We'll find him. In the meantime, is there anything we can do; anything you need?"

"There are only two things you can do. First, find Rusty. Don't worry about me. If you bring him back alive, that's all I need. And second, give all the help you can to Tanya Childers. She's going to need it. They hadn't been married very long. And her family isn't nearby."

Escobar acknowledged the request and thanked Melinda for her time. It was obvious that she no longer wished to continue the conversation. "We'll keep you in the loop on any progress we make in the search. And please, don't hesitate to call me if there is anything we can do to help you get through this."

They walked to the door. Escobar extended his hand and Melinda shook it. "Thank you for coming. I know it wasn't easy. Find Rusty. That's all."

CHAPTER 21

DAY 3

RAMON FOUND DIEGO Molina in Mexico City and requested that he promptly return to Hermosillo. The next morning, they met at Domingo Fuentes' home, picked up Rusty, who was now more or less awake, but securely restrained, and moved him to Ramon's apartment. Molina reluctantly agreed to remain there until a decision was made regarding Powell's future.

Rico once again presented his case to Fuentes with respect to a ransom demand. Breaking with conventional cartel practice was not a decision to be made lightly. But Fuentes wanted to rid his organization of a captive U.S. law enforcement officer. He was disappointed that Morales hadn't done away with Powell in the desert. He now was obliged to contact Sancho Lopez, his superior, and request his approval for the ransom demand. He decided to pay Lopez, who was presently in Guaymas on business, a personal visit.

The Sonoran beach town was about a ninety-minute drive from Hermosillo. Lopez typically drove himself, using his BMW 740i. This trip was no exception. One of his cocaine suppliers had a home in Guaymas. Lopez's cartel currently owed the supplier something over $1.8 million. Lopez had a cashiers check for that amount that he decided to deliver in person.

Fuentes had a mistress in Guaymas. He had not had the pleasure of her company for several months, so the visit to see Lopez would have a pleasurable side to it as well. He told his wife that he would return the following evening, and had Rico do the driving. Rico would be useful, should Lopez have any issues with the ransom decision. They departed at noon driving south on Mexico 15, from Hermosillo to Guaymas. Fuentes called Lopez's office assistant and secured an appointment for 3PM at the San Carlos Plaza Resort in San Carlos, a beach town nearby.

Sancho Lopez, although in his 80's, remained one of the most powerful and ruthless men in Mexico, and had maintained a soft spot for Domingo Fuentes. Both had fought their way up and through the drug production and distribution network in the Sonoran area of the country. They were responsible, collectively, for the deaths of more than two hundred competing cartel operatives, as well as numerous innocent bystanders. The Calimar cartel was presently operating at its peak; a $600 million enterprise. A decade earlier, it decimated the competing operations of three other entities. Its nearest competitor of any substance was located in Tijuana and was half Calimar's size. Running most of its smuggled narcotics up through the Nogales-Tucson corridor, its distribution reached fully a third of the western United States, from Texas to the California coast, and north to Colorado, Montana and Idaho.

Fuentes made a stop at his mistress's apartment, where he organized their dinner and overnight plans, before heading for San Carlos. Morales was asked to remain in the car. Twenty minutes later they were back on the road.

"Sancho, I am here to support Rico's idea", Fuentes said, as he and Sancho sipped coffees in the resort's bar by the pool. The location was chosen to separate the men from any tourists or hotel staff, at least for the time being. "It's not the money; he recommends $10 million. To me, it is a good test. We have never tried such an approach."

Lopez sensed that Fuentes had more to add to his diatribe, but decided to interrupt. "Do we need such a test, my friend? What will it prove? To me, it is not worth of risk of having the U.S. authorities, especially the FBI, breathing down our necks. Unless you can figure out a way to isolate us from direct involvement, it is not, in my opinion, a good thing to do. The $10 million would be a nice little bonus, but I am not sold. Tell me more."

Morales chimed in before his boss had the opportunity to respond.

"Señor Lopez, you make an excellent point. My idea, however, is one that will totally remove the Calimar organization from any association with the ransom offer." He went on to describe his proposed methodology for contacting the U.S. government and implementing the exchange of Powell for the ransom funds.

Fuentes added his support for the plan. "Morales has thought this through, Sancho. You must admit, putting $10 million in the Calimar coffers is very appealing. And requiring very little effort on our part."

Lopez pondered Rico and Domingo's defense of the idea. While not totally comfortable with the proposal, he was willing to go along. "Okay, if you believe our interests will be protected, then proceed. But I assure both of you that if this thing explodes in our faces you will have to pay the price. And the price may be a high one, so pray that all goes well. If you have any doubts at all before pushing the button, then my advice is to put this border patrol person down. No one will ever know of his fate. End of story."

Fuentes knew full well that his boss was, as usual, giving him sound advice. The option to do away with Powell was still on the table.

Chapter 22

SALLY HENKEL WRAPPED up a busy afternoon, filling out a deluge of reports on various cases yet to be solved. Drug lord fugitives were a dime a dozen, and missing person reports, also plentiful, needed diligent follow-up. Sally was a stickler for neatness in report preparation. As much as she disliked the administrative detail work, if it was headed to Phoenix or Washington, it was done right.

Henkel, Assistant Special Agent in Charge of the Tucson office, was a ten-year FBI veteran. Thirty-eight and a divorced single mom with a fifteen-year old daughter, Henkel was law school trained and joined the Bureau after a brief career with a Cleveland law firm. Born and raised in Akron, she earned both her undergraduate and law degrees at Ohio State. Smart, tough and a physically fit attractive brunette with striking green eyes, Henkel was destined for bigger things.

At 5:20PM, close to finishing the paperwork, Sally's cell phone, set to play an uplifting tune, signaled an incoming call. "This is Special Agent Sally Ann Henkel."

"Sally, it's Richard. How was your day?" Martinez made a concerted effort to check in with his location heads on a daily basis.

"Busy, boss. Not sure I accomplished a hell of a lot in catching the bad guys, but not a bad day overall. What's up?"

"Need you to pay a visit to Roland Escobar, the Chief Honcho for the Tucson Border Patrol Sector. We met yesterday, via conference call, regarding a missing agent and apparent homicide. Agent Randall Powell, who works out of Nogales, went off the grid, the day before yesterday. Not a good story. His partner for the day, Gary Childers, was found dead in their patrol jeep; a gunshot wound to the chest. Apparently they were chasing down a renegade van with New Mexico plates, allegedly moving drugs across the desert. A chopper was sent out from Nogales and spotted their Jeep somewhere near Arivaca, with Childers dead in the front seat. A Black Hawk later airlifted the vehicle and corpse back to Tucson."

"Sounds like a big-time bad day. Is Escobar expecting my call tonight?"

"If I were you I'd give him a buzz right now and set something up for first thing tomorrow, if you've got time. Frankly, I'd put a high priority on this. Go meet with him, open a case file and get it going. We'll probably need some help from our people in Mexico. The handwriting on the wall points to an abduction of a federal law enforcement officer, possibly by one of the cartels. Escobar is as surprised as I am that Powell wasn't found sitting next to Childers with a bullet in him as well. Go figure."

"I'm on it Richard. Once I meet with Escobar I'll check in. You need to let me know how involved you want to be in this thing."

"We'll talk after you have the meeting and are ready to recommend next steps.."

Henkel dialed the CBP Field Operations Office, located on Oracle Road. Escobar was in his office. An administrator working the duty desk transferred the call to him. "Roland Escobar speaking"

"This is Special Agent Sally Ann Henkel calling. Arthur Martinez called from Phoenix and briefed me topline on the Agent murder and suspected abduction. I'd appreciate a get-together tomorrow morning to move this case along. Will you be available?"

"I've got a meeting at 8AM; shouldn't last more than an hour. We could meet this evening, if that works for you. If not, how about 9:30?"

"I'd like to do it sooner rather than later, but unfortunately my ex-husband is out of town and my daughter needs a ride home from her band rehearsal. Anyway, you're booked earlier, so 9:30 in the morning will have to do."

Sally emailed her boss and let Martinez know that the meeting was set for the next morning. She lived on the east side of Tucson, and her

14-year old daughter Meredith was waiting for her mom to fetch her at the Alice Vail Middle School. August marching band practice has just ended. She was sitting on a bench near the football field when Sally arrived. "Let's go, princess. I'm hungry."

CHAPTER 23

DOMINGO FUENTES WASTED no time finalizing his decision to move ahead with the ransom demand. The next morning, after an evening of fine dining and heavy, satisfying sex, he headed back to Hermosillo, with Morales at his side. Fuentes decided to drive. The rain, having subsided for a day and a half, began to pummel the BMW, as they motored along Mexico Highway 15.

"We will ransom our wounded agent, and I want to get it done as quickly as possible." Fuentes, as usual, sounded self-assured and emphatic in delivering the order to his lieutenant. "Ten million is as good a number as any. Whatever the amount, I do not think the feds will hesitate for a moment to pay it. The challenge will be to pull off the exchange. You need to give this careful thought. And this must be your number one priority. Understand?"

Rico knew his place. When the underboss issued a command, there was no avenue for disagreement. "Yes, Domingo. I have some ideas already, but need to finalize the plan. Give me until tonight. I will call you with the proposed set of actions."

"Tonight; no later. Let's get this done. I have other, more important business matters on my mind."

On their way back to Fuentes' home, they stopped at Ramon's "guest apartment" on Paseo de la Cascada to check on their $10 million captive federal agent. They knocked on the front door. "It's Rico. Open up!" At first, no answer, but after a second round of pounding, Diego Molina woke up from his nap and let them in. He immediately nodded respectfully to Fuentes, as the two men walked in.

They walked to the bedroom, where Powell remained firmly tied down and gagged. His eyes were wide open as his captors checked on his overall condition. His left leg, still tightly bandaged with the tourniquet applied by Dr. Del Rio, filled Rusty's facial expression with the look of agonizing pain.

"He looks good", Domingo said. Keep him healthy, with food and water. I hope that he will be out of here very soon. In the meantime, Molina, I am counting on you to treat him well. I will make sure there is a nice bonus for you if you do." Fuentes then motioned to Morales that he was ready to go. "I want to hear your plan by 8PM tonight. In the morning we will get word to the feds. Understood?" Rico nodded and opened the door for his boss, as they departed the flat to finish the fifteen-minute drive to Domingo's home. It was a few minutes before noon.

****

Morales arrived at the Fuentes home a little after 7PM. Domingo had not yet eaten. His dinner was usually served around nine. No longer cooking for her husband and his frequent guests, their housekeeper of twenty years was charged with the responsibility, which she enjoyed. "Stay for dinner, my friend", Fuentes said. "Anita is a wonderful cook. No matter what she serves, it will be superb."

"Many thanks, Domingo. The invitation is greatly appreciated, but I have another engagement. However, please allow me to share my plan for the ransom of the Border Patrol agent. If you approve, we can implement it as soon as you like. The wheels are very easily set in motion."

"So, let's hear it. In any case, I must insist that Lopez and I have nothing to do with it.. Under no circumstances can the organization be associated with the transaction. You certainly can understand this."

"That is not a problem, Domingo. The caller will certainly use a fictitious name, we will employ untraceable vehicles, and the exchange will be made in a remote location. You and Sancho do not need to worry." Rico then explained, in detail, how the ransom would be communicated and the method of Powell's return would be handled, on the assumption that the ransom would be paid. He also proposed the specific manner of the agent's disposal, should the feds refuse.

Bringing an end to his comments, Rico was emphatic with regard to the eventual outcome. "There will be no loose ends, Domingo. I am confident that the American government will pay the ransom. If I am wrong, the matter will be concluded with minimal effort."

"You will have my decision tomorrow", Fuentes said, as he walked Morales to the door.

CHAPTER 24

DAY 4

SALLY HENKEL WAS a few minutes early for her meeting with Escobar. He was a few minutes late. At 9:40AM they met in the CBP conference room. They were alone. Henkel used her iPad to take notes.

Escobar briefed the FBI agent on the available facts, as presented to him, of the incident resulting in Childers' death and Powell's disappearance. Henkel decided to listen and take down the salient points before beginning a barrage of questions.

Escobar interrupted himself about five minutes into the meeting. "By the way, Special Agent Henkel, you're invited to the informal press briefing I have scheduled for 11PM this morning. I didn't mention this to you yesterday afternoon, because the decision wasn't made to have it until later in the evening."

Henkel was thrown off guard by the news. "I have some concerns about this happening today, but I assume it's too late to delay it. What motivated you and the CBP to want this briefing so soon?"

"That's easy; there was a leak from someone here in the Sector office. The media was on it like flies on flypaper. I would think you might agree that it will be better to deal with the press now, and head off any misinformation that permeates the airwaves and alarms the community. We have a dead Border Patrol Agent lying in the morgue, and another one missing, who might also be dead or missing at the hands of the drug traffickers. I simply want to tell what we know and what we don't know, with a commitment to deliver more when we have more to give."

"Understood. I won't be joining you for obvious reasons. Richard Martinez, my boss, who's based in Phoenix, will need to be informed that this briefing is happening this morning. He will not want to be seeing this on TV without a heads-up ahead of time. I suggest we call him now."

"Fair enough", Escobar said. "Go ahead and make the call."

Henkel dialed Martinez's direct line at the office, but only managed to get his voicemail. She then attempted his cellphone. He answered on the second ring. "Hi Sally, how was your meeting with the Border Patrol? It certainly was quick."

"It's not over, by the a long shot, Richard. I'm with Escobar in the CBP conference room. I'm putting you on the speakerphone. He can take it from here."

"Mr. Martinez, this is Roland Escobar. Sorry to drop in on your day like this, but Special Agent Henkel wanted me to let you know that we have an informal press briefing at eleven today. The word leaked out yesterday regarding Agent Childers' death and Powell's disappearance. We need to make sure the word gets out in a controlled, reasonably accurate way. The Arizona media is more or less used to reporting border violence, but this time there are two reportable events, not just one. We obviously don't want anything to get out onto the airwaves that might endanger Powell's life, assuming he's still alive."

"Got the picture", Martinez said. "Why don't you guys finish your meeting? Agent Henkel can catch up with me later. And at some point in the near future I'll be heading down to double team with her on this case. Looking forward to meeting you. Catch up with you later."

Sally Henkel wrapped up the conversation with Martinez. For the next half hour, Escobar provided a reasonably thorough background briefing on the Powell/Childers incident. With less than a half hour to go before the scheduled media briefing, Henkel made her questioning opportunity short and sweet.

"What do we know about the vehicle the agents were pursuing? I understand it was a non-descript van with New Mexico plates."

"That's about all we know as well. For some reason, quite possibly their location, our communication with the agents was non-existent for some time. When they didn't report back that evening we were more or less hogtied because of the lousy weather; couldn't get a chopper up on a search detail, and the Predator drone was grounded as well. A drone took some pictures earlier that day. They may show the actual plate detail. I should have them in hand later today."

"How are the wives taking things? Any idea?"

"I personally visited both of them yesterday. They're handling it, but what can you expect? These spouses are totally sensitized to the reality of being married to Border Patrol federal agents. But let's face it; when it happens it's a major blow. For Tanya Childers it's over. The grief is big time. But at least there's a degree of closure for her and the rest of the family. For Melinda Powell, it's a whole different ballgame. You guys work kidnappings every day. You know the drill."

****

Tanya Childers entered the Pima County Medical Examiner's office a few minutes after nine in the morning. Her husband's body was brought there by the Tucson Border Patrol Sector's personnel office the night before. Tanya needed to formally identify and take possession of the remains, however, Arizona state law required that an autopsy be done in case of a suspected homicide. She signed a few papers required of the decease's next of kin, and was advised that the autopsy would be performed the following day. Once the procedure was completed, a funeral home had been employed to secure the remains and conduct the cremation.

The Childers' family attorney joined Tanya there at her request, primarily to protect her interests and those of her fallen spouse. The entire meeting was concluded in less than an hour.

Gary's parents were on their way from Sacramento to Tucson to see their son for the last time and be with their daughter-in-law. They would be able to view the body later that afternoon. Tanya's mother was due to arrive the next day. Her father was in Japan on business, and would not be able to get there for several days.

Childers' death in the line of duty was now public information. The print and electronic media met first with Roland Escobar at the Sector office. The more or less informal press conference was held at 11AM and was attended by reporters from the Arizona Daily Star, the major TV and radio stations, and The Arizona Reporter website.

Tanya was advised the night before that late the next morning the media would have the story of her husband's death. Escobar was reluctant to let the story out before her parents were there to be at her side. But the information had leaked to one of the stations, KVOA, by an unidentified individual in the Tucson Sector office. This led Escobar to reluctantly schedule the press briefing. He was tempted to call a meeting of Sector employees and sharply condemn the inclination of anyone to go the press without explicit orders to do so.

In virtually every case, any communications with the media on Border Patrol matters were handled by public information officers located at each Sector office. In a number of sensitive cases, the matter was bumped up to CBP press relations or all the way to the Department of Homeland Security headquarters in Washington for eventual disposition. For Tucson, the public information officer was Jordan Poole, who contacted the various media people invited to the briefing. In this particular case however, Roland Escobar ran the session.

Lauren Fowler, the KVOA reporter, led off with the first question, asking for the details surrounding the death. "Agent Childers was shot and killed by an unknown assailant", Escobar said. "He and his partner, Agent Randall Powell, were on patrol, tracking a vehicle suspected of transporting illegal drugs across the border. Agent Powell is missing."

The next question, asked by a young male reporter from the Arizona Daily Star, pursued the aspect of Powell's disappearance. "So, are you saying that the other agent was kidnapped?"

Escobar was cautious about providing a definitive answer. "At present, there is no way we can come to that conclusion. An investigation is being launched into both the murder of Agent Childers, and Powell's disappearance. There are no apparent clues that might provide any leads. We have video that was taken by a Predator drone. It contains visual identification of the vehicle pursued by the agents. We will be turning this information over to the FBI as they begin their work on the case."

The ensuing barrage of questions was pointed toward the Border

Patrol's increasing number of agent deaths occurring along or near the border. Over the past two years, a total of ten killings were directly related to drug trafficking, with only two of them resulting in any arrests, and none of which had yet gone to trial. The Department of Homeland Security was taking increased criticism for its lack of success in dealing with the problem. Escobar adjourned the press conference a few minutes before noon.

CHAPTER 25

DOMINGO FUENTES NORMALLY was a calculating and cautious man. This situation, dealing with a kidnapped federal agent, was no exception. At the same time, however, his confidence in Morales, clearly one of his most trusted lieutenants, had never been misplaced. So Domingo's inclination was to go along with Rico's plan. After lunch with his wife on the shaded patio by their backyard pool, he called Rico's cellphone. He answered after the second ring.

"It is Fuentes. So, my loyal and faithful friend, you will now have my decision. I will endorse your plan for the $10 million ransom payment. In any case, the decision to pay such an amount will likely be made by a high level individual in the government. Perhaps even the President. This will be a very high profile matter. Are you ready to move on the implementation?"

"Yes, Domingo. All I needed was your decision. We will begin the process tomorrow morning. The sooner we get the agent out of our hair, the better. However, it will probably be a few days before the U.S. makes a decision and organizes the exchange at their end. I will keep you informed of our progress. You will no doubt want to let Sancho Lopez know when the issue has been resolved."

"By all means, Rico. And at any point that you see things going in the wrong direction, I am counting on you to deal with it in a swift, final manner. Do you understand?"

"Completely, Domingo. Nothing will go wrong. I will see you soon. Goodbye."

Chapter 26

Rico's plan was relatively simple, and was now being set in motion. Using an untraceable cellphone, he placed a call to the Washington office of the U.S. Department of Homeland Security. When connected with a senior level official, he would offer Agent Powell's release in exchange for $10 million dollars, deposited in a numbered HSBC Zurich private bank account, used by the cartel. With confirmation of the deposit, Powell, alive and well, would be delivered to a predetermined location in Nogales, Mexico.

The drop-off site was the parking lot of the Banamex (HSBC) bank office in that town. A friend of Rico's was the branch manager, who would see that Powell was safely transported to the Mexico side of the border station at Nogales, Arizona. He would then be able to walk, unhindered, to the U.S. side, where a pre-assigned Customs & Border Protection official would meet him. If Powell's left leg made it impractical for him to walk unaided, a taxi would be employed to deliver him to the border station.

Fuentes was somewhat skeptical of the notion that the U.S. Government would be amenable to delivering the funds without any absolute guarantee that Agent Powell would be freed. Morales believed that there was very little risk associated with the demand. Should the U.S. refuse to accede to it, he and Fuentes concurred, with Sancho Lopez's agreement, that Powell would be killed.

Rico's call to DHS was transferred to the office of Andrew Barnes, the Assistant Secretary for International Affairs, and the department responsible for interaction with the Mexican government.

"Mr. Barnes office. May I help you?"

"I must speak directly to Mr. Barnes", Morales said, using as dignified a voice and tone as he could muster.

"Might I inquire as to the reason for the call?" The assistant filling in for the vacationing admin made every effort to sound as a vigilant gatekeeper for the Assistant Secretary.

"I have the life of one of your border patrol agents in my hands. Please tell Mr. Barnes that he will have the man's blood on his hands if he does not come to the phone."

"I will relay the message. One moment, please."

Less than a minute later, "This is Andrew Barnes speaking. May I have your name please?"

"My name is of no importance, Mr. Barnes. You may call me Mr. Lucky. We will have very brief and to-the-point conversations from this moment forward. A Border Patrol Agent is being held somewhere in Mexico. The only way your country will get him back alive is to follow my instructions. Do you understand?"

Barnes, an administrator, with virtually no experience in dealing with such matters, was reluctant to continue the conversation without law enforcement support. "Mr. Lucky, I regret that you happened to be transferred to this office. There is very little I can do to address your demands. You should contact the Border Patrol headquarters here in Washington, or the FBI. If you like, my assistant can provide you with those contact numbers. Mr. Lucky?"

There was no response at the other end. Rico wasted no time and wanted no further dialogue with that office. He quickly grabbed his iPad and went online to secure the appropriate information, jotting down both the CBP and FBI headquarters phone numbers.

Barnes needed to make a decision; do nothing and let the caller make the next moves, or contact the FBI and allow them to begin putting the pieces together. He opted for the latter. "Maggie, place a call to the Border Patrol office here in D.C. I'll talk to the most senior person you can find."

CHAPTER 27

RICHARD MARTINEZ SAT, pensively, in his office at the end of the day, pondering his next move with respect to the Border Patrol murder and disappearance. He had every confidence in Sally Ann Henkel, but this was shaping up to be a very high profile case, and one in which the Bureau was destined to play a major role.

Sally emailed him the notes she took during the session with Roland Escobar earlier in the day. There wasn't much there to provide law enforcement with a clear direction to pursue. The Childers autopsy would no doubt confirm the cause of death. The disappearance of Rusty Powell was an entirely different animal. If he had been killed at the same hands of those who murdered Childers, his body would have been close by. Drug smugglers were unlikely to drag a Border Patrol Agent into their vehicle, wait until they reached their destination, and then put him down. They might, however, decide to kill him later and dump him somewhere else in the Sonoran Desert.

Martinez was experienced enough to realize that a number of different scenarios might have been played out that night in the Sonoran desert. Powell could have run and hidden somewhere in the brush, or made it to a mountain hideaway until drug runners departed the scene. But that was highly unlikely. Agents typically wouldn't run and hide; secondly, by now Powell would have somehow surfaced. The Predator drone had been making passes over the area for the past three days; he would most likely have been spotted and rescued.

No; to the trained investigator the most likely scenario was an abduction. While kidnapping was normally not a drug cartel modus operandi, it certainly was not outside the realm of possibility. Martinez and Henkel would necessarily have to consider that as a viable direction to pursue.

Tomorrow Martinez would climb into his F-150 pickup and head to Tucson, pick up Sally Henkel and drive to the Nogales border station. From there he planned to climb into the station's helicopter and fly to the crime scene. Nothing like a good walk-around of the area to get a feel for what might have happened that hot, arid evening in the August desert.

Approaching 6:30, he dialed Henkel's cell phone number, while beginning to gather his gear and leave for home. A bachelor since his wife's death, he lived in a newly built townhome complex in southern Scottsdale. The complex was jam packed with singles; there was no shortage of women, but Martinez didn't have much time for socializing this time around. The Phoenix division was one of the busiest FBI operations in the nation. And, at his age, the chase no longer had much appeal.

"This is Sally Henkel." She saw his name pop up on caller ID. "Richard, hi. Glad you caught me before my Pilates class. I'm on my way there now. What's up?"

"Sure don't want to screw up your day tomorrow, Sally, but I thought it might be a good idea to get down to Nogales and sniff around. Okay?"

"Copy that, boss. I'll call Roland Escobar and see if he's available. What time will you get to Tucson?"

"I'm thinking like around 10'ish. And if Escobar isn't available, we can hit the border station on our own. Just ask him for the name of the contact at the station and we can take it from there. Make sense?"

"I like it. Not sure how he'll feel about us going down without him, but he seems like a reasonable guy. I'll get back to you straight away."

Martinez locked up the office and headed for his pickup. "Call me on the other phone, Sally. Whenever."

As soon as they ended the call, Henkel dialed Roland Escobar's cell phone number. She got his voicemail and left a message for him to call back at his earliest convenience. Then it was on to the fitness center for her 7PM Pilates class.

The local TV news ran the story. Martinez recorded the 11PM version on Channel 5 (KPHO) the CBS affiliate in Phoenix. It was a pickup from the CBS channel in Tucson. The emphasis was on the death of Childers. Minor mention was made of Powell's disappearance.

CHAPTER 28

DAY 5

THE PIMA COUNTY Medical Examiner called both Tanya Childers and Sally Henkel with the results of the autopsy. The report was issued too late to make the Tucson morning paper. There was nothing unusual in the report. It indicated that Gary Childers was a healthy 27-year old male specimen at the time of the shooting; the cause of death was a rifle shot to the mid-thorax, just to the left of the heart. Severe blood loss ensued.

Childers' remains were transported to the funeral home selected by Tanya, with the concurrence and support of Gary's parents. His will, which he deemed necessary when he joined the Border Patrol, called for cremation. Gary's mother was unhappy with this. Raised in a traditional Midwest family, a proper funeral and cemetery burial was the only appropriate method of honoring the deceased. But she had no say in the matter. Tanya was compelled to adhere to her husband's wishes.

There were no immediate plans for a memorial service. The Tucson Sector Border Patrol Station was planning a brief service some time within the coming week. As soon as the day and time were finalized Tanya was prepared to invite a number of family members and friends to attend.

****

Melinda Powell was advised by Roland Escobar that the FBI had been called into the investigation of Rusty's disappearance, and would be leading the effort to find and bring him home. That was a clear indication to her that the government believed he was kidnapped. He mentioned Sally Henkel as the primary Bureau contact and let her know that Henkel would be in touch within the next couple of days.

Rusty's parents were living in Ft. Meyers, Florida. His dad, retired from the Marine Corps., wanted to be near the water, and convinced his wife of 32 years to make the move, after a military lifetime of frequent relocations. As soon as they learned of Rusty's disappearance they hopped on a plane and went to Tucson to be near Melinda until their son was found. They arrived the night before. Her parents were on their way from Poplar Bluff, Missouri, and would be staying with their daughter for as long as she needed them. The Powell home had two extra bedrooms, but Rusty's mom and dad opted to stay at the Airport Hampton Inn, less than 15 minutes away.

A little after 10AM, Melinda received a phone call from a reporter with KMSB, the local Fox affiliate, who was unable to attend yesterday's Border Patrol press briefing There wasn't much for Melinda to say, other than what appeared on Tucson TV the night before. "They'll find him"; I know it. He's alive and is very strong. I don't know what else to add."

"When was the last time you spoke with your husband, Mrs. Powell?"

"The morning he left for Nogales, four days ago. He would almost always give me a call in the afternoons while on duty, but I guess the communications were poor. The guys were out on patrol in the middle of the desert. Even the border station had lost contact with them. I'm so sorry about Gary Childers. I didn't know him or his wife, Tanya, very well, but it's a tragic loss. The agents know the risk when they head out on patrols, but it's never going to happen to you." The tears began to flow. Melinda strong veneer was slowly breaking down.

"Has the FBI contacted you as yet?"

"I'm expecting a call from them today. The Border Patrol also has a group of investigators, so they will no doubt get involved as well."

"They'll find your husband, Mrs. Powell. I'm sorry to bother you. Goodbye."

Melinda made her third cup of coffee and moved to the family room, where she turned on the TV. A local talk show host was interviewing Roland Escobar. No news, at least, as far as Melinda was concerned. She was anxious to speak with the FBI agents investigating the case. Their involvement couldn't come soon enough.

CHAPTER 29

MARTINEZ PARKED IN front of the building where the FBI had their satellite office in Tucson. As promised to Henkel, he arrived a little after ten. Sally had a cup of coffee ready for him as he walked in the door. He was dressed in a dark blue short sleeve shirt and khakis. He was purposely unarmed, preferring not to carry his Glock 23 unless there was a likely need for it in the field. Henkel, a conservative dresser, wore a starched white blouse and loose fitting, lightweight green slacks. Her medium-length blonde hair was, as usual, pulled back in a ponytail.

"So, Sally, anything coming from the Border Patrol guys this morning? I caught the news on TV last night; nothing really on Powell. No leads at all?" Sipping on the coffee, he perused the morning paper as Henkel shoved some paperwork into her briefcase and checked the time. Her weapon, the same as the one issued to her boss, was fastened with Velcro to the interior of the case. She was never on the job without it. And the briefcase never left her side.

"Not a word. We should go. They're waiting for us down in Nogales. Escobar said he would meet us at the border station before noon. The media is still bugging him, but there obviously isn't much he can say. Bring the coffee. I have a thermos with more if you want it before we get there."

They headed out, with Sally driving her black Explorer, toward I-19 South, and the short one hour drive to the border. It was another scorching, hot August day in southern Arizona.

Martinez was reading the scant Bureau file on the case. "Not much here, Sally. I think we're going to need some blanks filled in, by Escobar, as well as our friends in Mexico. There probably isn't much time for Agent Powell. If one of the cartels has taken him alive, they won't wait very long to get what they want, or they'll put him down. What's your gut tell you about this?"

"Well, unfortunately they've moved the vehicle from the spot where Childers was shot. We can inspect the Jeep; it's been compounded up in Tucson, but there probably isn't much there to go on. I have New Mexico DMV running a check on the van, but it was probably stolen. I don't know, Richard; let's see what we can learn in Nogales."

Martinez wanted his young lieutenant to lead the way. Henkel was smart and intuitive, but didn't have her boss's experience. Together, they were a formidable team, but this case would be a tough one to crack.

A few minutes before noon, they pulled into the Nogales border station, and showing her FBI ID, Henkel asked an agent where they might find Roland Escobar.

"I believe he is in the office Ma'am." Pointing over his left shoulder, he added, "You can park in one of those spaces against the fence."

Sally parked the Explorer. They walked to the office door, where Escobar, noticing their arrival through the window, opened it and smiled, as they walked in. He extended his hand to both visitors. "Special Agent Martinez, I presume; and Agent Henkel, good to see you again. Come on in."

They walked to a small conference room in the rear of the station office. A host of various specialists were there. Seated at the table, and waiting for them, were Agents Page and Cooley, the two watch commanders that were on duty while Powell and Childers were out on patrol.

In attendance was a Border Liaison Officer, assigned to support both CBP and the FBI team on the case. Border Liaison was comprised of both U.S. and Mexican law enforcement agents. Also present was Anthony Reese, Immigration and Customs Enforcement (I.C.E.) investigator from the Tucson office. Martinez requested their support. Escobar introduced all parties and the questioning began.

The number of agencies and units represented was typical for a comprehensive crime investigation like this one. In this case, the FBI was taking the lead.

CHAPTER 30

RUSTY'S LEG WAS painful, enough so that the heavy doses of oxycodone could not completely mask it. Confined to the small bedroom, with arms and legs tied with leather straps, he passed his waking hours wishing he could make contact with Melinda and let her know he was still alive.

Diego Molina, his reluctant guardian, watched TV and spent hours on the phone with his girlfriend. Every few hours he would open the bedroom door and check to see if Powell needed to visit the bathroom.

Molina's girlfriend arrived at noon with some chicken legs and a burrito. Diego inhaled his portion and delivered the balance to Powell, along with a bottle of water. Molina then sat, with pistol in hand, and watched his charge consume the food and water before retying the arm restraints and leaving the room.

Molina's cellphone rang. "How is our guest doing, Diego?" It was Ramon, calling in to confirm that Molina had not left Powell alone in the apartment. There was little chance that this would occur, given that such a flagrant disregard of cartel orders would lead to an almost certain end to Molina's life.

"He appears to be okay, Ramon, but you need to put an end to this thing. I agreed to be this watchdog for only a day or two. Why don't we just kill him and get it over with?"

"Later today we will start the wheels turning to get him out of the way. Be patient for one more night and you will be finished with the task. And we want the gringo to be in decent condition when we get him out of there. So make sure he gets enough food and water to keep him alive."

"Okay, but just for one more night, please. I am supposed to be in Monterrey tomorrow evening. Otherwise, I will be in trouble with my wife and her family. It is her birthday."

"You have my word, amigo. One more night and it will be over. Then you can make it to Monterrey for the birthday celebration."

Rusty was sufficiently lucid to make out Diego's end of the phone conversation. "What does one more night mean?" He asked himself. "If they wanted to kill me why didn't it happen by now? Rico or Manuel would have put me out of my misery before we reached Hermosillo. Let's just get this over with, one way or another." His leg was throbbing, swollen and discolored. He needed a doctor soon, or it would possibly have to come off.

Molina's girlfriend left the apartment. He returned to the TV and managed to doze off for his afternoon siesta. Ramon reported back to Fuentes that their captive federal agent was still in tow and ready for anything that he and Rico had in mind.

Fuentes agreed with Morales that Ramon was the best man for the transfer. He was a huge human being, with the strength of an ox. Handling the border agent would not be easy for an average size person, but for Ramon it would be of little consequence."

"Ramon, you need to get in touch with Rico tonight. He has a job for you involving the young man. He will ask you to make yourself available tomorrow afternoon, but he can give you the details."

"Domingo, you know I will do whatever is necessary. But to me it is an order coming directly from you." Ramon and Rico were not the best of compatriots. Both were considered viable candidates to take over a significant element of the cartel's organization. There was a distinct possibility that the loser would not survive.

CHAPTER 31

"DID CHILDERS AND Powell have the right experience for that kind of patrol?" Martinez was responding to Carroll Page's briefing on the assignment the agents were given that morning. On his watch that morning, Page had ultimate responsibility for the teams and their ability to deal with particular situations.

"No doubt about it. They were both highly capable people. Childers was an excellent handler of firearms and Rusty Powell was a first-rate tracker. Let's keep in mind: their initial assignment was to locate and take into custody a group of suspected aliens that were seen traveling on foot past the border since daybreak. Powell and Childers took the handoff from two other agents when they reported for duty. The individuals being pursued were never spotted. Once the agents caught up with the guys in the white van, that was their focus."

Escobar added his perspective. "The agents operating along this stretch of border are subjected to just about every type of risky situation. Remember that this station is the largest single CBP border post in the nation. There are rarely less than forty to fifty agents on duty at any given point in time. Human and drug trafficking through this corridor goes on all day. These agents are ready for just about any situation. I'll vouch for any one wearing the badge."

"No criticism intended", Martinez said. "We're just trying to grab onto any piece of information that might help. My guess is that the drug drop, if there was one, had already been made. Right now, it's all about bringing Agent Powell home. Full stop. Anybody disagree?"

The entire conference room was quiet. Richard Martinez had a commanding presence, and not only because of his physical stature. He was fluent in Spanish and his credibility on matters concerning illegal aliens, drug trafficking and other crime along the border was unassailable. Special Agent Henkel scanned the players sitting at the table and smiled. Her boss knew his stuff.

Roland Escobar recognized the need to acknowledge the question. "Speaking for the guys, Richard, there's no disagreement. They know Rusty Powell and want him found, alive and well. Tell us what we need to do. We'll do it."

"For now, just telling us what you know is enough. Sally and I believe, based on what we know at this point, that Agent Powell is likely a hostage of one of the cartels. These drug lords typically don't hold anyone for ransom. It's not their style. But the old cliché may apply here. There's always a first time. Let's hope this is it. Just a few more questions and we'll let you guys go."

Henkel took the lead and asked a handful of routine questions, before the meeting broke up. The two Bureau agents thanked their CBP hosts and departed the station. Martinez used his MacBook Air to make notes during the drive back to Tucson. They then made a visit to the vehicle barn where the recovered Jeep was stored. The vehicle was covered with a tarpaulin and marked as off-limits. Prints and photos had been taken as soon as it was returned from the desert. Nothing of any value, from a forensic standpoint, was found. However, Martinez wanted a first-hand look at it before releasing it as a crime scene location.

When they reached the Tucson Bureau office, it was a few minutes after 3PM. Henkel made some notes on her Dell desktop and asked Martinez to email her a copy of his. He phoned his Phoenix office line for messages. Maggie French, his admin, reminded him that he was scheduled to fly to Washington that night for a 2PM Director's meeting the next afternoon. He was booked on a Jet Blue redeye that departed Sky Harbor at 11:30PM and was scheduled to arrive at Washington Dulles Airport at 10:20 in the morning.

"I'm leaving here in a few minutes. There's a suitcase already packed in my office, so there's plenty of time. I'll drop by for it by around six. Just leave any worthwhile mail on my desk. See you when I get back."

"Sally, I've got to get going. I'll give you a call after tomorrow afternoon's meeting in D.C. In the meantime, give Pepe Sanchez a call in Mexico City. He's one of the Mexican government's drug task force experts. Maggie can give you his contact information. Just let him know what this case is all about. I'd bet real money he'll have a good idea which cartel might hold Powell for ransom. Cheers." He waived as he ran out the office door.

It was about a two-hour drive from the Bureau's Tucson office to the one in Phoenix. Martinez dropped by, picked up his bag, as well as some files he would need for the meeting, and then drove over to his favorite Chinese restaurant in South Phoenix before heading to the airport. Arriving there just before eleven, he felt deserving of an upgrade to first class. Checking in at the Jet Blue service counter, he was disappointed to learn that the forward cabin of the Airbus was full, but was able to change to an exit row aisle seat. Ten minutes after the plane was airborne, Martinez was sound asleep.

CHAPTER 32

DAY 6

PEPE SANCHEZ; FIFTY-THREE, short, pudgy, bespectacled and very smart, turned off his alarm clock a few seconds before his cellphone signaled an incoming call. It was 8AM in the morning and raining in Mexico City. "Sanchez here. Who the hell is this?"

"This is Special Agent Sally Henkel. I'm calling from my Tucson office on the advice of my boss, Richard Martinez. We need your help."

"Ricardo, my friend! Why does he not call me himself? He must still be in bed with one of his young señoritas. Anyway, what can I do for my friends at the FBI?"

"My boss is traveling at the moment. He asked me to brief you on a case that may very well involve a drug cartel operating in Sonoran Mexico. I'm sorry to call so early this morning, but there is a fair amount of urgency attached to our request."

"So, Special Agent Henkel, does this have anything to do with the missing Border Patrol Agent based in Nogales? We do not live with our heads in the sand, señorita. The news media here has reported the matter. How can I help?"

"Richard and I have reason to believe that one of the northern Mexico cartels may have abducted Border Patrol Agent Randall Powell. There has been no word of his whereabouts as yet, but we expect to hear something fairly soon."

"Don't hold your breath Ms. Henkel. If this Agent Powell is still alive, and that may be wishful thinking, it isn't likely that his captors are in any hurry to claim they have him to bargain with. They typically enjoy keeping authorities in the dark. Comprende?"

"That certainly would not be surprising, Mr. Sanchez. But if you could help us in this matter, it may very well save Powell's life. If you are not already aware, the agent apparently was taken by some men in a delivery van with New Mexico license plates, some time after Agent Gary Childers, his partner on the patrol, was shot and killed. At the moment, this is all we know."

Sanchez grinned at Henkel's summation of the limited facts, climbed out of his bed and began to find his way to the kitchen. "Go tell your boss that I will make some inquiries and get back to him within the next couple of days. I already have an idea about where he might be, but it has to be confirmed. The Sonoran region of northern Mexico has only two drug cartel organizations of any consequence. We actually have people embedded in both, so this shouldn't take very long. There's a project called Revolution Six. We work with your people all the time. It is a joint effort to attack the narcotics problem on both sides of the border. And please be so kind as to remind Señor Martinez that he still owes me on a bet we made a few months ago. Now, please excuse me. It's time to get dressed and get to work, so I will say farewell."

Henkel politely signed off and dialed the Phoenix FBI office to leave a message on Martinez's voicemail. It was a rather cryptic one, with a confirmation that she had spoken with Sanchez only a few minutes before. She then placed another call; this one to Roland Escobar. It was time for another round of questions, and ahead of a prep session for the personal visit she planned to make later in the day to Melinda Powell.

CHAPTER 33

At 10:35AM, DHS Deputy Director Frank Amelito was advised he had a phone call coming through from someone identifying himself as Mr. Lucky. The caller mentioned Randall Powell's name. Amelito punched one of the buttons on his phone to answer the call. "This is Deputy Director Amelito. Can I help you?"

"I will make this very brief, Mr. Amelito. My associates and I are holding one of your Border Patrol Agents. I believe his name is Randall Powell. He has an injured leg, but is otherwise in good health. If you wish to see him released without further harm, it will cost the United States Government ten million U.S. dollars. Do you understand?"

Amelito was fully aware of Powell's disappearance and Childers' death. He was not, however, empowered to deal with a potential abduction and ransom demand. Thus he could only respond as any department deputy could under the circumstances. "I believe, sir, that you have identified yourself as Mr. Lucky. I can only state, Mr. Lucky that it is not my purview to deal with you directly on this matter. If you will please provide me with adequate contact information, I will direct it to the appropriate authorities within the U.S. Government. Do I make myself clear?"

Morales fully expected this sort of runaround treatment, but decided to play hardball with Amelito. "I cannot do this, sir, as it will possibly jeopardize the positions of me and my associates. You must give me the name, title and telephone number of the individual who is in a position to handle things directly and authorize the payment of the funds. Otherwise, I am afraid that your agent's life will most certainly and rapidly come to an end. You may put me on hold for up to ten minutes, which should allow you to accommodate my request. No need attempting to trace the call, as you will not be successful. The ten minute window begins now."

Amelito knew that his choices were few. He opted to provide the contact information for the Director of the FBI. Within a matter of thirty seconds, he returned to Rico's line and gave him the name, phone number, street address and email address for Lowell Fox. "Mr. Lucky, I believe Director Fox is the person that can address this matter to its conclusion. Good day."

Amelito then contacted Fox's office directly. He was transferred to him, almost immediately after the purpose of the call was delivered to his desk. "Director Fox, I regret that no additional information was made available to me by this individual. Given the urgency of his request, I decided to contact you without delay."

"You did the right thing. I'll request White House authority to deal with this to its conclusion. Under the circumstances, I have little doubt that the President will authorize the action. Thanks. We'll take it from here." The line went dead.

"Tiffany, get me the White House."

Fox's assistant got through to the President's Chief of Staff. He asked to speak to his boss, who had just adjourned an intelligence briefing in the Oval Office. President Donald Forrest came on the line. "What's up Lowell?"

"Mr. President, I understand you're familiar with the Border Patrol incident in Arizona that resulted in one agent's death and another's disappearance. Homeland Security has requested that I be the point man for negotiations with the cartel. One of their soldiers contacted Frank Amelito and announced that Agent Randall Powell is being held for ransom. The caller mentioned $10 million. I would like your authority to deal with them. Hopefully we will succeed in getting Powell back."

The President, who was well aware of the Nogales situation, asked a couple of relevant questions, but without any hesitation he approved the FBI Director's authority of up to $10 million to secure Powell's release.

"I don't like the idea that we have to negotiate with drug dealers, but it seems to me that the American people would want us to bring the man home. Good luck with it Lowell. Keep us posted." Fox then awaited Mr. Lucky's call.

CHAPTER 34

IT WAS A few minutes after 1PM when Sally Henkel arrived at the Powell's home in West Tucson. Melinda greeted her at the door, wearing a white warm-up outfit, with her hair pulled back in a ponytail. She looked tired and stressed out, but smiled and after requesting identification she welcomed her in from the August heat.

"Mrs. Powell, I am truly sorry about your husband's disappearance. My boss, Special Agent in Charge Richard Martinez, and I will do our very best to find him and bring him home. As I said on the phone, I need to gain as much information about Rusty as you can give me. It could be a huge help in getting a fix on his location and the approach we might use to get him back."

Melinda asked her into the family room and offered a coffee or cold drink. Henkel passed on both. "Naturally, I'll do whatever I can. As I understand it, you already have his physical description from the Border Patrol people. What other information do you need?"

"As much as you can give us. Does he have any health issues? What's his personality like? Is he easily angered? If being held as a hostage, would he likely try to escape? Anything along those lines would be great."

"He's very healthy. The only thing I can think of along those lines is his reluctance to eat red meat. He doesn't handle it well, for some reason. Also, Rusty does have some sleeping problems. It's pretty unusual for him to sleep through the night. But since he hates taking any medication, he just lives with it. As far as his personality is concerned, he's a friendly, no BS kind of guy. He makes friends easily and likes to stay in touch with them on a regular basis. When he makes a commitment he keeps it."

"And how do you think he would act if he was kidnapped and somehow restrained."

"I would say that he would probably make an effort to get away, but he's smart enough not to risk getting himself killed in the process. Rusty's a survivor. It's partly his nature, and also partly the training he got in the Marine Corps. We're expecting our first child, so I would say that he would do whatever he can to improve the odds of getting free and back home in one piece. Does that make any sense?"

"Perfect sense, Mrs. Powell; and congratulations on the pregnancy. I hope it all works out well for you. How far along are you? You don't seem to be showing any signs as yet."

"Only three months. No signs like morning sickness yet. Hopefully it'll go smoothly. But it's hard to think about it without Rusty in the picture. Do you think there's a chance he's still alive? Everything I have heard and read about the drug lords doesn't bode well for my husband's safety."

"I would say that there's a reasonable chance that Rusty is still alive. If they were going to get rid of him they likely would have done it when they shot and killed Agent Childers. My advice to you is to think positive. And don't hesitate to call me if there's something you think the FBI should know that could help us find him." Henkel got up and began walking to the front door. She turned and shook Melinda's hand. "We will be in touch. Any progress we make, we'll let you know right away. Thanks for seeing me this afternoon."

Melinda said goodbye as Henkel left the house and walked to her Explorer. She called Richard before driving off, leaving a voicemail with the salient points of the visit. Martinez was in Washington for meetings with Director Fox and the other western region agents in charge. Being there he would learn first-hand about Rusty Powell's dilemma.

CHAPTER 35

MORALES PLACED THE call to Lowell Fox. The executive assistant to Fox received it, put Rico on hold and alerted the FBI Director that a "Mr. Lucky" is on line one. She then went back on the line. "Mr. Lucky, Director Fox will be with you momentarily. He has someone in his office and needs to end that meeting before coming to the phone. It will be only a moment or two."

Rico decided to hold, giving Fox two minutes to come on the line. "Miss, I am extremely busy and can hold, but only for a few minutes. If your boss doesn't answer by then, I will be forced to take other measures. Do you understand?"

The assistant was about to respond when Fox came on the line. "Mr. Lucky, I am well aware of the reason for your call. Secretary Amelito provided the information. I'm prepared to deal with you, but under the circumstances you will have to provide very specific information that we can act on with certainty. Our primary interest in this matter is the safe return of Agent Powell."

"Our demands are quite simple. In exchange for your agent's return, my organization will require the deposit of 10 million U.S. dollars in a bank account of our choosing. I will supply that bank account information when and if you decide to proceed. When that deposit is confirmed, we will provide you with specific instructions to follow in connection with the agent's return. Do I make myself clear?"

Fox was somewhat taken aback by Rico's command of English. It sounded as though he may have been schooled in the U.S. "Mr. Lucky, you are crystal clear. But my government is, as I would hope you can understand, somewhat reluctant to release such a large amount of funds with absolutely no assurance that Agent Powell would be safely returned."

Rico was prepared for such a response. "I fully understand, Mr. Fox; however, you and your government have little choice in the matter. If these instructions are not followed to our satisfaction, in other words the funds have not been wired as directed, I am afraid that your agent will be eliminated in short order. You should know that his left leg needs urgent medical attention, so it would not be in his best interest to wait much longer. He is becoming a nuisance to us, so we want this transaction to be concluded in the very near future."

"What, sir, is your definition of *near future*?"

"Let us say, by midnight tomorrow. The United States Government should have no problem in transferring the funds within that time frame. Am I correct in that assumption?"

"Mr. Lucky, your assumption may be valid, but until I can receive some assurance of Agent Powell's release and safe return to the U.S., it will be difficult to accommodate your request."

"Mr. Fox, apparently you are unable to understand. This is not a request. If the funds are not sitting in our account by midnight tomorrow, your agent will be killed. I will give you the account information now, and tomorrow I will call again, probably somewhere around midday, to see where we stand. To repeat my earlier statement, once the transfer has been confirmed, I will call once again with the instructions regarding the agent's return."

Fox hedged his bet, realizing that he had little bargaining leverage. "Very well. Please give me the bank account information. You will know for certain, when you call again tomorrow afternoon, what we agree to do."

Morales very clearly relayed the Swiss bank account wiring information, and then added: "It is in your hands, Mr. Fox. We will talk again tomorrow. Goodbye."

Fox knew he had to comply with the demand. In less than an hour, the 2PM meeting with his senior agents running the Bureau's western offices would get underway. He was well prepared from an agenda standpoint, and looked forward to the productive dialogue he frequently had with these people. Importantly, he wanted some additional time with Richard Martinez, in order to brief him on where things stood with the Rusty Powell case. Martinez knew nothing of the "Mr. Lucky" calls. His agents, led by Henkel, were continuing their search for clues. Bottom line, given the President's blessing, Fox had every intention of wiring the funds. The Bureau's Tucson office would most likely play a role in the agent's recovery.

CHAPTER 36

Fox's MEETING STARTED on time, at 2PM. A variety of subjects were covered, including Congress's approval of funds to hire additional agents in the southwest offices. This was music to the ears of his senior team, as they had been requesting more manpower in the growing markets of Arizona, New Mexico and West Texas.

Frequently an item on Fox's meeting agenda was an input session on a specific topic, pre-announced to give the agents some time to prepare. The topic this time dealt with the issue of the Bureau's coordination with Immigration and Customs Enforcement (ICE), as well as the Drug Enforcement Agency (DEA). Both of these agencies were regularly involved in chasing down the same people that the FBI had on their open case lists. The interaction between the three was often disjointed and resulted in wasted time and money.

Several good and workable ideas were put on the table. Fox promised to follow up with his counterparts running ICE and the DEA. The formal part of the meeting ended at 4:30. Fox then had individual sessions with two of his Senior Agents in Charge, also attended by his deputy directors. Then, close to 6PM, he sat down with Richard Martinez and laid the status of the Powell case on the table.

"So, here's where we stand. This Mr. Lucky will call again sometime tomorrow afternoon. At that time I will confirm that the funds are ready to be wired to the bank. I will also demand that some proof of Powell's condition be provided, even though they could easily have taped something earlier and then finished him off. But we'll have to proceed with the money transfer. I want you and Henkel to be directly involved in securing Powell, once we know how it will happen from their end. I'll tell Mr. Lucky that this is the way it needs to go down. At that point I believe he'll cooperate with the request."

Martinez was dumbfounded. "You mean we just write these guys a check for $10 million and hope that they let Powell go? I realize you don't have much leverage on this, Lowell, but shit. It's a pig in a poke. You're a pretty damn good salesman if you got the President to buy in."

"No kidding. I guess ten million doesn't mean much to presidents anymore, since they now talk in trillions every day. In any case, if we don't pull this off and bring Powell home for that amount of dough, you guys may be getting a new boss. So say your prayers, either way." The last statement was obviously tongue in cheek; both men flashed a smile.

"Lowell, the one positive thing about this is that Sally and I are no longer on a wild goose chase. That's assuming the transfer takes place and we have Powell back safe and sound. If we don't, then we'll almost be back to square one. Obviously Mr. Lucky has another name. And my bet is that one of the cartels is where we will need to look. We've got Pepe Sanchez plugged in. He's still our best Mexican contact for getting good intel on the drug boys. Henkel spoke with him yesterday. He'll be helpful."

"Pepe's a good man. Let me know if he gets back to you before I release the funds. Are you headed back to Phoenix tonight?"

"I'm on the 7:45 flight in the morning. If I need to stay longer; not a problem."

"No, go ahead and stick to your schedule. I'll keep you posted from this end. You do the same."

"Will do. And I promised you feedback on Sally Henkel. She's a keeper. I've been impressed with her work on a number of cases. But if you want her someplace else, and it's a promotion, I won't hold her back."

"No need to make any moves in the short term. We can talk about her later. In the meantime, let's get Agent Powell back home."

They chatted a bit longer before Martinez left for a dinner date he had with an old friend at the Justice Department. Later, in the room at his hotel, he called and left a voicemail message for Henkel. He suggested they talk when he returned to his office the following afternoon. The ballgame changed. He needed to get to her with the news, but wanted to deliver it firsthand.

CHAPTER 37

DAY 7

PEPE SANCHEZ AWOKE to the chimes of his cellphone. It was 8AM in Mexico City. Miguel Castro, a close ally in the battles against the cartels, and an undercover CIA operative, not often befriended by the FBI, was on the line.

Sanchez had called him the day before and suggested he sniff around the Sonoran cartel playgrounds to see what he could find on the Powell disappearance. Pepe wanted to get back to Henkel and Martinez with something of value.

Castro wasted no time getting to his brief intel report. "This is only what I hear; not what I know. A close contact of mine plays football on the weekends with a few of the guys in the Calimar organization. One of them mentioned a pretty good pot score that was temporarily interrupted by some border patrol agents not far from Ajo."

"It sounds like they popped one of the agents, but the other one is still alive. I asked him what he knew about that guy, but he wouldn't say. You ask me; they either hauled him off somewhere and chopped him up, or maybe they still want him alive. It doesn't make much sense, but that's it, at least for now. You want me to keep looking around?"

"I do, amigo. See if you can dig a little deeper on this Calimar thing. It sounds like it might have some legs. Let me know."

Sanchez dialed Martinez's office and got the office assistant. "Special Agent Martinez is not available. Would you like him to return the call when he returns?"

"I would like his cellphone number, please. This is pretty important."

The assistant said that she was not authorized to do so without Martinez's permission. She suggested that Sanchez leave a voicemail on his direct landline. He did so, but then called Sally Henkel, who had given him her cellphone number. She answered on the second ring.

"So Agent Henkel, this is your new friend, Pepe Sanchez. I am working very hard on your behalf. Would you like to know what I have young lady?"

Her answer was obvious. "Let's have it, Pepe."

Sanchez shared the scant intelligence and suggested that more may be coming in short order. "You tell your boss that we will break this one open. Richard is a great guy. And he is half Mexican! He is smart, and tough as well. I knew his father. Also a wonderful man." He abruptly ended the call.

Sally was well aware of the fact that her boss was in the air, but nevertheless she called his voicemail and left a message, so he would know, even before they talked later in the day, that Sanchez had some intel that sounded worthwhile. She also rang Roland Escobar with the update. He answered and was encouraged, but not overly optimistic that it would pay off.

"I'll keep the lid on this for now. There's not a hell of a lot to go on in any case. Let's see what Richard suggests as a next step. He's on his way back from D.C."

Escobar asked Sally if she had met with Melinda Powell. "I did, Roland. Had a good session with her. She seems to be holding together pretty well. These Border Patrol wives are amazing."

"All the spouses are. They know the score. Just about every day they hear about the injuries and the death. That being said, more and more of our new recruits are single. Not surprising. It's rough out there."

CHAPTER 38

RICO MORALES, ALIAS Mr. Lucky, was anxious to get Agent Powell off of his "to do list". The next step entailed getting the confirmation from the bank in Zurich that the $10 million was there. To do it, he needed Fuentes to have the cartel's principal moneyman initiate the contact. It was a few minutes after nine in the morning. He dialed his boss's cellphone number. Fuentes answered on the second ring.

"Domingo, the American Attorney General did not resist. I believe the money will be there by midnight tonight. I am calling his office again in an hour. When the Americans say the money has been wired, can you please have this verified? If it is, we can begin the process of getting rid of our excess baggage in Ramon's apartment. If it is not, we can still get rid of it. This can be done before the sun goes down."

Fuentes had no problem with the request. "Let me know and I will get the ball rolling, my friend. Like you, I am looking forward to getting this thing behind us. We have much to do in other areas of the business. There is another shipment of material that needs to be delivered within the week. I would like you to supervise the operation. This time, it is the white powder. There is much more at stake. Stay by your phone Rico. Goodbye for now."

Morales was at home. His wife of 22 years was on the beach at Mazatlan with her sister. He waited until 10AM, or 1 o'clock in Washington, to place the call to Fox.

The FBI Director was having lunch in his office when his admin assistant alerted him that Mr. Lucky was on the line.

"Mr. Lucky, as I indicated to you yesterday, the United States Government is prepared to accede to your demand. I must, however, insist that you provide some form of proof that Agent Powell is alive.

I am sure that you can understand our reasons for making this a requirement to precede the release of the funds."

"Mr. Fox, I will acknowledge your request as being a reasonable one, however you are not in a position to make any demands if you wish to have your agent returned in one piece. Do I make myself clear?"

The Attorney General had no more chips to play, but made one last attempt at getting the caller to acquiesce. "Again, Mr. Lucky, I ask you to provide some sort of tangible proof that you are holding Agent Powell and that he is, in fact, alive. I can then assure you that the funds will be transferred. We certainly have the mechanism to complete the transaction by midnight, as you requested."

Morales hesitated, but finally gave in. "Very well; I will send to the recipient of your choice a dated video confirming the agent's condition and state of captivity. This will be done within the hour. You will not hear from me again until the transfer of funds has been confirmed. Do you understand?"

Fox responded affirmatively. Rico saw no need to stay on the line. Instead, he rang Ramon's apartment, where Diego Molina had agreed to spend one more night looking after their hostage.

"Diego, it's Rico Morales. I need for you to video our agent and email it to me within the next half hour. If your cellphone is not able to make a video recording, then just take a photo, but get it to me right away. Agreed?"

Molina had an iPhone. "I will do it, but the agent is asleep. Do I need to wake him and get him to say something?"

"Yes, you will need to wake him. We need to see him moving, and if you can get him to talk that would be good as well. He can still be tied securely. Okay?"

Molina acknowledged that he understood. "In half an hour then." Morales gave him his email address and that was it.

****

A 30-second video of Powell squirming in bed, and mumbling something unrecognizable, was emailed to Morales at 1:45PM. Using a scrambled email masthead, masking the source of the forwarding message, Rico sent it to the address provided by Fox. He expected no response, and decided to await confirmation that the wire transfer was made.

•

Part III

A Deal is Done

CHAPTER 39

Martinez's plane landed at Sky Harbor Airport at 2:05PM, Arizona time. After a quick trip to the men's room, he jumped in a taxi and arrived at his office 25 minutes later. Priority number one was his call to Sally Henkel. He was greeted by her voicemail message, but was confident that she would return the call in short order. Henkel checked messages regularly and seeing that it was her boss would mean a quick response. Within five minutes Richard saw her name on caller ID. He picked up while leafing through the pile of mail on his desk

"Richard, how was your meeting with Fox?"

"Are you sitting down, Special Agent Henkel?"

Sally wasn't sure she wanted to hear what was coming next. "Okay, let me have it. Are you being transferred to London or someplace exotic. Or am I on a slow boat to Siberia?"

"Relax. Nothing so ominous. We have a bead on your Border Patrol Agent, Rusty Powell. Wanna hear about it?"

"Just tell me he's alive and we can get him back."

Martinez gave her what he knew. Realizing that the deal wasn't done until Fox and Mr. Lucky had at least one more conversation, his tone was somewhat subdued. "Don't get too excited. In the first place, we don't know if this Mr. Lucky will deliver. It's a crapshoot that the President is willing to bet $10 million on, flat out. If it's legit, then we have a good chance to get Powell back in one piece."

"It's a hell of a lot better than bringing him back in a box. So what's next? What do we do in the meantime?"

"Just wait. Fox's office will call with the high sign. Lowell wants us to handle things, once it's a go. He's supposed to talk with this Mr. Lucky this afternoon. There isn't much we can do right now. I wouldn't say a word to Escobar or Melinda Powell at this juncture. No sense getting anybody's hopes up just yet."

"Copy that. I have to appear in court first thing in the morning. It's that interstate flight to avoid prison case that needs the judge's decision before the end of the month. He wants our statement again. Should be out of there by ten or so. By the way, earlier today I heard from your friend, Pepe Sanchez. He tells me that the Calimar cartel is likely the bunch that's holding Powell."

"Okay, I'll pass that on. Anyway, my guess is we will hear something before the end of the day. It's nearly 5PM in D.C."

Less than five minutes after their phone call ended, Martinez was told that Attorney General Fox was on the line. "It's Washington calling, sir. The A.G. is picking up on his end."

"Richard, it's Lowell. It looks like our agent is alive. Just got a video that looks genuine. Seems to have been taken a few hours ago. I have asked the Secretary of the Treasury to authorize the release of the funds to the account the Mexicans have provided, and to complete the transaction by midnight. Diplomatically, there's virtually nothing that the President can do to convince the Mexican government to intervene. They're powerless in dealing with the cartels. So that's where we are. As soon as I get word from these guys regarding the actual release, I'll let you know."

Richard chimed in. "Just got a little piece of intel from our contact in Mexico City. Our friend Pepe Sanchez says it looks like the Calimar cartel is holding Powell. It blows me away that these guys are actually doing this for some bread. Maybe business isn't as good as we think."

"I wouldn't count on that. But, go figure. At least we might get our man back in one piece."

After the call ended, Martinez phoned Henkel and briefed her on Fox's update. "I still think we wait until the Mexicans let us know how the release will go down before calling Escobar and paying Melinda Powell as visit. Agree?"

"Sounds right. Let me know. I won't sleep much tonight anyway."

CHAPTER 40

WHILE WAITING FOR Fox's feedback and instructions on securing Powell's release, Martinez decided to contact Bennett Frost in Mexico City. The CIA operative never responded to the FBI's request for assistance in finding the missing agent. This wasn't particularly surprising. The Bureau and "The Company", as the Langley, VA based CIA was affectionately called, were rarely in lockstep. But Richard had a reasonably good relationship with Frost.

"Bennett, old man, you never call, you never write. What's your problem?"

"Richard, what can I say. No news is no news. You have anything for me to go on? And how is my old girlfriend, Sally Henkel."

"She's fine. But shit, if we had to depend on you guys for intel, we'd be up a creek. Anyway, here's what we know, and it's probably too late to do anything about it. Our missing Border Patrol Agent is being held by a cartel, most likely the Calimar boys, for $10 million in ransom money. Hold on to your undies: the White House has agreed to pay it, so Lowell Fox is making it happen. When the funds get to the cartel's Swiss coffers, they will tell us how we can get him back. Comprende?"

"So tell me, my fine Bureau friend, how the hell do you know it's the assholes at Calimar? They're bigger than hell. Why would they pull something like this?"

"No telling. My buddy Pepe Sanchez made the call on Calimar. And even *he* isn't totally sure. Can't you run these guys down?"

"I know Sanchez. Good man. He's got people all over these cartels. I would bet he's right on with the Calimar tag. Let me sniff around. What's the timing here?"

"What time is it? You're a little late with the helping hand. If this deal doesn't go down by midnight, they may chop up poor Agent Powell and serve him to their troops for dinner. I just wanted you to know what was going down. On second thought, you guys better stay away. We don't need for this thing to get screwed up."

"No problem. But if things turn to shit, let me know. Sayonara."

The click at the other end of the call let Martinez know it was over. But he was glad he let Frost know what was about to happen. The CIA couldn't complain that they were left out of the case. They had an early opportunity to get in the game. It didn't happen.

At 5:25PM, Sally Henkel got a call from Roland Escobar. They hadn't touched base for a while. He needed to report back to his superiors with an update on the FBI's progress. The CBP investigation had led them nowhere.

"It's Escobar. Anything you can tell me about my agent? It's almost a week. If he's still alive, we need to get him back."

Henkel was tongue-tied. Whatever she told him now would open up a can of worms. If only he had waited a few more hours, but the normal business day was coming to an end. Smart enough to buy at least a little time, she provided a guarded response.

"Something's in the works, Roland. If I could give you something hard to go on, I would. What I can tell you is that the FBI Director is on it in a big way. We're waiting to hear from him, so give us a little more time."

"Okay, but what's a little more time? The FBI's definition is probably a lot different from mine."

"Can't argue with that. Only trust me a little bit longer. I won't hold back. You'll get it straight away. All I can say is; the night is young."

Escobar had nothing meaningful to say. He got the message. End of conversation.

Henkel was reluctant to leave the office. Her daughter had a ride home from band practice. She decided to wait until seven to head out. That would be 9PM in the nation's capital.

At seven she gave up. Calling her daughter, she started for home.

They agreed to have some pasta at an Italian restaurant close to home. Heading to her Explorer, she rang Martinez's cell phone and got his voicemail.

Chapter 41

Rico Morales was normally a patient man. But this night was dragging on. He had people standing by to make the delivery of Rusty Powell a foregone conclusion. After this week a brief vacation was in order. But Fuentes already let him know that another important delivery would require his involvement. He missed his wife, and his mistress was sick in bed. But he kept his cool.

At 7:40PM his cell phone vibrated in his pocket, as he finished the last few bites of his dinner. It was Fuentes.

"It is done. I received a message that our bank account in Zurich is $10 million to the good. I salute you, my friend. You have earned your salary and then some. Now you can get rid of the gringo and sleep well tonight."

"Maybe not quite yet, Domingo. While we certainly can forget our promise to the Americans and finish off the border agent, I don't think we would want them to eventually find us out and bring us down. They don't like being screwed."

"Agreed; so go finish it. Your plan is well thought-out. I wish you well. Please let me know when it has been done."

Morales agreed, said good night to his boss, paid for his dinner and left the café. He immediately left for Ramon's apartment and called Ramon's home to let him know that he would need to get to the apartment himself and pick up the border agent sometime over the next few hours. Reaching the apartment, he checked Rusty's condition and let Diego Molina know that his agent-sitting job was coming to an end, as soon as they could get Ramon and Powell on the road.

****

Martinez got the call at 8:35. Fox had left for the day, but an agent at Bureau Headquarters relayed the message that the bank transfer was confirmed and a man using the name Mr. Lucky would be calling him to arrange Powell's return. He immediately phoned Sally Henkel, who breathed a huge sigh of what was only temporary relief. She asked her boss what role he wanted her to play in the process of getting Rusty home.

"Not sure yet, Sally. Fox directed this guy who calls himself Mr. Lucky to contact me and describe the steps they would take to release Powell and get him to the border station in one piece. We don't know where he's being held, but it's believed he's somewhere in or near Hermosillo, where the Calimar cartel apparently has its base of operations. I have no idea when Mr. Lucky will call. It's getting late; will be dark in less than an hour. We'll just have to sit tight and wait for the process to unfold."

"I don't care what time it starts. I won't sleep well anyway. Don't keep me in the dark, once this thing gets underway."

"Don't worry; you're my right arm on this thing. And I need you to keep Escobar and Melinda Powell informed. They have a right to know, and we'll necessarily need the Border Patrol involved at some point in the agent's return. Stay tuned.

****

Ramon reached his apartment a little after nine. Powell was still asleep, his usual condition over the past several days, having been kept drugged with oxycodone at regular intervals. Morales and Molina sat in the small living room, awaiting the arrival of Calimar's giant strongman when he walked in the door.

"Ramon, you know the plan. Diego, you will help get the gringo out of here and into his vehicle. Then you can go. Fuentes is much appreciative of your help in watching the American over these past few days. He has asked me to show you his gratitude. Morales pulled an envelope from his shirt pocket. Molina didn't dare open it in Rico's presence, but smiled and shook his hand.

Morales then dialed Martinez's cellphone to describe, step-by-step, how and when Rusty would be transported to within a short distance of the border station at Nogales. He introduced himself as Mr. Lucky and laid out the plan in simple terms.

"It is rather straightforward, Mr. Martinez. Someone will notify the people at the Nogales border that the agent is on his way to the crossing. I cannot tell you when exactly that will happen. His left leg is pretty bad. You may want to have a doctor there, or maybe an ambulance to take him to a hospital."

"Is it a long distance from where he is now to the border station? Martinez needed to gain some sense of how long the process might take before Powell would reach his freedom."

"Maybe a few hours. When the station is called it will be much less than that. Your Director has asked that an FBI agent be present when the man reaches there. I do not know why exactly, but that was his request."

"Can you not tell me the name of the individual who will be calling the station? In fact, I would prefer that the person call me directly, given that the FBI is responsible for Agent Powell's safe return. Can you arrange for that to happen?

"I cannot make that commitment, Mr. Martinez. It may be too late to make the change in arrangements. But I will try. In any case, you need to let someone at the border station know that their agent will be released and brought close to the checkpoint within the next several hours."

Martinez acknowledged Morales' last request. Rico ended the call without any further comment. It now sounded as though Powell could well end up at the border station sometime before the sun rises; eight days since he was shot and taken by the cartel.

Martinez immediately got the word to Sally Henkel a little after ten, asking her to phone Roland Escobar with the news. The border station needed to be on alert for their estranged agent to be welcomed home. Escobar also had to be told that the handoff at the border needed to be handled by the FBI.

CHAPTER 42

RAMON AND DIEGO lifted Rusty from the bed after undoing the restraints. Powell was semi-conscious, making it even more difficult to transfer him from the bedroom to Ramon's Nissan Xterra. It took nearly ten minutes to negotiate the move. Rusty was dressed in the same garb that Morales provided when they arrived at the Fuentes home. Rico, leaving the apartment as well, walked to his own car, feeling confident that the operation was moving ahead according to plan. Molina departed the scene, disappearing into the evening.

Once they had him secured in the back seat of the vehicle, Ramon placed new shackles on Rusty's arms and legs. Climbing into the driver's seat, Ramon closed the door and switched on the ignition. As the engine roared to a start, the Xterra began to shake. It was clearly not just a short-lived, normal shaking motion caused by the engine starting up. It was sudden, violent and continuous.

The ground beneath them was erupting. The tarmac was splitting apart. The SUV began to quickly drop through the expanding crevice. It was an earthquake. And a big one.

Now only a few steps away from his BMW, Morales lost his balance and fell backwards onto the rolling, cracking sidewalk. His head began to bleed and he soon lost consciousness. Seconds later, the apartment house they had just left exploded; steel and glass flew in all directions. Flames and dense smoke ensued. Paseo de la Cascada, once a quiet residential street was, for all intents and purposes, destroyed.

Within minutes, a significant section of eastern and central Hermosillo had ripped apart. It was 9:45PM, Wednesday, August 13, 2014.

PART IV

Devastation

CHAPTER 43

MEXICO'S NATIONAL SEISMOLOGICAL Service came on the air at 9:52PM, with a special announcement:

"A major earthquake has caused catastrophic damage across the northwest and central regions of the country. Measured at 8.4 on the Richter Scale, the center of the quake appears to be located 90 miles northeast of Guerrero Negro and 125 miles west of Hermosillo. The initial temblor occurred at 9:41PM. Aftershocks of up to 6.5 continue to aggravate any efforts to respond to emergency calls across the region. We repeat, this is a very destructive quake. Please remain in your homes until and unless emergency services or law enforcement advise you to do otherwise. All future announcements regarding this quake will be made by both your local authorities and the National Weather Service."

A quake with a similar epicenter shook the region two years earlier. There was no major damage or injury in the Hermosillo area, but at that time the temblor measured a magnitude of only 6.9. This one was an all-time record for Mexico.

Sirens blared continuously throughout the city. Emergency vehicles found it nearly impossible to reach many neighborhoods, owing to the falling buildings, downed power lines and street collapse. The only communications of any consequence was cellphone-based, although a large number of cell towers had already fallen.

Domingo Fuentes was returning from a meeting east of the city, which although heavily damaged still had many passable streets and major roadways. His car swerved when he felt the road shaking, briefly lost control and ran into a guardrail on Mexico 15. Not going very fast, he avoided injury, but the vehicle suffered some minor cosmetic damage where it scraped along the rail.

His first instinct, after regaining a modicum of composure, was to call his wife. Unfortunately, the landline at home was the only way to reach her. He dialed, but nothing happened at the other end. Maria Fuentes was a stout and hardy woman, but Domingo obviously feared for her safety, not knowing if the quake damage was severe in the vicinity of their home. Maria did not own a cellphone, but that wouldn't have made any difference.

Having no mechanical damage, Fuentes steered the car back onto the road and continued on Mexico 15, having every intention of getting home in short order. He tuned the radio to one of the local stations. The only sound was that of a blaring emergency siren. It lasted for a good thirty seconds, followed by a recorded message that warned the listeners of the dangers throughout the city and strongly urged its residents to remain in their homes, unless there was obvious structural reasons to get out.

Domingo once again made an attempt to use his cellphone, this time placing a call to his strongman, Ramon, who was lying trapped, and unconscious, in his Xterra, now partially buried in the fissure created by the street collapse. His cellphone was inoperative at the time. Rusty Powell sat, still tightly cuffed, in the back of the vehicle, and was badly injured when the SUV dropped into the hole. Blood trickled down his face from the side of his head. He too was out cold.

A few minutes past 11PM, the news of the monumental quake and the resulting damage made its way across North America. Associated Press picked up a local Hermosillo transmission and immediately contacted the station to gain a better fix on the extent of the devastation. Most U.S. networks released the initial AP reports, as well as making contact with Mexico City affiliations for more detailed updates. All reports at this point were too general to provide a realistic picture of how bad the situation really was.

Sally Henkel was watching TV, awaiting the call to get to the border station and assist in Powell's return. The local Tucson stations were just beginning to pick up on the AP reports. KVOA, the local NBC affiliate, broke into their regular programming and announced the news. Sally jerked her head up from the pillow and looked on in horror as the initial photos AP had wired across the country splashed onto the screen. She remembered Pepe Sanchez's report suggesting that the Calimar cartel might have Powell, and that their de facto headquarters was in Hermosillo. Given that Martinez hadn't received any additional information on Rusty's release, Sally assumed that the earthquake was the reason.

CHAPTER 44

DAY 8

THROUGHOUT THE NIGHT numerous aftershocks ripped through the already devastated Hermosillo environs. Early the next morning, smoke filled the heavy summer air as police, fire fighters and emergency medical personnel began to blanket the city in search of victims. Shattered window glass from homes and stores was everywhere. Buckled and cracked residential streets made getting to trapped victims a difficult and dangerous task.

Fuentes made it home around 2AM, finding both his wife and property in reasonably good condition. There was no city electricity, gas or phone service. The home did have a generator, but it had just begun to work. Without it, the heat of a typical August evening would rapidly turn the house into a sauna. Maria was shaken and uncertain of what the light of day might bring, but Domingo was relieved that she was unharmed. Their twin daughters were away at The American School of Pueblo. There was no way to know if that area, just east of Mexico City, was impacted by the quake.

Domingo found a battery-operated radio in a bedroom closet and tuned it to the first Hermosillo station that he could find that was on the air. The news was bad. Seventy percent of the city was in shambles. Only the eastern and southern outskirts were spared the heavy property damage and loss of life found almost everywhere else.

Paseo de la Cascada, the street where Ramon's little apartment once stood, was located in the center of the city, where damage was extensive. Gas leaks were particularly bad in this immediate area. The city shut down gas distribution just after midnight, but the smell and continuing risk of fire and explosions continued. It would be some time before emergency services would be able to get to the victims, including Ramon and his charge, Rusty Powell. Rico Morales, just a hundred feet away from them, was dead.

By noon, a number of emergency shelters were being organized throughout the city and would soon open to the public. Generators were brought in to supply the power. The Red Cross was alerted and began preparing to harness their capabilities of delivering food and water to those locations.

****

At 7:10 in the morning, Special Agent Henkel was awakened by a ringing cellphone. It was her boss. "Sally, have you heard the news? A major earthquake nearly flattened Hermosillo. Didn't Sanchez tell you that Calimar was based in Hermosillo?"

"He did. No word yet on Powell's whereabouts? I thought we were going to get word last night that he was on his way to the border station."

"Mr. Lucky was unclear on that point. I called the station about twenty minutes ago. They haven't seen hide nor hair of Powell. So you or I, or both of us, going down there last night would have been a waste of time. They've got their $10 million. I was afraid of this."

"Hold on Richard. Maybe they had every intention of letting Powell go. The quake probably threw a monkey wrench into the operation."

"No doubt. But we don't know how to reach Mr. Lucky. And trying to find our wounded agent will be a bitch and a half; unless that is, if Rusty somehow got loose, or was let loose in the middle of the chaos. In that case, CBP might hear directly from him any time now. Hell, I don't know. This is a tough situation. Any ideas?"

"Not a clue."

CHAPTER 45

MELINDA POWELL WAS pouring her second cup of coffee when the phone rang. She grabbed the handset on the wall-mounted extension by the kitchen counter. "Melinda, it's FBI Special Agent Sally Henkel calling. Hope I didn't wake or disturb you."

"Not a problem. What's up Agent Henkel?"

"You may or may not have heard the news this morning. We were hoping that Rusty would have been returned to us at the Nogales border station last night, but a major earthquake struck in northwestern Mexico. We believe that your husband was being held somewhere in the vicinity of Hermosillo, a city that was hit pretty hard. We're trying to get more information, but communications in and around the city are still not very good. I just wanted to give you an update, but unfortunately there isn't much to report."

Melinda hadn't had the TV on, but was about to read the morning paper when Henkel called. "Thanks for calling. I haven't had a chance to read the paper. Is it okay if I call you Sally?"

"Absolutely. I hate titles anyway. At this point, Melinda, our first priority is to get more information on just what's happening down there. It might take a few days, but our contacts in Mexico will be trying to get some on-the-ground intelligence that might lead us to Rusty and get him safely home. At least we were led to believe that he was alive as of yesterday afternoon. There's no reason to believe he isn't still okay."

"Sally, I know you guys are doing the best you can to get Rusty home. I have my parents here in town and they're doing what they can to keep my spirits up. Our Christian faith is very strong. Praying is about all we can do at this point. So keep at it. If Rusty's still alive, he'll find a way to get back home."

"Melinda, all I can say is that my boss, Richard Martinez, is the best. He won't give up until we can close this case with Rusty back home safe and sound. Everyone at the Border Patrol is backing us up every step of the way. You already know it, but they don't give up either. I'll call you the minute we have any further news to report. Take care."

Henkel saw Richard's name on caller ID as she was ending the call with Melinda. "Richard, hi; I was just talking with Melinda Powell. She sounds okay, her parents are there with her for support. I obviously didn't have any hard facts to give her. Any news from Mexico?"

"Nada, but I spoke with Roland Escobar at CBP. He managed to make contact with someone on the Hermosillo police force. The town is a disaster. If Mr. Lucky was having Rusty brought to the border from Hermosillo he might not have made it out of town before the quake hit. At this point, our only hope is that Powell finds a way to make contact with the border station, or his wife, and tells us what we need to do to get him home."

"I'm going to give Pepe Sanchez a call." Sally was running out of ideas. "If he can make contact with anyone close to the Calimar operation, maybe we can get some actionable intel. Like finding out who this Mr. Lucky is for real."

"Why not? Give it a go. And I'll see what Bennett Frost can suggest. Who knows? The CIA works in mysterious ways. And let me know when you want me to head down there. I've got two very hot fugitive cases up here, but one of my agents can ride herd on them if I'm in Tucson or Nogales."

"I'm not sure you can do any good down here right now Richard. With nothing hard to go on, it would be a waste of your time. Go catch your fugitives. I'll let you know if things heat up."

CHAPTER 46

BENNETT FROST MAINTAINED a cadre of well-placed informants more or less embedded in the major Mexican drug cartels. These individuals, all men, led extremely dangerous lives, living and operating under the thumb of the drug lords, although usually two or three levels down in the organization.

Martinez reached his Langley friend at a little after ten in the morning, Phoenix time. Frost was actually at the CIA's headquarters when he called. "Bennett, I need your help. You've obviously heard about the quake last night in northwest Mexico. Since I haven't heard a peep out of you for the past few days, I assume you don't have much to report."

"Right you are, Richard. Yeah, I know all about the quake. Not good. Hermosillo, clear over to the Baja; it's bad news. So what can *you* tell me? No word from your missing border patrol agent?"

"Not a peep, directly that is. I spoke with someone down there who calls himself Mr. Lucky. After Lowell Fox managed to get the President to wire 10 big ones to a bank in Switzerland, this guy committed to ship Agent Powell back to the Nogales border station, safe and sound. My guess is that Powell was being shipped from somewhere around Hermosillo and the earthquake stopped him in his tracks."

"What makes you think he was coming from Hermosillo?

"Pepe Sanchez; you know Pepe. His intel is rough around the edges, but he thinks that the Calimar cartel may have grabbed Powell. You have anybody embedded there?"

"Can't tell you that, but I will tell you that the head of that mob is a guy named Sancho Lopez. He's getting pretty old, but still runs the operation with a heavy hand. His second in command is Domingo

Fuentes. Very dignified, classy individual, and just as ruthless as his boss. If it was the Calimar bunch, I'd be very surprised if your border patrol agent is still alive. But go figure."

"Bennett, however you do it, I sure would hope that you could somehow find out who this Mr. Lucky might be. He's the key link with Agent Powell. If we find him, we can draw a bead on Powell and hopefully get him home."

"That's a tall order, my friend. Obviously your Mr. Lucky has another name. But I owe you a couple of favors, so sit tight and let's see what we can see. Keep in mind, Hermosillo right now is apparently a shit heap. We might not be able to get much intel out of there for a number of days. Say hi to Sally."

"Understood. Not asking for miracles. Do what you can."

****

Henkel got Pepe Sanchez's voicemail. At 10:40 he returned the call. "Sanchez here. I always return the calls of my friends in the FBI. Young lady, what can I do for you today?"

Sally got right to the point. "Mr. Sanchez, Richard and I need more information about the Calimar cartel. If you believe that Border Patrol Agent Powell was taken by their people, we need to know who would be the likely point man for the operation. All we know is that a man named Mr. Lucky contacted our government and made the deal to return Powell in exchange for a hefty ransom payment. Powell was supposed to be returned late last night, but it didn't happen."

"Not surprising. Hermosillo has been leveled by an earthquake. But you probably already know this. I understand that there are many dead people throughout the city. And thousands more are believed to be trapped under fallen buildings and other wreckage. It may be days, even weeks, before the bodies are all accounted for. Your Agent Powell may be one of those casualties. Right now, it is impossible to know."

"Anyway, Mr. Sanchez, whatever you can find out will be greatly appreciated. We are working with other sources in Mexico, but no one knows the cartels like you do. If Calimar has Powell, it must be one of the cartel's key operatives who is either Mr. Lucky, or knows who Mr. Lucky is."

"Miss Henkel, I would do anything for my friend Richard Martinez. I will do my best, but you shouldn't expect much until the dust clears somewhat in Hermosillo. Goodbye."

CHAPTER 47

LATE MORNING ON a sunny day in northern Mexico shed even more light on the horrific scene that reached across much of the city of Hermosillo. There was no telling the amount of human carnage that lay beneath the rubble. Of the more than 700,000 inhabitants of the capital of Sonora, there was little to convince the shocked and rattled city government that anything less than 100,000 were already dead and many thousands more were injured and needing medical treatment.

The Hospital CIMA, a state-of-the-art facility on Paseo Rio San Miguel, was heavily damaged itself, but receiving scores of patients by the hour. Many arrived by foot; literally hundreds of others were transported there by emergency vehicles, picking up the injured along the way.

The other hospital of any size, the Hospital Hermosillo, located not far north of Hospital CIMA, was dealing with a similar influx of injured people. Their smaller emergency room was packed to capacity. The medical staff began bedding overflow patients on the large terrace just behind the main building.

Domingo Fuentes began the search for his cartel comrades, after seeing that his wife Maria had a decent breakfast, "Let me make you something to eat. I have a feeling that this will be a difficult day. We will both need our strength, as well as our courage." They dressed and went to the large kitchen, where a live-in maid and cook was usually at the ready. But the woman was on vacation and not expected to return for another week.

The home was equipped with a generator that had been installed several years ago. It provided adequate power to handle the air conditioning, some small appliances and refrigeration needs of the large residence. Domingo made coffee and eggs rancheros for Maria, went to his home office and proceeded to make phone calls to a handful of his lieutenants. Only one of them was able to answer his cellphone; a senior cocaine crew manager in Santa Ana. That Sonoran town, just northwest of Hermosillo, surprisingly received only minor damage from the quake.

None of the other five calls were answered. While clearly disconcerting, Fuentes was not surprised. Cellphone coverage across the city was spotty at best. Landlines were affected by power outages that were widespread. While he normally required daily contact with his senior people, the present circumstances clearly necessitated Domingo's patience.

The issue of the border patrol agent's status was on his mind, but of no great concern. Having had no word from Rico Morales since early yesterday evening, there was no way to know if and when the agent was released for transport back to the U.S. Domingo had received confirmation that the $10 million had been wired to the cartel's bank in Zurich. Bottom line, Fuentes couldn't care less if Powell was dead or alive. He was, however, concerned about the condition of Morales, his best drug transporter, and Ramon, his strongman. He decided, however, to let things lie for a day or two, hoping that Hermosillo would begin to at least regain some of its power capabilities.

Maria asked her husband to accompany her to mass. Not a church-going Catholic for many years, he wasn't very comfortable doing so, but given the uncertainty of conditions out on the streets, he agreed to go. The nearest church was less than a mile away. They decided to walk.

On the way, the couple ran into several neighbors, many who were outside for the first time since the quake. Most nearby families were not as fortunate as the Fuentes' to have a generator supplying power to run things. Many were outside to escape the heat that was steadily building up in their homes.

Mexicans, 80% of them Roman Catholic, continued, for the most part, to be true to their faith and typically made it to mass at least once a week. It was Thursday. The church was full.

CHAPTER 48

RICHARD MARTINEZ SAT in his office after having a casual lunch with two of his Phoenix-based agents. He was angry with himself. Something that one of the agents said over his sandwich stuck in Richard's gut, and he didn't like it. Usually an obsessive fact digger and thorough case plodder, the question asked by the agent had to go completely unanswered.

"How's the border patrol agent murder investigation going?"

Legitimate question. Bottom line, he and Sally Henkel were completely focused on getting Rusty Powell home, safe and sound. The fact that a murder was committed; the shooting of Gary Childers, had somehow taken a backseat.

Richard dialed Sally Henkel's cellphone number, and was sent to voicemail. "Sally, it's Richard. Give me a call. It's Thursday, around 2PM."

Twenty minutes later, Sally returned the call. "Hi Richard, it's Sally. What's up?

"I'm coming down in the morning.

Henkel had thought about it a few days earlier, but the push on finding Powell was deemed to be priority number one.

"I agree, but there are certain steps that need to be taken that probably fell between the cracks. We need to backtrack to day one and make sure we haven't missed some important pieces of the murder puzzle."

There probably weren't too many steps they would need to take at this point. But at the very least they needed to run through the checklist they routinely followed in a pure murder investigation. "I'll see you later. I'm out the door."

Sally agreed as they ended the call. She was in the middle of a mail fraud investigation, but a few hours with Martinez might help in that case as well. Not yet having any lunch, she walked to a nearby Subway and bought a small veggie sub to eat back to the office. She also phoned Roland Escobar at the CBP office and asked him to be on call in case she and Richard needed to meet with him before the end of the day.

Martinez arrived at the Tucson FBI office at 4:15PM. He had packed and brought along an overnight bag, on the assumption that another day down there would be worthwhile. On the way he stopped and booked a room at a Hampton Inn fairly close to the office, where he had stayed once before.

"I asked Escobar to make himself available, in case we run into some questions that we need Border Patrol input for." Henkel pulled a second chair up to her desk while Martinez grabbed a notepad and felt tip pen.

"I think we went over this stuff before, but there were no prints on the Jeep other than those of Childers, Powell and a maintenance man at the border station garage. Also, we ran a DMV check on the van with New Mexico plates. The plate number didn't match up with the vehicle itself, so they were probably put on by the bad guys."

Martinez knew that there wasn't much else to go on. "I guess we haven't missed anything critical. If we're successful in getting Rusty Powell home, there's a good chance he can fill in some of the blanks. Then we'll have to rely on our friends on the Mexico National Police Force to help bring whoever did this to justice."

Henkel was a realist. "Richard, you know damn well that Mexican law enforcement is scared to death of cartel big wigs. They make some arrests of low level people, but when it comes to the heavy duty operators they keep their distance."

"This is true, but their new administration has just added 10,000 new positions and created an elite national police force to go after the cartels in a much bigger way. This would be a terrific case for these people to handle."

"Wish we would get something to go on from Sanchez or Frost", Sally said. "Otherwise this is going to be an almost impossible manhunt.

If they do have Powell holed up somewhere in Hermosillo, it'll be fortunate if Powell makes it out of there. Hate to say it, but it's not looking good."

"Now, now, Special Agent Henkel. Positive thoughts, please. We *will* bring Powell back alive. Do you read me?"

"Loud and clear. Do we need Escobar? If not, I'll take him off point for the present. I can't think of anything he could add."

"Yeah, tell him we'll be in touch down the road. The Border Patrol can't help us in Mexico. That's where the effort has to be focused. Buy you some dinner?"

"Sounds good. Meredith is staying with a girlfriend tonight. I'm all yours.

CHAPTER 49

DAY 9

HERMOSILLO EMERGENCY CREWS were beginning to make progress reaching devastated neighborhoods and rescuing trapped residents. It was slow and tedious. In some cases, frontend loaders were needed to move large chunks of debris from the fractured streets and sidewalks. Most storefront businesses in the hardest hit areas were not yet reopened. There was limited electric power to 30% of the city.

Domingo Fuentes was concerned about his favorite lieutenant, Rico Morales. There was no word from him since the quake rocked the city. And Fuentes knew that the residential neighborhood where Powell had been held was in extremely bad shape.

Morales lay dead alongside his BMW on the Paseo de la Cascada. There was no way to get to his body. The street was still inaccessible to emergency personnel.

Frustrated, and feeling the lack of control he had over the situation, Fuentes decided that his number one priority should be his wife. Their marriage was often on shaky ground, given Domingo's position in the cartel and his almost fanatical devotion to Sancho Lopez. Realizing that Lopez was aging rapidly and delegating more and more of the Calimar activities to his subordinates, Fuentes needed to keep a firm hand on his power and influence within the organization.

On this hazy, humid morning, he made breakfast for Maria and retreated to his office, making renewed efforts to contact his key operatives. He hoped that most were unharmed and working to assure that planned cartel activities would remain on track.

****

Miguel Castro, CIA Informer, placed a scrambled call to his boss, Bennett Frost, before heading to the beach for a long weekend. Castro had some hard information to pass along. He had just spoken with a contact in the middle ranks of the Calimar cartel. Although the call was scrambled, Castro never communicated with Frost using his real name.

"Frankie, I have something for you on your long lost relative. The number two man collected some money for him. I hear that he was on his way to the border when the big shake came. No one knows where he is at present. It is suggested that he may still be somewhere in town. I should have more to report after the dust settles. That is all I have right now."

Frost was encouraged, but not overwhelmed, by the news. None of it was actionable, at least in the short term. Deciphering the message, he concluded that Powell was still in Hermosillo, but decided, for the moment, not to pass the information on to Henkel or Martinez. He opted to wait for corroborating intelligence before doing so.

In the meantime, FBI personnel in Mexico City, receiving specific direction from Martinez, were implementing additional, under the radar fact-finding efforts to locate Powell. They had very limited resources in northern Mexico. With power and telephone communications still in limited supply, the process was frustrating and slow.

CHAPTER 50

THE HOLE IN the street was a little over ten feet deep. There was a fair amount of air to breathe, given that the windows of the Xterra were shattered; but the glass littered the bottom of the hole. No emergency personnel were able to reach the vehicle as yet, due to blockages at either end of that particular stretch of Paseo de la Cascada.

Ramon remained comatose. For the first time in two days, however, Rusty Powell opened his eyes, taking his first look at the huge hole carved by the earthquake. Blood was caked around his eyes and forehead, but he felt no immediate pain. Still bound, feet and hands, and propped up in the rear seat of the vehicle, he managed to wiggle himself upward and glance at Ramon, whose chest was pinned up against the steering wheel. Powell's first thought was that this man was probably dead. He did not know his name.

In fact, he had no idea who *he* was, or how he managed to get himself into this precarious situation. The condition, however, did not dissuade him from his immediate priority; that of getting out of the vehicle and out of the hole. Without food or water for almost two full days, he had little strength in his arms or legs. His head was pounding and he desperately needed some fresh air. He began to yell. "Is anybody up there? Somebody help! Please help me! I'm trapped in a car, down in this hole! Please help! Help!

Two things were working against his urgent cry for help. First, no one was within shouting distance; the nearest humans at the moment were more than a mile away. Secondly, he was yelling in English. That wouldn't help. In any case, he continued to yell, as loudly as he could, until the siren coming from an emergency vehicle broke the silence, some distance down the road, and nowhere near the hole.

"Can anyone hear me? Help… help, please! I'm trapped down here in a hole!"

The next ear-piercing sound that reached Powell in the hole was that of some sort of earthmoving vehicle that was crunching its way down the street parallel to Paseo de la Cascada. The diesel engine noise was getting louder, giving Rusty some hope that it was headed in his direction.

It was a few minutes after ten in the morning. Rescue work was slow; emergency crews were shorthanded. But there was life out there. Powell was hopeful that his yelling would eventually pay off. He waited a few minutes between the calls for help. His energy level was low and sinking fast. And he realized that his leg hurt like hell.

Suddenly, there was a man's voice. It sounded a few hundred feet away, but nevertheless, a voice. The words weren't clear to Powell. There were now two men speaking. One seemed to be shouting instructions to the other. Then the machinery roared to life again, drowning out the voices. Rusty yelled again. "Help me please! I am trapped in this hole! Please help!"

Then a voice rang out. "La voz viene de alli! El habla ingles." Rusty heard one of the men loud and clear. And he understood! It was Spanish. They were coming his way.

In less than a minute, the two men appeared at the rim of the hole. They spotted Rico's body, lying next to his BMW, less than a fifty feet away, but it was obvious that he was dead. Looking down into the fissure, they saw the two men. Rusty was the only one moving.

"Let's get a rope. If he can grab on to it, we can pull him out."

One of the men disappeared, supposedly to find a piece of rope and drop one end down to Powell. The other man seemed to be searching for way down, but the pieces of asphalt were jagged, so he opted to wait for his partner and the rope to pull Rusty out.

"We will get you out, amigo. Not to worry. We will get you out. Are you hurt?"

Powell used very limited Spanish to respond. "I'm okay. My leg feels very bad, but I'm okay." Rusty looked down at his left leg. It was swollen, disfigured and painful. He had no idea how it got that way.

His head was aching and he felt lightheaded. Stuff was floating around in his brain, but nothing seemed to make sense. But he was alive!

The second man reappeared; this time with a rope. He looked down at Rusty, hogtied in the back of the Xterra, and smiled. Lowering the rope, he motioned to Powell to grab onto it. The tight straps binding his wrists made it difficult to do, but he managed to get a hold on it, as both men pulled on the other end to lift him out of the vehicle and up through the hole in the street. No knowing if Powell understood Spanish, the older of the two men used his limited English to encourage Rusty as they got him to the surface. They removed the wrist and leg restraints and let him lie down, offering him some water from a bottle that was hooked on to the younger man's belt. Without hesitation, Powell took three large gulps and returned the bottle with a grateful smile.

"You will be okay amigo. Do not be afraid. We want to help."

Rusty responded in Spanish, to the man's delight. "Thank you. I think I need to go to the hospital. Can you help me get there?"

The older man pulled a cellphone from its holster and made a call.

Ramon looked to be dead. And Rico Morales' lifeless body was still lying beside the badly damaged BMW.

CHAPTER 51

RICHARD MARTINEZ' OFFICE received a call from the FBI Director's office in D.C. Lowell Fox wanted an update on the missing Border Patrol Agent. Martinez was in Flagstaff, working with local law enforcement to locate a mail fraud suspect they believed was holed up in the area. The Phoenix office admin tried Martinez's cellphone number.

"Richard, I have Director Fox's office on the line. Figured you would want to take it right away." Without waiting for an answer, she put through the call. Fox's assistant immediately transferred it to his desk.

"Richard, it's Lowell. Just wanted to touch base on the status of our missing agent search. Anything to report?"

"Nothing yet; unfortunately, not a word. We were expecting him to show up on the grid two days ago, but we can't learn anything from our sources in Mexico. The earthquake has wrecked Hermosillo. That's where the CIA believes he was being held."

"So where do we go from here? The President asked me about this yesterday afternoon. He's concerned that if the word gets out we paid big bucks to spring the guy, and he doesn't show up, we'll look pretty bad. We need to have a plan."

"I'm with you Lowell. It's just that communications have completely broken down between our guys and their contacts in the Hermosillo area. It might take a few more days to get something we can move on. Sally Henkel's on it. I'm not sure we can do much right now."

That didn't seem to satisfy Fox. The Bureau was taking heat for a number of difficult cases that weren't getting solved. "Richard, I understand, but I repeat; we need a plan. Give me a call tomorrow morning. Okay?"

Martinez had little choice but to acquiesce to his boss's request.

"Will do. I'll get with Sally and we'll be in touch." He didn't wait for an answer and ended the call. Without letting any time go by, he dialed Sally Henkel's number. Leaving a voicemail message, he returned to his meeting with the Flagstaff sheriff and two of his deputies. It was 11:20AM.

Henkel returned his call a few minutes after noon. Martinez was on his way back to Phoenix and had stopped at a Wendy's for some lunch. "What's up Richard.? Aren't you up in Flagstaff today?"

"On my way back. Got a call from Fox this morning. He sounded a little impatient about our missing Border Patrol Agent recovery. Seems the President wants to know how we're going to keep this off the airways; you know, the ten big ones albatross. He wants a plan. Any ideas?"

"No further word from Frost or Sanchez. It's not surprising. Northern Mexico is a disaster. I felt the ground shaking here in Tucson. Hermosillo is in ruins. If that's really where Powell was being held, he could be dead. I'm not trying to be negative, but it's estimated that more than 10,000 people were killed and another 20,000 are unaccounted for. It's going to take days, maybe even weeks, to learn the extent of the loss of life and the destruction down there. So that's what we're dealing with. If Powell was on his way back to the border, he must have been stopped dead in his tracks."

"So, no ideas." Martinez was coming to the conclusion that his ass was on the line, meaning that drastic measures were in order. "Guess I'll have to go down there. Not sure where to look, but my boss's neck is on the line."

"Richard, what are you talking about? Which piles of rubble do you plan looking under? Have you seen the TV reports from Hermosillo?"

"Yeah, some of them. But I know the country and the language. We're not doing a bit of good sitting here and hoping that Rusty Powell is somehow going to magically appear at the border station. I have to go find him and bring him home."

"Sorry for having to say this, boss, but you've lost it. If Powell's still alive, we should let him surface. I have to believe that the Calimar people would just as soon get rid of him for good. They probably have enough problems digging themselves out of a hole. Please think this through, Richard. And by the way, if you go down there, you realize that I have to go along? I can't let you go alone."

"No way, Sally. I know this is also *your* case, but it's too risky. Our agents from Mexico City will come up and give me support. You need to stay in Tucson and keep the Border Patrol under wraps."

Henkel knew that an argument at this point would be fruitless. "Just sleep on this another day or so. Would you please? Then decide."

"One more day. Then I'm headed south. End of story."

CHAPTER 52

THE AMBULANCE MANAGED to get within fifty yards of where Powell and his rescuers on the front-end loader awaited its arrival. The broken up street and sidewalk wouldn't allow it to get any closer. Two EMT's exited the vehicle and walked to the site of the massive hole in the pavement. They carried a stretcher.

On the way, they approached Rico's body. It was obvious he was dead, but one of the EMT's checked his vital signs, then made the sign of the cross on his own chest out of respect, while his partner moved directly to Rusty and his new found friends. The EMT by Morales' corpse used his cellphone to call for assistance in removing it. He then joined the group by the side of the hole.

One of the front-end loader men spoke to the EMT's. "This man needs to get to a hospital. It looks like his leg is in pretty bad shape. The man still in the car down there looks to be dead. We can pull him out with the rope."

The man appearing to be the EMT in charge looked down into the hole. "Pull him out and we will check his vital signs. It looks like his head and chest may be crushed."

They managed to get Ramon out of the Xterra and up onto street level. "We have to get back to our work now", said one of the loader men to the EMTs. You can handle things from here."

Both EMTs nodded, as the other two men smiled at Powell and returned to their vehicle. Ramon clearly was unresponsive and no longer breathing. "What is your name?" The senior of the two EMTs asked Rusty.

Powell answered in Spanish. "I do not know. I speak better English, so I must be American. My head hurts and my leg is swollen and very sore." They could see the dried blood on the side of Rusty's head, and the swelling of his left leg was also apparent.

"We will get you to the hospital. But they are all very crowded. It may take a long time for you to get medical·assistance. I am going to give you an injection to reduce the pain. Can you walk?"

Powell hadn't done so in quite a while. "I think so. We can get moving. I will do my best." Clearly weak and disoriented, he took a few steps and fell. They immediately placed Rusty on the stretcher and slowly carried him to the vehicle. Loading him into the ambulance, the senior EMT glanced at his watch. It was 2:18PM.

Negotiating the narrow streets, cluttered with debris, they turned on the siren, but were unable to move very quickly, weaving their way around the devastation to the nearest full-service medical facility; Hospital San Jose. It was five miles away. The trip took nearly twenty-five minutes.

The ambulance drove up to the emergency entrance, but was unable to get within 200 feet of the doorway, owing to at least five other emergency-type vehicles parked in front of them. Orderlies were hurrying to unload patients. Powell's ambulance inched up to the entrance as the unloaded ones moved away. In a few minutes a hospital employee walked to rear of the vehicle and opened the door. He was joined by one of the two EMTs and pulled the stretcher out and on to a hospital gurney.

"What is his problem?", the orderly asked.

"Looks like a busted leg, and a head injury as well. He was trapped in a street hole for some time. Looks dehydrated as well. BP is 110 over 60. Heart rate is 135. Can you take him?"

The orderly didn't respond, but began moving the gurney toward the ER entrance. Rusty was awake and reasonably alert, as he was wheeled into and through the morass of patients and medical personnel that filled the small ER lobby. A nurse greeted the EMT as she quickly examined the paperwork she was handed. "It will be at least an hour before a doctor can see this man. We have several critically injured people and I am the current triage nurse on duty." Looking down at Rusty, she forced a weary smile. "We will do the best we can, sir. Try to relax." She stuck a thermometer in his mouth and took his pulse. One of the doctors called to her; she moved away.

About half an hour later, the nurse returned. "Doctor Valdez will check you out in a few minutes. He will look at your head and the leg. "You have a temperature of 102 and a pulse of 130. You will need some IV fluids." She motioned to an orderly to move Rusty's gurney into a small alcove next to one of the treatment rooms.

The senior EMT that brought him in, finished his paperwork and shook Powell's hand as he prepared to leave. "Best of luck amigo. I hope they can fix you up and bring your memory back. We have to go back to work."

Rusty forced a smile, held out his right hand and spoke to him in Spanish. "I will do my best. Thank you for everything. Say goodbye to your right hand man." Just then, someone moved the gurney again, this time to a treatment room close by. Sometime later, a young man with a handlebar moustache and a stethoscope around his neck approached and said, "good afternoon, my name is Dr. Hector Valdez. Welcome to Hospital San Jose. You have no identification. The nurse says you are an American."

Switching to English, Rusty said, "Yes I am. But I can't remember my name."

Valdez switched to English as well. "Well, let's have a look at you. From this EMT report, it looks like you had a fall and banged your head. And I see that your leg is also a problem. Did that happen when you fell?"

"No, I think it's been this way for a while. I don't know exactly when it happened, but it feels like it's broken."

"As soon as we can get you in for some x-rays we will be able to assess the extent of your injuries. It may be some time, so try to relax. The nurse is going to insert an IV and we will give you some fluids. I noticed that your Spanish is pretty good. But we have several English-speaking nurses and technicians here. Whichever way you feel more comfortable is fine with us. I will see you a little bit later."

Shortly thereafter, of the nurses came in and took off his filthy clothing, sponging him down and bit and enrobing him in a clean hospital gown. She then found a vein in his arm and began the IV.

It was several hours later when an orderly wheeled Powell to the radiology department. A rotund, but pleasant looking woman, speaking Spanish, instructed him to move from the gurney to the x-ray platform, where she proceeded to take several pictures of his injured leg. Another woman then moved him to an adjoining room with an MRI, where his head was examined. After those pictures were taken, Rusty was returned to the ER, but placed in an actual treatment room.

Scores of new patients were brought in over the next few hours, crowding the hallways and adding to the difficulty of seeing to everyone in a reasonable amount of time. Corpses were taken directly to the already overwhelmed city morgue. Several additional facilities were set up around the city to handle the dead. The August heat was making conditions extremely difficult. The smell of death and destruction filled the already heavy Sonoran atmosphere.

It was close to 6PM when Dr. Valdez returned. "Sir, have you had any luck remembering your name?"

"No, not yet. The dizziness has not gone away. What did you see in the x-rays, doctor?"

"Well, there is good news and some not-so-good. You have a brain concussion, but fortunately the swelling is not severe. There are no blood clots, and that is very good. The MRI can't tell us exactly why you are experiencing memory loss. This is not an unusual reaction to this type of brain injury. In time, your memory will likely improve. In the meantime, the more serious problem is the leg. The bone is shattered and it appears that a low-level infection is taking hold. This could explain your elevated temperature. We need to get you to surgery, or there is a growing risk that you could lose the lower half of the leg."

CHAPTER 53

RICO MORALES'S BODY was brought to one of the temporary morgue facilities in the center of the city. There was ample identification on his person. From this information, a firefighter working in the tent was able to pass on the information to the Hermosillo police; now a requirement in the wake of the disaster.

Morales's wife was still at a beach resort. Hermosillo residents not in the city when the earthquake struck were ordered not to return until the authorities deemed it safe to do so. Elaina Morales made a number of attempts to contact her husband but was unsuccessful. At this point she felt compelled to try and contact his boss, Domingo Fuentes, in the hopes that he would have information on Rico's whereabouts.

She reached him on the second ring. "Señor Fuentes, it is Elaina Morales. I am very worried about Rico. There has been no word. Has he contacted you since the quake? Do you know where he is?

Fuentes knew Elaina, but not very well. Rico never discussed his wife, or any aspect of his personal life, with anyone in the cartel. "I have not heard from Rico. Communications are very poor. Landlines are mostly out, and only a few cellphone towers are operating in the city. It may be a few more days before your husband can make contact with you. I suggest you wait before calling the authorities. They have their hands full."

"I know this, but Rico would have figured out a way to make contact with me by now. I fear that he is injured, or even worse, and I cannot eat or sleep until I know for sure, one way or the other."

"Certainly, Elaina, but you must have faith. Keep saying to yourself that Rico is okay. Pray for his safety. That is all you can do at the moment. If he is alive he will get word to you soon."

Elaina thanked Fuentes, gave him her cellphone number and asked him to let her know if he got word on her husband's condition.

****

All four of the surgical suites at Hospital San Jose were in use, with a number of critical cases waiting in the wings. There was little chance that Powell would get an opening for an operation anytime soon. This was exacerbated by the fact that no one was there to make any pleas on his behalf. Virtually all of the other critical and serious patients awaiting surgery had someone from their immediate family present.

Another two hours passed before Dr. Valdez paid Rusty a visit. "How are you feeling, my young patient?" Valdez took a quick look at Powell's chart. "I see that your fever has gone down; the heart rate as well. I would guess that the antibiotic and other fluids are beginning to do the job."

"I feel a little better. What about the leg?"

"An orthopedic surgeon is necessary to take a better look at the x-rays and plan for the surgery as soon as possible. Unfortunately, there is only one such surgeon available and he has been operating for almost two solid days without a break. I have contacted Hospital CIMA, the largest facility here in Hermosillo. There is a chance that we could secure one of their orthopedic surgeons to attend to your leg. But you would need to be transported to CIMA and that might take some time. They will let us know if and when that could take place. In the meantime, we will continue with the antibiotics to attend to the infection in the leg."

"Thanks Doctor. I can understand what you are dealing with, even though the extent of the disaster hasn't been made clear to me. I don't remember a thing before the men discovered me in the hole. I had only been conscious for a few minutes before they came."

"There was a major earthquake that struck a few days ago. It has destroyed much of the western and central parts of Hermosillo. Many are dead, thousands are injured and an unknown number of people are missing. It is the biggest earthquake on record in this country. Our hospitals are struggling to keep up. My wife, vacationing with our three children in Cancun, is unable to return to the city. It is a terrible situation. No doubt your family has no idea where you might be."

"I have no idea where my family is. I don't even know if I have a family. But at least I'm alive. Right now, that's about all I can say. My head is really aching like crazy Doctor. Can they give me something for the pain?"

"Certainly. I will have one of the nurses come by to take care of that. We want you to be as comfortable as possible. Keep your spirits up and say a prayer that Hospital CIMA can get you a surgeon to work on the leg. I will check in on you later."

Powell thanked Valdez, who walked out of the treatment room to find a nurse.

CHAPTER 54

RICHARD MARTINEZ RETURNED to his Phoenix apartment, following a dinner with some neighbors, when the grandfathers clock in his small study chimed the 10PM hour. He was dog tired, having been up since 5AM and in federal court most of the day. Checking the mail, as well as messages on both his landline and cellphone, there was nothing of great importance, so he changed into his skivvies and dropped into bed.

Tomorrow morning, he was to decide on making the trip to Mexico, hoping against hope that his missing Border Patrol Agent was found and on his way home. He wasn't about to see his boss take it on the chin and have nothing to show for the $10 million he bet on Powell's return.

He flipped on the TV, as the local news had just begun. Sally Henkel had let him know that a memorial for Gary Childers was going to be held that afternoon at the Nogales Border Station. She told him that she would attend, representing the Bureau, but standing in the background as just one of the crowd. The station showed a brief clip of the ceremony. It was an extremely subdued affair. Childers' murder was the third such killing to take place in the line of duty over the past six months.

The ensuing weather report was for continued very hot days with the chance of rain every evening. He went to his iPhone and checked the forecast for northern Mexico. It was much the same. If he decided to head south, he would do so by late morning, giving himself the better part of the day to get to Hermosillo. It was normally about a six and a half hour drive, but not knowing what he might encounter once he got close to the city, he allowed himself additional time.

He had no idea where he might stay, but the plan was to meet up with Dan Bolger, a Mexico-based FBI special agent at the U.S.

Consulate General Office by 7PM. His car's navigation system would help get him there. Reports indicated that the office experienced only minor damage from the quake.

After a few more minutes of news and local sports, Martinez turned off the TV and was asleep five minutes later. The peace and tranquility was interrupted shortly thereafter. His cellphone rang at 10:25. It was Sally Henkel.

"Richard, I hope you gave very serious thought to your insane idea about heading down to Hermosillo tomorrow. Tell me you decided it was not an intelligent thing to do."

"Sally, I love you; really I do. But playing the mother role with your boss is also not too bright. It's like I told you: In the morning, if my head says to do it, I'll be on my way by ten. But a little sleep tonight would do wonders. So good night, lovely lady. I promise to call you with my decision, either before ten, or when I'm on the road." Martinez hung up before Henkel had an opportunity to respond. She feared that he would make the trip, and walk into a situation he would not be able to control.

Richard had no trouble falling back to sleep. A short time later, the rain began to fall; first as a soft shower, an hour or so later as a heavy downpour. It would rain all night and into the early hours of the morning.

CHAPTER 55

DAY 10

THE DRIVING RAIN pelted the outside of the small window in the treatment room where Rusty awaited some word on a surgeon for his leg. It was a little past five in the morning when a different on-duty ER physician looked in on the patient. Powell had slept for a few hours, but was half awake. The new doctor appeared to be in his early forties; tall and thin, with an infectious smile.

"Sir, my name is Dr. Alex Montoya. Dr. Valdez left me a note last night. We are still awaiting word on an orthopedic surgeon to look after your leg. Nothing yet. Sorry to bother you so early in the morning. How are you feeling; any memory improvement?"

"Not too bad. The pain medication seems to be hanging on. No improvement as far as the memory is concerned. If possible, I would appreciate something to eat."

"I will ask one of the nurses to find you some food. Your fever continues to go down. It is close to normal. I understand you may be an American. Would you prefer that we speak in English. My medical training was at UCLA."

Powell tried to sit up a bit, but he was still quite weak. The IV continued to drip an antibiotic and some fluids into his bloodstream. "Either way is fine with me, doctor. For some reason, my Spanish is pretty good. I sure wish I could figure things out. My head feels better, but the memory banks are still asleep. I don't even know how I ended up in the back of the SUV at the bottom of that hole. How the hell did I wind up in this town in the first place?"

"Good questions. But take it easy. You need to get your strength back. That will speed up the healing process in your head. Right now, let's concentrate on getting that leg fixed. I have a good contact at Hospital CIMA. She's on your case. We'll either get you over there for the surgery or if we're lucky we can get it done here. I'll see you in a little while. And we will certainly get you something to eat."

Montoya left the treatment room in search of a nurse to scrape up some food. It was too early for the regular breakfast trays to come around, but there was always something in the hospital kitchen to help a patient in need of some solid food.

Powell had no idea how long he had been in the hospital. His mind simply was not processing any information dealing with the past. Hopeful that the condition would improve over time, his limited ability to focus was centered on his lower left leg. Rusty's fear at the moment was that he would lose it. Unable to conjure up any real emotions, he stared at the ceiling and waited for someone to come by with a little food.

The ER seemed to quiet down a bit. There were fewer moans and screams. Rusty could hear nurses and doctors conversing in the hallway, but there didn't seem to be as many new victim arrivals as there was the day before. He wasn't sure what to make of the change in the level of chaos, but it helped to calm his nerves a bit.

About half an hour later, the voice of a new nurse entering his room provided some hope that food might be on the way. Turning his head to see her, his tired eyes sprang fully open at the sight. The woman, probably in her late twenties, was possibly the most beautiful human being he had ever seen. Somewhat petite, but lean and shapely, she had lustrous jet black hair, pulled back in a ponytail, and possessed the most striking clear blue eyes.

"My name is Angela. You will have some food in just a few minutes. I will be your nurse for a while. Apparently you are going to be transferred to Hospital CIMA in a few hours." She approached Rusty's gurney and took his vital signs, as his eyes continued to be awestruck by her magnificent face."

"That's good news. Thank you. If they are planning to transfer me, it must mean that a surgeon has been found to work on my leg."

He spoke in Spanish, as it seemed that Angela might not be English speaking. He was wrong.

"They tell me you are American. I would like to practice my English with you. Is that okay?"

"It's fine with me. Where did you learn to speak it?"

"I went to a private school in Monterrey. English was a required course. Then, when I graduated from high school, my mother sent me to Tucson to live with an aunt while I waited to be accepted to nursing school. I loved living in the states. Someday I would like to go back and work there in a big hospital."

Rusty was mesmerized by Angela's beauty and wonderful personality. She turned and left the treatment room, but returned in a few minutes with a tray of food. "Here are some eggs they made you in the kitchen. And some toast and coffee. I hope you enjoy it." She moved the rolling bed shelf in position and set the tray on it. The food looked great. He hadn't eaten in almost three days. It took him less than five minutes to finish it all. Angela left again to tend to other patients. He couldn't get her out of his mind.

CHAPTER 56

MARTINEZ WOKE WITHOUT the need for his alarm clock. It was 6:30. He switched off the alarm and went to relieve his bladder, when the phone rang. "Who the hell is calling at this hour?" He asked, as finished his tinkle and ran back to answer it.

"Richard, it's Lowell Fox. Glad I got to you before you hit the road. Are you coherent?"

Martinez was literally caught with his pants down. "Lowell, what's up? Everything okay?" It was 8:30 in D.C., so he thought for a moment that Fox forgot about the three-hour difference.

"Everything's fine here, Richard. But a little birdie told me that you might be getting ready to do something really dumb. Is this a fact?"

Martinez was mad as hell that Sally would call the FBI Director and tattle on her boss. "So Special Agent Henkel ratted on me. Last time I confide in a subordinate. What can I say? A man's got to do what he has to do."

"What the hell are you talking about? I thought you had more brains than that. Why would I want one of my key people throwing himself in the middle of the biggest natural disaster in the history of this hemisphere to find a missing man in a mountain of rubble? Sorry, but it doesn't make any sense."

"Lowell, I've got this thing wired. Dan Bolger is driving up from Mexico City. We're going to meet at the U.S. Mission in Hermosillo and start chasing down some leads. We'll check all the hospitals, and the morgues, as well as follow up on some intelligence I dug up from Bennett Frost at the Agency and Pepe Sanchez with the Mexicans Drug Task Force. If we strike out, we'll head right home. We owe the guy that much. He risked his life to enforce the law."

"Richard, these cartels kill and chop people up for the fun of it. They won't think twice about taking you out if they smell you snooping around on their turf."

"Sanchez tells me that the Calimar people are in a state of total panic and disarray. With the town a pile of rubble, their drug shipments are on hold and several of their key people are either missing or dead."

"I know why you're doing this. It's the $10 million that you're worried about. I briefed the president and he totally understands the situation. We'll be giving hundreds of millions to the Mexicans for disaster relief. If this Agent Powell is still alive he'll find a way to get back to the U.S. So you very well may be wasting your time. See what I'm saying? It's not worth it Richard. That's the bottom line."

"Guess you can fire me if you like. I'm going down there. One promise: if after three days we're still in the dark, with no leads to follow, I'll head home. I spoke with the Red Cross yesterday. The city is still a disaster, but rescue and cleanup are under a full head of steam. We'll have some police protection. I'll be fine."

"I have nothing more to say." Out of sheer frustration, Fox ended the call.

Martinez sat on the edge of his bed and pondered his next move. He could call the whole thing off; phone Bolger and tell him to stay home, wait a few more days to go down, or simply abort the whole mission. He was confident that Lowell Fox would support him in any case. It was something he had to do.

He shaved and then jumped in the shower. His choice of wardrobe was easy: white cotton shirt, sand-colored khakis, and a pair of rubber-soled chukka-style boots. His reliable tan-colored Tilley hat and horn rimmed sunglasses completed the picture.

For breakfast, he pulled a package of Aunt Jemima pancakes out of the freezer and popped the short stack in the microwave. The coffee brewer was already going. He poured an oversized cup and worked on it as he straightened up the apartment and checked emails before heading out the door.

The rain was easing up as Richard walked to his F-150. At 8:45 he was on the road.

CHAPTER 57

A FEW MINUTES after ten in the morning, Dr. Montoya paid Rusty a visit. The activity in the ER had picked up a bit following a rather quiet period earlier. Powell dozed off after his much-appreciated breakfast and the amazingly beautiful nurse's visit.

"Sir; I regret that we can't refer to you by name. In any case, I have some good news. You will not have to be transferred to Hospital CIMA. That facility is still overwhelmed with patient activity and its operating facility is at capacity for the foreseeable future. Two orthopedic surgeons are arriving from Chihuahua to help alleviate the backlog in surgical patients. I understand that they are on the way and should arrive in Hermosillo in a few hours. One of the two is coming directly here. You are scheduled as one of his patients for surgery this afternoon or this evening."

Powell was unsure of what lied ahead. "Good news, I guess. In any case, I really appreciate your efforts, Dr. Montoya. I would imagine that there are many people who are in need of medical help and in much worse shape than I."

"Not for you to worry about. And by the way, we have given you a name. It's needed for identification and recordkeeping purposes. Until you regain some memory, the hospital will refer to you as David Smith. Try to remember it, in case someone on the staff calls you by this name. In the meantime, we have no option but to leave you here in the ER. No regular patient rooms are available. Hopefully, after your surgery we will have a room to put you in for recovery. I regret that this is the best we can do."

"Understood. Your nursing staff here in the ER is outstanding. They have made it as comfortable as conditions might allow. My headache seems to be easing up a bit. Maybe this is a good sign that my memory will be returning soon."

"That could very well be the case. So, David Smith, if I do not see you again before you head to surgery, best of luck. My understanding is that both of the surgeons coming to Hermosillo are first-rate. I am confident that you will receive very good care." Montoya shook Rusty's hand and went on his way.

A few minutes later, Angela returned to take Powell's vital signs. His heart rate went up as soon as she appeared. She smiled as she fastened the blood pressure cuff and placed the pulse monitor on his finger. "How are you feeling, Mr. Smith?"

"I see the news of my new name has gotten around. I'm feeling okay. As soon as this torn up leg is fixed I'll feel much better."

"Your new name is now on your chart. You see; we are very organized here. I am also supposed to give you some more pain medication. Dr. Montoya said it was okay." Angela reached over to the table, picked up a syringe and injected something into the IV. "Is there anything else I can do for you, Mr. Smith?"

Several thoughts ran through Rusty's mind as he pondered the wishful notion of having sex with this ravishing young woman. "Guess I'm okay. Thanks for asking."

"I understand that you will staying here in the ER until they call you for surgery. So I will see you again." Her spectacular smile surfaced again, as she turned and left her patient lying there in a euphoric state."

Ambulance sirens continued to break into Powell's consciousness. It sounded as though the ER was once again facing an influx of quake victims. Rusty was yet to totally comprehend the extent of the disaster, but his shaken brain was struggling with something of importance to only him; discovering who he was and what he was doing in there in the first place.

A few minutes later, the pain medication dripping into his bloodstream made him very drowsy. Dozing off, his mind drew a vivid picture of Angela and her perfectly shaped breasts peeking through her starched white uniform. A wonderful vision to lull him to sleep.

CHAPTER 58

MIGUEL CASTRO HAD an update on the Calimar situation in Hermosillo. As promised he placed a secure call to his boss, Bennett Frost, who was on assignment in Acapulco.   The CIA's chief operative in Mexico was tailing a suspected al Qaida organizer planning an attack in that Mexican resort town sometime in the near future.

"Mr. Frost, it is Miguel. I do not know how important this is, but this morning I received a message from a contact very close to the Calimar leadership. The organization operating in the Hermosillo area has been decimated by the quake. Sancho Lopez, the headman, is okay. He spends most of his time at his beach house near Guaymas. That town was shook by the quake, but there were no deaths or major damage. Domingo Fuentes survived. His house in Hermosillo was also spared.

I have heard that half a dozen of his key lieutenants were killed. One of the drug runners told me that the American border patrol agent never got out of Hermosillo. The ransom money was paid, but no one knows where the border agent is. There is a strong possibility that he is dead as well. Apparently he was being held by some of Fuentes' men."

"Good stuff, Miguel. I think it might be time to let my friends in the FBI have access to this information. Keep your eyes and ears open my friend. If you hear anything at all about the patrol agent, get back to me right away. Comprende?"

"Okay, but it is very difficult. Hermosillo is a mess. The hospitals are full. Power is slowly coming back to some parts of the city. It will take months, maybe years, for the place to recover. You know it is bad when the drug traffic slows to a crawl. I will do my best."

Frost wasted no time dialing Richard Martinez's cellphone number. While he didn't have any really hard intelligence to share on Rusty

Powell, he thought that Martinez would appreciate the update. Richard was on I-19, just north of Tucson, when the phone signaled an incoming call. Caller ID was unavailable. "Martinez here."

"Richard, it's Bennett Frost. What's happening, my friend?"

"Not much. I'm on my way down to Hermosillo. Need to find my border patrol agent. Have anything for me?"

"No, not really, but what the hell are you doing? You must have a few screws loose! Nobody in their right mind would be headed down there unless they were asked to come by the authorities. The only people they want are emergency types. What do you think you can accomplish?"

"Help the Bureau out of a jamb. We need to find Agent Powell and bring him home. If he's dead, then we'll bring him back in a box. End of story. Now what have you got?"

Frost passed on what limited information he had. It didn't take very long. "So that's about it. Your missing border agent can be anywhere, but the town is in such bad shape even the bad guys can't get their act together. If you want a place to start, I would try the hospitals or the morgues. Word is that they've set up several locations to handle the bodies. Last report I got was that more than 15,000 people are dead, and another 50,000 missing under the rubble. Lot's of luck."

"Thanks for the info and the kind words of encouragement. You hear anything that sounds interesting, let me know. Running into quite a bit of traffic going into Tucson. Gotta go."

Martinez heard sirens. He figured there was an accident up ahead. Traffic on Interstate 19 was backing up at a time when there was normally not a problem. Lunch hour was usually not this bad. It was 11:30. As the southbound traffic inched along, Richard got another call. It was Sally Henkel.

"So you're actually going down there. You clearly need to have your head examined."

"You, you turncoat! Going over my head a couple of levels." Martinez was playing with Henkel. He fully understood her motivation to contact Lowell Fox, given the hazards of the trip and the lack of knowledge to guide his search for Powell. "I'm surprised you didn't call the president. Maybe he just wouldn't come to the phone."

"Get serious Richard. Where are you now?"

Martinez was reticent about letting her know exactly where he was. She might try to hook up with him. That was the last thing he wanted. Stretching it a bit, he provided a misleading answer. "I'm almost to the border. Should be in Hermosillo for a nice Mexican dinner."

"Right. Listen, you let me know what's happening down there. Where are you staying, in case we need to come and dig you out?"

"I have no idea at the moment. Dan Bolger is meeting me at the U.S. Mission. He said he would book something he could find that was open for business. I'll let you know. How did the service for Childers go? Did you meet up with Escobar?"

"It was okay. Pretty sad scene. You know what those things are like. I didn't try to see Escobar. He needed to be with his troops. I kind of stayed in the background. Let's hope we don't have to attend another one anytime soon."

"We're going to find Powell. I have this feeling that he's alive; maybe injured and lying in one of the hospitals. If he is, we'll find him and get him home. Talk with you soon."

Traffic began to move as Martinez approached the center of Tucson. Patrol cars, an ambulance and fire engine appeared on the shoulder. A wrecked pickup truck and a banged-up Toyota were there as well.

CHAPTER 59

ANGELA CONTRERAS WAS twenty-six years old. Still single, after finishing nursing school and working for four years in hospitals in Monterrey and Hermosillo, she lived with a roommate, also an RN, in a small two-bedroom apartment east of the city. Their immediate neighborhood experienced only minor damage. Their only inconvenience was being without power and running water for two days.

Having lived in Tucson for a short time, she was not unfamiliar with American men, many who were immediately attracted to her beauty and magnetic personality. Coming from an extremely conservative Mexican family, she was, unconventionally at her age, a virgin. Only a total commitment to a man would be her rationale for submission. This was certainly an unusual attitude for a young single woman in the 21st. century.

David Smith, her patient at the moment, ignited emotions in Angela that perhaps equaled what he experienced when in her presence. There was a level of electricity that was palpable and powerful in its intensity. The fact that David Smith was Rusty Powell and did not, for the moment, know that he had another woman in his life, and a wife at that, was inconsequential. Only time would allow the facts and consequences to play themselves out.

A few minutes before 4PM, Angela entered Powell's treatment room, where she found him sound asleep. Not wanting to wake him, she left and returned to her nurses' station, where a distinguished-looking, dark-complexioned, middle-aged gentleman was conversing with an ER physician. The head nurse on duty made the introduction.

"Angela, this is Dr. Manuel Ortega. He has just arrived from Chihuahua, and will be performing several operations this evening.

Two of the patients have already been admitted and will precede our special ER guest, David Smith. I suggest you alert Mr. Smith that sometime later tonight he will be in surgery."

Excited by the news and anxious to let Rusty know, Angela excused herself and went back to his treatment room, where he remained in a deep sleep. Again hesitant to wake him, she thought it best to follow the head nurse's direction and began to wake him up.

"Mr. Smith, wake up. It is Angela. I have some good news for you. Mr. Smith?"

Powell quickly opened his eyes. "Angela. Good to see you. What's up?"

"Sometime tonight you will be in surgery. Dr. Manuel Ortega has arrived from Chihuahua and will operating here for a few days. I know that Dr. Montoya advised you that an orthopedic surgeon was on the way. He is here now. At some point I imagine he will come in to see you before you move to the O.R. This is very good news."

Rusty was still half asleep, but the sight and sound of Angela, coupled with the fact that his leg would soon be in a surgeon's hands, gave him a sense of warmth and encouragement that filled his senses.

"That's great, Angela. Thanks for coming in to tell me. You're the best. What's going to happen to me when you go off duty or I get assigned to a regular room?"

"Somehow I will find you. By the time you are out of surgery I will be off duty. The information desk will give me a report on how you are doing. Then we will see. It may not be until tomorrow morning before we can see each other again."

At that moment, Dr. Ortega politely rapped on the side of the treatment room entrance and walked in. "Mr. Smith, I am Manuel Ortega; pleased to meet you. I understand you are an American, so permit me to practice my rusty English."

"Good to meet you, doctor. My left leg will be even more pleased to make your acquaintance. English or Spanish; either way is fine with me."

"I have just had a look at your x-rays, Mr. Smith, and by the way, I know that this is a name the hospital gave you for the time being.

Hopefully your memory will return very soon. As for the surgery, you have a compound fracture of both the tibia and fibula. There are major bone fragments and a bullet fragment that must be removed. And we will have to insert a few metal supports. This could be a long and difficult operation, and there will be substantial trauma as a result.

Pain management will be an important aspect of your recovery. And to be honest, once we get in there, the decision will have to be made to either proceed with the reconstruction, or to remove the leg below the knee. I am afraid that this is the best information I can provide at the moment. I hope you can understand. What I *will* promise you is that I will do whatever I can do save the leg."

"I understand Dr. Ortega. Thanks for taking the time to speak with me. I'm sure you have other patients to attend to in the meantime. You're very kind."

"You will probably not see me again until you are in recovery. Goodbye for now."

Angela returned a few minutes later. "Dr. Ortega has ordered some medication that should relax you for the next few hours. Someone will come by to take you up to the O.R. I go off duty in about an hour. If I can, I will stop by before then.

"I'll be thinking about you until we see each other again." Powell gently put a hand on her arm. She smiled, as she injected the medication into his IV. Before leaving the treatment room she bent down and kissed him on the forehead. It was totally unexpected, and clearly against hospital rules. For Rusty, it was heaven.

CHAPTER 60

MARTINEZ DROVE THROUGH the Nogales Border Station at 1:05 in the afternoon. He showed his FBI identification to the guard at the crossing gate. He was waved through without delay.

Picking up speed as he entered Mexico Highway 15, he used his cellphone's Bluetooth connection to call Dan Bolger, who had planned to arrive in Hermosillo by this time and find his way to the U.S. Mission. Bolger, a seasoned Bureau agent, went through the FBI Academy with Martinez, and requested international assignments. His most recent one was to London, where he worked with Scotland Yard on security plans for the 2012 Summer Olympics. Immediately thereafter, he was transferred to Mexico City.

Agents assigned outside the U.S., are known as Legal Attaches, or Legats, and are usually based at the host country's embassy or consulate. There was also a Legat based in Monterrey, but Bolger was more senior and very experienced in kidnapping cases.

Dan was still on the road when he answered the call. "Ricardo; glad you called. Where are you now?"

"Just entered Mexico. Ran into an accident on I-19. It was slow going for a while. Where are you amigo?"

"I flew into Guaymas; got there about an hour ago and jumped in a rental car. Hermosillo airport is still closed. The terminal building is in shambles. Should get to Hermosillo in less than an hour, but no telling how difficult it's going to be to get over to the U.S. Mission. The folks there know that we're coming; I called them this morning. Two of their senior employees are dead. But they say they're operational. The building had minor damage."

"I roll in about three hours from now. You should have some time to kill before I get there. How about calling the coroner to see if they have Powell's name in their system. I understand they have temporary morgues set up all over the city, so it may be a shot in the dark. If you strike out there, try the hospitals. If we're lucky, he's in one of them getting treatment. We found Powell's blood in the Jeep they took on patrol. There's no way to know how badly he was hurt."

"Will do. I'll see you at the Consulate; guess around 4:30?"

"Sounds about right. Find a place we can chow down afterwards. I'm buying."

Martinez then rang Sally Henkel's cellphone, getting her voicemail. "Hey Sally, it's me. I'm on Mexico 15, probably around three hours from Hermosillo. Give me a call when you get this message."

Henkel picked up as soon as she could, after seeing Richard's number on caller ID. "Boss, I'm here. Sorry I couldn't answer right away. I had the Pima County Sheriff on the line. What's up?"

"I need you to get with Roland Escobar, as well as Melinda Powell. If the cartel henchmen got rid of Rusty's uniform and other forms of ID, I need to know if he had any distinguishing body scars, birthmarks, and the like. If he is deceased, Dan Bolger and I will need that kind of information. Take it easy on his wife. She's got to be a basket case. Okay?"

"Copy that. Anything else? Have enough clips for the Glock?"

"No problem, but I don't expect to need it. The cartel is in disarray; the population's trying to survive on a day-to-day basis. It's not likely that anybody will be gunning for us."

"Alright. Be careful. You never know. I'll get back to you as soon as I can get what you need."

Chapter 61

Sally immediately phoned Escobar, who answered on the second ring. "Special Agent Henkel, how are you? Any news on Agent Powell?"

"Afraid not. But we hope to have some very soon. My boss is on his way to find him."

"You mean you know where he might be?"

"Not really, but we have every reason to believe that he is somewhere in Hermosillo, hopefully still alive. Knowing Richard Martinez, if Rusty is down there, he'll find him."

"That'll be quite a trick. All the news reports show the city is still a disaster. Martinez must have some clues. No?"

"We have pretty good contacts down there. Let's wait and see what he learns. In any case, I'm calling to see if you can provide any information on Agent Powell's physical anomalies, if there are any. Do your records show that kind of thing?"

"Usually not, unless an agent is injured on duty. Then the medical staff puts a notation in their file. I can check on it and let you know. How soon do you need the information?"

"If you can get it within the next couple of hours, that would be great. Worst case, we may have to identify Powell's body if he's deceased and turns up in one of the locations they set up to handle the dead."

"No problem, Agent Henkel. Have you talked with Melinda Powell?"

"My next call. Hope to hear from you soon."

Henkel dialed Melinda's home phone. Her mother answered, while preparing dinner in the kitchen. "This is FBI Special Agent Sally Henkel calling for Melinda. Is she available?"

"I believe she is. Please hold and I will see if she can come to the phone. Melinda's mom put the call on hold and went to the patio, where her daughter was watering some plants. "Honey, an Agent Henkel is on the phone. Can you take it?"

"I'll be right in, mother. Thanks. Melinda turned off the garden hose and went back into the house. The cordless phone handset was on the island in the kitchen.

"This is Melinda. Agent Henkel, can I help you? Any word on Rusty?"

"Good afternoon Melinda. Please call me Sally if you like. No word as yet on your husband, but Richard Martinez, my boss, is on his way down to Hermosillo. If anyone can find him and bring him home, Richard is the man."

"My God, Sally, you think Rusty might be alive in that battered city? Every time I turn on the news they talk about how bad it is down there. And how do we know he wasn't taken somewhere else?"

"We don't know Melinda, but we do have a number of contacts down there who have gotten information that gives us some hope that Rusty is somewhere in the city, and may be okay." Sally wished she could take back the last comment. There was no information to suggest that Powell was indeed okay. "Let's keep hoping for the best, Melinda. In the meantime, I do need some information that could help us in the search."

"What kind of information?"

"Are there any distinguishing marks on Rusty's body that would help in an identification; things like scars or birthmarks? If his paper identification was somehow removed or damaged, this kind of information would be needed."

"You mean, if he's dead."

"Yes, but also if he's unconscious or otherwise not able to prove his identity. That could be problematic, if we are trying to get him home without having difficulties with the Mexican authorities. Anything you can share with me?"

"He has a couple of scars; one on his right shoulder and the other on the right side of his neck. And he has a birthmark on his butt. That's about all I can remember. I think that's about it."

"Great stuff, Melinda. Let's hope we won't need it, but at least we'll be prepared. Thanks and keep saying your prayers. Richard Martinez is the best hope we've got. Any news and we'll get to you right away. Take care."

Immediately after ending the call, Roland Escobar's name popped up on caller ID. "Roland Escobar here. Just checked Powell's personal file. There was one notation about a scar on his neck. Apparently it was caused by a run-in with a barbed wire fence. It happened on the job in Nogales. That's about it."

"Thanks, Agent Escobar. That confirms the information I just got from Rusty's wife. There are a few other distinguishing marks, but they're typically not visible, and probably happened before he joined the Border Patrol."

"Very well, Agent Henkel. Let me know as soon as you draw a bead on Powell. We're praying for him to get home in one piece."

"Will do. That's it for now. Talk with you soon."

Henkel made the call to Martinez, who was within a couple of hours of Hermosillo. She gave Richard the information and reminded him to be safe.

CHAPTER 62

DOMINGO FUENTES RECEIVED an unexpected phone call from Diego Molina. It was almost dinnertime for Domingo and Maria. Most nights they ate around seven. She had been making one of her husband's favorite chicken dishes when the call came through on the landline.

"Señor Fuentes, sorry to bother you, but I was told that you were looking for Rico Morales. I wanted to tell you what I know about his whereabouts."

"Diego, it is good to hear from you. I am pleased that you have survived our disaster. Many our colleagues unfortunately have not been so fortunate. What do you know about Rico? Is he alive, or injured? Do you know where he is?"

"I regret that I do not know, but when I left Ramon's apartment Rico and Ramon were taking the gringo to Ramon's Xterra and were going to deliver him to the Banamex HSBC Bank according the plan. Rico told me it was okay to leave, as I needed to head to Monterrey to meet my wife. As I headed to my car, which was parked close by, the ground began to shake. I did not know it was an earthquake and went to open the car door, when everything went black. I guess I fell and hit my head. It was some time before I woke up, but by then Ramon's apartment and the Paseo de la Cascada were totally destroyed. No one could get through. I wanted to see if Ramon had driven off with the gringo, but there was no way to reach them.

I began to walk, not knowing exactly where I was going. Everything was still shaking; I guess they call it aftershocks. Anyway, I managed to get out onto a road that was still in one piece and kept walking to the north. A police car picked me up and took me in the direction of my house, dropping me along the road, so that they could help some injured people. I eventually made it to my home.

I am sorry, Señor Fuentes, but I am not able to tell you what happened to Rico or Ramon. I understand that the Paseo de la Cascada is not yet open to traffic. They may have gotten away, but none of the men have heard from them, so it does not look good."

Fuentes looked somewhat perplexed, but understood why Molina felt he needed to tell the boss what he knew. "Diego, I understand. Do not feel badly. There was nothing that you could do under the circumstances. Rico's wife called me from the seashore. I told her that the conditions in the city were so bad that many people were missing or dead. She was advised to stay away from Hermosillo until the authorities considered it to be safe to return. Rico and Ramon are in God's hands."

It was clear to Domingo that the drug running into Arizona and beyond would be stymied for some time. Until he re-solidified his senior reporting structure, communications and specific distribution directives would have to wait. Production of cocaine continued in a number of the cartel's locations, but the inventory would necessarily sit there for a while. In the meantime the $10 million bonus to return the American was a nice addition to the working capital reserve.

PART V

The Search Is On

CHAPTER 63

MARTINEZ REACHED THE outskirts of Hermosillo around 4:40PM. Federal police were intercepting Mexico 15 highway traffic at several checkpoints going into the city proper. Richard was stopped, showed his identification, and was politely permitted to pass through. The GPS navigation in his F-150 indicated he had eight miles to go before the U.S. Mission facility. He dialed Dan Bolger' cellphone number, but the call went to voicemail. Several streets on the way were still in bad shape and blocked by wooden barricades. The obstructions drove the navigation voice crazy, making numerous attempts to adjust the route along the way.

Bolger was doing some dinner reconnaissance, per Martinez's earlier suggestion. There was a very limited selection in the immediate area. Several restaurants had been boarded up, seemingly due to structural damage.

He did manage to secure two rooms at the Hotel San Alberto, just a few blocks from the U.S. Mission building, home of the Consulate General. The San Alberto was nothing special, but the rooms were clean and there was virtually no damage to the building. A cafeteria was the only food service in the hotel. The Caffenia Rosales, an excellent coffee shop nearby, was also open for business.

The University of Sonora was only a few blocks away. The school was closed, due to damage in a number of buildings on the campus. Oddly enough, the cafeteria was open, serving a limited lunch and dinner for students living in the dorms. It was another option, if all else failed.

Bolger returned Richard's call ten minutes later. Martinez was a few minutes from the U.S. Mission building. "Where are you now? Can you find the building?"

"Navigation says I'm within a few blocks of there. If you see the white F-150, I've arrived. Any problem getting through the gate?"

"There is no gate. It was leveled by the quake. There's a security guard just outside the door. Show your badge. I'll be in the lobby."

The consulate building was visible in short order. Martinez turned off of Mexico 15 and on to Monterrey Avenue. He pulled his pickup into the parking lot by the main entrance. Dan Bolger waved as Richard walked toward the door, where a contract security officer greeted him. Holding up his FBI credentials, he was waived through and into the lobby.

Bolger smiled and grabbed Richard's hand. "So, you made it. What do you think of this once beautiful city? Quite a mess."

"Never been here before. What a pity. I understand it was one of the most cosmopolitan cities in Mexico. Ford has a big plant here. It's going to take a long time to bring it back. So give me the lay of the land. Found a place to stay?"

"Yeah, not the Ritz Carlton, but it'll do. The food choices are pretty meager, but we'll survive. We can walk to most everything we need. That's a real plus. You don't want to be cruising around in the pickup if you can avoid it. A hell of a lot of streets are still torn up. Fortunately, this is one of the least damaged areas of the city."

"Any luck with the phone calls?"

"Nada. As far as the hospitals and the morgue locations go, Border Patrol Agent Rusty Powell doesn't exist. I didn't get through to all the hospitals. But the bigger ones couldn't help. I think it's going to take some legwork to check these places out."

"Sounds right. Let's grab a bite to eat and then pay a visit to the police. We're probably going to need them somewhere along the way."

"Fine with me. First, though, I think you should meet the Consul General. His name is Philip Boyce. Good guy. Guarantees me he won't be in the way."

"Lead on McDuff."

The two men walked to Boyce's office. He was meeting with two women at the time, but seeing Martinez and Bolger he excused himself and walked to the door. "Special Agent Martinez, I presume. Welcome to Hermosillo. Sorry our fair city is a little worse for the wear these days."

"Pleasure to meet you. It's Richard, please. For all the wrong reasons, this place is now world famous. And I'm guessing that our work's cut out for us, trying to find our border agent. Thanks, by the way, for letting us use the facility as our little command post."

"Our pleasure, Richard. Whatever we can do to help, let us know. In the meantime, you and Agent Bolger must want to check into your quarters and grab a bite to eat. He tells me he's scouted out some options. I'm about to head home, but again, please don't hesitate to call on us for assistance. Any idea how long you guys will be in town?"

Martinez took the lead. "My guess is; if we can't find our man within the next 72 hours, we'll be out of here. That doesn't mean we'll give up, but we might have to bark up another tree. See you tomorrow."

The two G-Men left Boyce's office and walked back to the lobby. Bolger grabbed his suitcase and they left the building. Martinez left his F-150 at the Consulate compound. The walk to the Hotel San Alberto took less than ten minutes.

Chapter 64

A few minutes after ten, an ER nurse entered Rusty's treatment room with an orderly. Powell was awake, but still groggy from the sedative. "Mr. Smith, it is time. Miguel will take you to the OR. Good luck. Here is an extra blanket to keep you warm."

The orderly began to push the gurney toward the elevator. Surgery suites were on the second floor. Weaving their way down the corridor, Powell noticed the patients lining the halls. The overflow was choking the ER. Nurses and support staff were exhausted. Many of them were working around the clock.

Powell's gurney was moved into one of the elevators. The orderly pushed the second floor button and smiled at his charge. "We will take good care of you, señor. Do not worry." The door opened and Miguel was met by a pleasant nurse who accompanied them to Operating Room 4. She spoke very little English, but was told that Rusty knew Spanish as well.

"Mr. Smith, my name is Tina. I believe you have met Dr. Ortega. He is a wonderful surgeon. I am going to give you an injection now to put you partially to sleep. It will be several minutes before the operation will begin. The doctor is finishing with another patient. The anesthesiologist is Dr. Campo. He will be here shortly to talk the procedure and then put you to sleep."

"I'm ready. Anything they can do to mend the leg will be a blessing. It has been hurting for as long as I can remember, which in fact, isn't very long. Do you think I can have a drink of something. My throat is very dry."

"We're not supposed to give you any liquids, other than what is flowing into your veins. Don't tell anyone, but here is some ice. It will help the dryness." She handed Rusty a cup half-filled with ice. "A little bit will be okay, but don't take it all." She then injected the sedative into the IV.

Powell chewed on a few pieces and handed the cup back to the nurse. "Very much appreciated. Thanks.

"Just relax here for a while. The medication should begin to make you very sleepy in just a few minutes. In the meantime, here comes Dr. Campo. Good luck Mr. Smith."

He looked to be in his twenties, but was actually quite a bit older. "Señor Smith. I am Martin Campo, your anesthesiologist. Are you ready for a nice nap? Once you wake up, it will be all over. Dr. Ortega is on his way. He just completed three long operations, but looks to be in fine condition. You are extremely fortunate. I can tell you firsthand; he is a gifted surgeon." Ortega signaled to the scrub nurses and Powell was shifted from the gurney to an operating table. "In just a few minutes I will start the anesthesia. Then it's pleasant dreams."

It didn't take very long. Once Campo initiated the anesthesia, it was lights out. As soon as Rusty was under, Dr. Ortega entered the operating room, addressing the team as they circled the table. "Okay, let's go to work. I want to save this man's leg. Any objections?"

Dr. Campo and the nurses visibly chuckled through their masks. Campo barked the vital signs: BP 133 over 70; pulse 118. Good as gold." Ortega took one last look at the x ray film. "Lights, action, camera." They began.

Chapter 65

Martinez and Bolger grabbed a quick meal after checking in at the hotel. Both were tired after long trips. They agreed that first thing in the morning would be soon enough to start moving ahead with the search. They went to their rooms, but Martinez wanted to make some additional calls to the hospitals Bolger hadn't yet contacted. Hospital CIMA was the first one he tried.

"I am looking for an American who was injured several days ago and brought to Hermosillo. His name is Randall Powell. Someone may have already asked you about the same person. I just want to make sure he is definitely not a patient there."

He was speaking to the admissions department supervisor on duty. She spoke reasonably good English, even though Martinez addressed her in her native tongue. "Sir, I did tell another gentleman earlier that we have no one registered here by that name. Are you certain that this individual was sent to this hospital? The earthquake has put all of the city's medical facilities under tremendous stress. This Mr. Powell you are looking for may have given up trying to get help, and went home."

"Ma'am, I'm afraid that Mr. Powell lives in America. He was brought to Hermosillo against his will. If by chance he should show up at your facility, I would appreciate a call as soon as possible. My name is Richard Martinez. I am an FBI agent, and can be reached at 623-581-2269."

The woman politely thanked Martinez for the call and said she would make certain that Powell's name would be posted at the admissions desk for the next several days. Richard then placed a call to the second hospital on the list: The General Hospital of the State of Sonora. The main switchboard was his first stop. He was then transferred to Admissions, where he spoke to a gentleman that was simply minding the store. "I'm sorry sir. The Admissions Department has closed. The hospital is completely full and we are not taking ER patients as well. I suggest you call again tomorrow morning."

Richard then tried the front desk, asking the attendant if there was a patient named Randall Powell already registered as a patient. "Sir, we have no patient by that name registered as of today. And the Admissions Department is closed."

Thanking the woman taking the call, Martinez went to the third hospital on the list, but was very close to calling it a day. It was Hospital San Jose.

Reaching the Admissions Department, a pleasant-sounding woman took the call. She was a part-time employee and was substituting for a regular clerk. "Ma'am, I am trying to find someone named Randall Powell. Do you have anyone by that name that was admitted anytime over the past several days?"

Absent for a few minutes, the woman came back on the line. "I am sorry sir, but we do not have anyone registered here by that name. Can I help you with anything else?"

Unfortunately, Martinez, dog tired, neglected to ask if there was an American by any other name registered there as a patient. He would have been given the name David Smith, which may or may not have made him suspicious and prompted him to ask some additional questions before hanging up. But he ended the call, turned out the light in his bedroom and fell immediately to sleep. Not long thereafter, his cellphone rang. It was Sally Henkel.

"Richard, I hope I didn't wake you up."

"Oh no, I was just getting ready to hit the sack. Are you just checking up on me, or what?"

"I just wanted to make sure you got there in one piece. I assume you found a hotel okay. Did you find anyplace to eat?"

"Yes, and yes. Dan Bolger scouted out the places for us. We're good. I've called a few hospitals, but Powell isn't registered in any of them. If the cartel took him, they may have used a different name. In any case, we'll be back at it tomorrow. Should be fun and games. You wouldn't believe how torn up this city is. It looks like an atom bomb was dropped here. Tomorrow we're going to check out the morgues."

"Be careful boss. And call me if anything turns up that you consider a lead. I'm on pins and needles up here. Do you understand?"

"Understood Sally. Not to worry. We're fine. Now, I *would* like to get some sleep. Talk with you tomorrow. Bye."

CHAPTER 66

ONCE OPENED, IT was obvious that Rusty's lower leg was in pitiful shape. Bone fragments were everywhere. The fibula, which took the brunt of the bullet's damage, was in three pieces. The tibia hadn't fared much better. It took more than an hour to clean out the fragments, remove the shell fragments and assess the likelihood of saving the leg below the knee.

"We have a pretty bad situation here", Ortega commented to the team. "But let see what we can do." Metal screws and other support pieces were handed to the surgeon at his direction. Fractures of the tibia and fibula shafts are often treated with an intramedullary nailing of the tibia. This involves placing a long rod or nail inside the tibia bone through the fracture fragments. In Rusty's case, the breakage was extensive. But Ortega had a remarkable amount of experience dealing with these severe cases.

The biggest problem was the length of time that had elapsed since the bones were shattered. But Ortega believed it was worth trying to connect the bone sections and giving the intricate assembly time to heal. Bottom line, the surgeon realized that the future held only two options for Powell's left leg.

Best case: the healing would allow Rusty to keep the lower leg, but given the reduction of bone and the extensive muscular damage around it, he would walk with a severe limp, and require a cane for stabilization, probably for the rest of his life. Worst case: If the patchwork failed, or if a major infection ensued, the lower leg would have to be removed at a later date.

The operation lasted nearly five hours. It was 4:45AM when Powell was wheeled into the recovery room, where he would remain for several hours. Ortega ordered a nurse to stay with Rusty until he returned to check on his patient. Painkiller was being pumped into his body at a steady rate. Still under anesthesia, he would be coming out of it gradually over the next half hour. Since there were no family or friends awaiting the results of the operation, Ortega had no one to whom he needed to report the outcome and provide a prognosis.

There was one nurse, now off duty, who returned to the hospital around six and waited for word of Powell's condition. Angela was now in street clothes, but was recognized by several staffers as they passed by the surgery lounge. One of the night duty nurses, recently transferred from the E.R. to the O.R. floor, recognized Angela and entered the lounge. "Angela, hi; what are you doing here at this hour?"

"One of my E.R. patients just had surgery. He has no family here, so I just wanted to be here when he comes to. They won't let any visitors into recovery just yet; he may still be coming out of the anesthesia."

"Is this the American who lost his memory? I heard about him from one of the other E.R. nurses."

"Yes, it is. He was very worried about losing his left leg. I wish I knew how he was doing. I'm hoping they will let me in to see him soon, even though we are not related."

"Angela, let me see if I can get some information for you. They will let me back there. Hang on, I'll be right back." She smiled, gently squeezed Angela's hand and walked toward the recovery room.

Rusty was coming out of the anesthesia. Slowly opening both eyes, he noticed the oxygen tube running into his nose. The attending nurse wiped his brow. She addressed him in Spanish. "Mr. Smith, you are in the recovery room. Just try to relax. Dr. Ortega will be here shortly to talk with you about the surgery. The tent over your left leg is normal. The doctor will explain everything. Can I get you something to drink?"

Still very groggy and disoriented, Powell was slow to respond. "Yes, thank you. I feel a little sick in my stomach, but water or ginger ale would be nice."

"Let me see what I can do. I will be right back."

Looking down at the semi-circular tent over his lower leg, Rusty was panic-stricken. Given the heavy level of pain medication he couldn't feel much below his waist. And the leg was immobilized. He immediately assumed that it was gone. The nurse who spoke with Angela saw Powell from a distance, and noticed the stressed-out look on his face. But she decided not to come any closer. The attending nurse returned with a cup of water and a straw. She immediately recognized Powell's concern.

"I couldn't find any ginger ale. This is just water, but it should help the dryness in your mouth." She reached over and handed him the cup, which had a lid. He took it and began sipping the water, as the nurse wiped his forehead again with a wet towel. "Are you worried about the leg, Mr. Smith? It is still there. Again, try to relax. Dr. Ortega will be here soon."

Rusty's frown turned into a smile of relief. For the moment, his fears faded away. However, it would be close to an hour before Dr. Ortega appeared. He had been summoned to briefly assist in another operation and was wrapping up that assignment a few minutes after six.

CHAPTER 67

DAY 11

THE RISING SUN flickered through the venetian blinds of Richard's hotel room window. No alarm was set, or wake-up call requested, but Martinez opened his eyes at 6:45 nevertheless. It was fifteen minutes later than he normally awakened. Pulling on a pair of skivvies he grabbed from the suitcase, he made his way to the bathroom and attended to all necessary bodily functions before taking a quick, cool shower.

He made himself some coffee with the small appliance supplied in the room. It tasted like hell. Following a quick shave, he threw on a pair of khakis and a purple golf shirt, before dialing Dan Bolger' room. "Up, up and away, good man. It's time to hit the streets."

Bolger had been up for some time and found an open convenience store that sold a wide assortment of fresh donuts. "Breakfast is served in my room, ready or not."

"I'll be right over. This better be good."

The duo inhaled three donuts apiece. Bolger also bought a quart of orange juice, which quickly disappeared. By 7:30 they were ready to go to work. The first stop was a temporary morgue located less than a mile from the hotel. The Consulate had provided them with a list of these locations; there were ten of them spread across the decimated city.

By noon they had visited all but two of them, with zero success. None of them had any corpses that were bore any resemblance to Powell, and most had some form of identification. Each location processed a minimum of two hundred bodies. All were local citizens. Martinez was beginning to suspect that they were wasting their time, but both men agreed that they needed to visit the last two and bring closure to that

190

phase of the search. They had phoned the main morgue and the medical examiner's office. Neither had a record of an American named Randall Powell, or of any unidentified males.

The next stops that afternoon were to three hospitals not yet checked by either Richard or Dan. Victims continued to be brought in to each hospital on the list, so there was a chance that Powell might appear later on. Each facility contacted was provided with a photo of Powell, as well as the FBI agents' cellphone numbers, in case anyone coming close to Rusty's description happened to show up.

Richard called his office for messages. There were six voicemails on his office landline phone. None required immediate callbacks. Checking emails, there were only two that needed his response. One was from Lowell Fox, who had resigned himself to the fact that Martinez was headed to Hermosillo. The other was from a Phoenix police captain who needed Richard to question a suspect charged with assaulting a federal judge.

He replied to Fox's email, indicating that the search for Powell was proceeding, but that nothing of value had turned up in the process. He thanked his boss for the concern about his safety and promised a daily report until returning to the States. His call to the police captain went to voicemail. He left a message. After a quick sandwich back at the hotel, he and Bolger split up. Martinez headed to office of the Hermosillo police chief. Bolger visited the Federal Police headquarters on Boulevard Garcia Morales, quite a distance from the Consulate. He was driven there by a Consulate employee.

The local police had their hands full with looting and labor-intensive traffic control. Having lost a number of junior officers to the quake, they were cranky and somewhat uncooperative. The Chief, a sixty-year old veteran of the force, was now convinced that he needed to retire. He was reasonably polite to Martinez, but offered no tangible assistance in the search for Agent Powell.

Bolger had marginally better cooperation from the Federal Police. Typically shying away from anything that even remotely involved the cartels, the officer in charge of the station was fond of the FBI and wanted to display a modicum of support for the search effort. He graciously offered the assistance of one of his officers to provide security and ongoing transportation resources for both Bolger and Martinez during their stay. The offer was eagerly accepted. Bolger was then driven back to the Consulate, where Richard awaited his return.

"So, Bolger, what have you got?"

"Not a hell of a lot. The good news is we have dedicated transportation for as long as we'd like it. The station chief loves the FBI. What about you?"

"Not a thing. Those guys are up to their eyeballs. The police chief is ready to throw in the towel. Half of his force has been decimated by the quake. I don't think they'll be much use in looking for Powell. Can't say I blame them. It has to be extremely low on their priority list."

"So what's next, fearless leader?"

"I think we need to actually pay the other hospitals a visit. It's probably a wild goose chase, but there's at least a remote possibility that our Agent Powell is lying in one of the emergency rooms. Who knows, for whatever reason he may not be identifiable to the folks working their tails off around the clock. What do you think?"

"It's worth a try. Let's split up the remaining list of hospitals and check them out. After that, your guess is as good as mine. It might be time to call it quits and head for home."

"We'll see. Looks like we each get three hospitals. Wait; on second thought, let's stick together. We've got one driver and transportation will be key. We should be able to make the rounds of all six by sometime tonight or tomorrow morning. A number of them are apparently pretty small. Then we decide to either fish or cut bait."

CHAPTER 68

RUSTY WAS GETTING anxious. Ortega was running late and it was close to 7:30 in the morning; two hours after Powell was moved to the recovery room. He called for a nurse. "Any sign of my surgeon? I was hoping to see him by now. Is there a problem?"

There was a shift change. A different nurse appeared; a pleasant-looking middle-aged woman with "Olivia" on her name tag. "Mr. Smith, how are you feeling? Can I get you anything to drink?"

"That would be fine. Actually, I am feeling a little hungry. Would it be possible to get something to eat as well?"

"As soon as the doctor comes in I will ask him. I have not yet met him, but I understand he has been in surgery for fourteen hours straight. Maybe he is taking a nap or getting some breakfast himself. In the meantime, I will bring you some water. Oh, here comes someone in a white coat. I do not recognize him. This must be Dr. Ortega."

"Well, Mr. Smith; how are you feeling?"

Powell was feeling some pain in the leg, but didn't think it was worth mentioning. "Not bad, doctor. I understand you've been a busy man. Anyway, what can you tell me about the leg? Good news or not so good?"

Ortega lifted the tent from around Rusty's leg, moved aside the blanket and exposed the substantial bandage that appeared to be wrapped around a rigid object. Only his toes were exposed. "Not much to see right now, and the leg is swollen, which is to be expected. You had quite a bit of bone damage, Mr. Smith. And there is a fair amount of nerve damage as well. We had to do quite a bit of work to clean it up and wire it all back together, so to speak. You have quite a bit of hardware in there. Security will have a field day with you at the airport."

"So, what does all that mean. The leg's still there, which I guess is good news. What's the prognosis? Just level with me, doctor; it is what it is."

"Okay. Here it is. I believe you are going to keep your lower leg. It was touch and go for a while. But I see no reason why it will not heal fairly well in time. That's the good news. On the other hand, the healing will just go so far. You will need crutches for a number of weeks, and a cane after that. I'm afraid that the cane may be a permanent thing. You will walk with a slight limp from now on. The reason is quite simple. Taking off the splintered edges of both bones and joining them back together, the leg is now slightly shorter than the other one. There were not any options available to save the leg."

Powell had a feeling all along that the end result wouldn't be perfect. At the moment, he was relieved and thankful to the surgeon for saving the leg. "I understand, Dr. Ortega. I really appreciate the effort you and your team successfully made to keep me whole. What's next? Where do we go from here?"

"The next step is an easy one. We need to let the leg heal a bit. Once the swelling goes down you will be in a cast and on crutches for several weeks. Then there will be some extensive rehabilitation, to retrain you to walk, albeit with the support of a cane. My guess is that you are in for at least a six-month period of recuperation. After that, well, it will be what it will be."

"Thank you again, Dr. Ortega. I know that you will be leaving the hospital when you're no longer needed here. Will another surgeon be treating me after that?"

"They will certainly assign another orthopedic specialist to handle your case. But Mr. Smith, you will be going home in a few days, once we are comfortable that there is no infection, and the cast is put in place. I understand you have a memory problem, so where will you go? You will need someone to help you get around and handle routine things. You will not be able to go it alone."

Powell had no answer, either for Ortega, or for himself. "Doctor, I don't know. Ever since I came to and was brought to the hospital I've had no idea what my real name is or how I got to Hermosillo in the first place. So I really don't know where to go from here. One of the ER doctors told me that in most cases, after the trauma from the brain concussion recedes, the memory should return. So far: nothing. That's about all I know."

"Mr. Smith, I will speak with one of the social workers here at the hospital. He or she will come and see you after we get you up to your room. Then I guess you will need to take one day at a time. My guess is that your memory will return quite soon. I wish you the best of luck. In any case, I expect to be here at the hospital for the next few days, and will continue to be available to you when I am not in surgery."

Powell again thanked Ortega, who left the recovery room after giving some instruction to the head nurse on duty. Rusty was now fully alert, and expecting to be moved to a regular room for some unspecified period of time. He assumed that once the cast was put on and was given instructions for his immediate care outside of the hospital, he would be released. But where he would go from there was the sixty four dollar question.

CHAPTER 69

BOLGER AND MARTINEZ worked through the afternoon, visiting four of the six hospitals on the list. All four were small facilities, and all were jam-packed with patients, but there was no one even remotely fitting Powell's description. With two more to check out, they were losing their enthusiasm, as well any hope to find Rusty anywhere in Hermosillo.

A light bulb went on in Richard's head. "You realize, Dan, that we may be looking in entirely the wrong place. I keep forgetting that as far as we knew at the time, the cartel was moving Powell to another location, where he was to be driven close to the Nogales Border Station and released to finish the trip on his own. That was what Mr. Lucky said would go down. So when you think about it, our man could be anywhere between here and the border."

"So where do we go from here?" Bolger asked. We've only got two more places to check. Sounds to me like you've had it with Hermosillo. It's your call."

"I originally thought we might need three or four days here to feel like we've done our job. But I think we're wasting our time. We called the other two hospitals and struck out on each one. My gut says; you go home, and I head back to Arizona, but make some stops along the way. There are a few towns between here and the border worth checking out. That includes Nogales, on the Mexico side. You don't need to be headed in that direction. I really appreciate your help. You've been great. Go home and make love to your wife."

"Guess there's no reason to argue with you, my friend. You usually get the last word."

Bolger signaled their police driver to drop them at the hotel. They stopped at a roadside stand and downed some tacos. Checking out of the San Alberto, the two Bureau veterans said their goodbyes. Bolger went on his way toward Guaymas, where he would catch a flight back to Mexico City. Martinez drove the F-150 out of the Consul parking lot, made his way to Mexico 15 and headed north on the federal highway. Out of town.

One of the two remaining hospitals they decided not to visit was the Hospital San Jose.

CHAPTER 70

POWELL WAS MOVED to Room 316 on the surgical patient floor. It was a semi-private room, but oddly enough there was nobody in the other bed. A small message board on the wall noted that someone named Marita was the on-duty RN assigned to the room. She had not yet appeared when a young-looking, bearded man walked in and introduced himself, speaking English.

"Good afternoon, Mr. Smith. My name is Fernando Perez. I am the hospital social worker. Our visiting surgeon, Dr. Ortega, asked me to pay you a visit. How are you feeling?"

"Pleased to meet you Mr. Perez. I am doing as well as could be expected. Thank you for coming to see me. Did Dr. Ortega explain my dilemma?"

"He did, indeed. I am very sorry that your memory has not returned. In the past I have worked with a number of patients with temporary memory loss. It is not uncommon in severe head injury cases. I can only recall one such case where the woman's memory did not return. I only say that because to my knowledge it did not return. It is very likely that you will begin to recall things sometime soon. Hopefully this gives you a reasonably good feeling about the future."

"That's certainly encouraging, but in the meantime, I will have a problem once the hospital throws me out and I need somewhere to go. Dr. Ortega thought you might be able to suggest some solutions to this problem. Any ideas?"

"Let's not worry about this right now. I am told that you will be staying here a few more days to tend to the leg and prepare you for rehabilitation. In the interim I will do some exploring of various options for you to consider. Since you had no identification when you arrived, the only thing we can surmise is that you are indeed an American, and somehow arrived in Hermosillo at the absolutely worst possible time. The local government is in disarray, so it isn't very likely that they will be of any assistance on your behalf. The federal government does provide support for this hospital, and although you have no known source of medical insurance, I believe we won't be throwing you out on your ear. I understand that is an American expression; out on your ear."

"Okay; so I guess we will talk again soon. Thanks for coming. By the way, how can I get in touch with you if I need to?"

"The supervising nurse on duty has my contact information. Just tell your room nurse you would like to see me or speak on the phone and she will take it from there. For now, get yourself feeling better and we will talk again soon."

Perez left the room. A few minutes later, Marita showed up. A pudgy redhead with a lively gait, she smiled as she wheeled in a cart of varied pieces of medical gear to take Rusty's vital signs. "Ah, señor Smith, a pleasure to meet you", she said, intimating that Spanish would be their primary mode of communication. While fastening the blood pressure cuff, she continued. "We will take very good care of you. How is the leg feeling?

"As good as can be expected. Thank you for asking."

"Do you need something for pain? Dr. Ortega also said you can have anything you want to eat or drink. Your blood pressure is 130 over 70; very good." Holding his right hand to feel his pulse, she rambled on. "Would you like some magazines or newspapers to read?"

"No thank you, I'm fine right now. Can you please turn on the TV? I would like to hear the news."

Marita handed Rusty a remote control. "Help yourself. We get CNN International, so you can watch it in English. I know you are American. I love America. My sister lives in El Paso. She wants me to learn English, but I am afraid. I am learning French, and that is much easier. Your temperature is normal. That is very good; no infection. Just push the top button on the remote control if you need me."

"Thank you Marita. I would just like to take a nap right now."

She smiled and left the room. Rusty watched a few minutes of CNN and fell asleep.

CHAPTER 71

ON THE ROAD and about an hour outside of Hermosillo, Martinez used his Bluetooth to phone Sally Henkel, who had sent him an email requesting a status report. She answered on the second ring.

"Hey, it's me" Richard said. "I'm headed north. Hermosillo was a dead end."

"Bloody hell! No clues at all? The guy just disappears?"

"Yeah; looks that way. We checked all the morgues and hospitals. Dan and I just came to the conclusion that Powell wasn't there. I'm going to check a few places on the way back to see if anybody has seen or heard anything. But I'm beginning to think that he was either trampled to death by the quake, or the cartel boys did away with him for the fun of it."

"Well, you gave it a try. Come on back to Arizona. The high temperature in Tucson yesterday was only 98. I almost put on a sweater; not really."

"Give me another day or so. It won't take me long to check out a couple of towns. I'll give you a buzz when I get across the border. Buy you a beer."

Richard's first investigative stop was in Santa Ana. There was one hospital there, The Health Center with Hospital, and a small morgue. He also planned to visit a couple of bars to see if anyone might recall seeing an American with Powell's description, although that was really a long shot.

The front desk at the hospital had no record of anyone that could possibly fit Rusty's profile. The town did suffer a fair amount of damage from the earthquake, so the facility had been busy for several days. No luck at the morgue, so Martinez dropped in for a beer at a bar nearby.

The bartender was lonely. At four in the afternoon the place was empty. Once Richard got the conversation going, it was a twenty-minute affair. Bottom-line, nothing doing. He did promise to ask around town and took Martinez's cellphone number just in case.

Next stop was Magdalena, just up the road on Mexico 15. There were several hospitals there, and in two of the larger ones there were Americans being treated there. Richard checked both men out. One was in a car accident the day before and was soon to be released. The person in the General Hospital of Magdalena was a woman who had to have her baby delivered there. It was an emergency, as she broke her water and went into heavy labor. She had been on the road, traveling home to Phoenix.

He checked the town morgue as well. As in Santa Ana, he stopped in a local bar, ordered a beer and chatted with the bartender and a couple of patrons. No dice. The town sees many Americans traveling to and from Mexican points of interest, but Powell's description failed to strike a chord with anyone.

He was now only about two hours from Tucson. He could make it there for a late drink with Sally, a quick dinner and perhaps head home from there for a good night's sleep. The only other town he was tempted to check was Altar. It was off to the west and didn't have any medical facilities to speak of. Its residents would either use Santa Ana hospitals or those in Caborca, several miles to the west of Altar.

He opted to forego Altar and head up to Nogales, the one on the Mexican side, for one last look around. It was on the way home, and a little over an hour from Tucson. If he struck out there, he planned to give Henkel a call and see if she could meet for a drink.

Nogales had only two hospitals where Powell might have been a patient: The General Hospital of Nogales, and the Hospital Socorro. Stopping at Socorro first, there was no record of Rusty being there at any time. It was a small catholic facility, with limited patient care resources. The General Hospital, while quite old and somewhat run down, was the more likely option.

Martinez struck gold. The head of nurses was brought to the lobby to address Richard's inquiry. She asked to see his FBI credentials. Speaking fluent English, she was chosen by the gentleman at the information desk for the assignment. "Mr. Martinez, my name is Diana. I am the senior nurse on duty this evening. How can I help you?"

Martinez explained his mission. "I went to Hermosillo and was unsuccessful in finding Agent Powell. He was to be returned to the Nogales Border Station, but it appears that the earthquake got in the way. Do you have any American patients here at the moment, or over the past several days?"

"Mr. Martinez, this is your lucky day. Unfortunately, we do not have anyone here that fits his description, but your Border Patrol Agent was to be brought to my husband's office the night of the quake. It is the Banamex HSBC bank facility that is used by many business people in the region. My husband is the assistant manager there. From the Banamex office, the agent was to be driven to the border and released to walk to the border station and into the United States."

Martinez immediately put two and two together, recalling Mr. Lucky's description of the methodology by which Powell would be set free. "But if I understand what you're saying, Agent Powell never arrived. So he is still missing and unaccounted for."

"That is my understanding. My husband waited until midnight for the agent to arrive. After hearing the news about the earthquake he attempted to call his contact in Hermosillo, but he was unable to get through. He has heard nothing since."

Diana, I would very much like to speak with your husband. He may be very useful to our government in dealing with this affair. Would that be possible?"

"Mr. Martinez, if you will wait here, I will call him and see if this would be a possibility."

"Yes, of course. It would be much appreciated. Thanks."

Maria left the lobby to make the call. A short time later, she returned, but with a negative expression on her face. "I am sorry, Mr. Martinez. My husband will be unable to meet with you, or even discuss the matter over the phone. He fears for his life if certain individuals learn of the conversation. I hope you can understand."

Richard was reluctant to press the issue. It now was apparent that the cartel was delivering Powell in return for the ransom money. If necessary at a later time, the FBI could petition the Mexican government to subpoena the man in an attempt to get at the people responsible for Rusty's abduction and Childers' death. But that would be a long shot, given Mexico's reluctance to fool with the cartels.

Thanking Maria for her time, Martinez departed and began the short trip to the border. Calling Sally Henkel's cellphone, he left her a voicemail, indicating that he would be in Tucson area in less than two hours, and invited her, if it wasn't too late, to have a drink or a bite to eat. It was a few minutes before 7PM.

He passed through the Nogales Border Station at 7:45: shortly thereafter getting a callback from Henkel. "Boy, am I relieved that you're back on U.S. soil. Any luck at all?"

"One little piece of information, but it only confirms what we've thought all along. Apparently they were on their way with Powell to deliver him to an intermediary in Nogales. It looks like the earthquake stopped them dead in their tracks, maybe literally as well as figuratively. Who knows? In any case, we still don't know if Rusty is dead or alive. So what about a drink? I could use one. And if you haven't eaten, can you hold on for another hour or so?"

"For you, boss; no problem. I just fed my daughter, so you've got a date. Give me a ring when you get close."

It was a clear, starry night in southern Arizona. With virtually no traffic on I-19, it was an effortless 50-minute drive to the Tucson environs. Richard gave Sally a heads up and they agreed to meet at Henkel's favorite Italian restaurant. They arrived just in time to grab a glass of wine, order some pasta and get served before the place closed. Sally gave her boss time to finish his meal before asking about the Hermosillo adventure.

"We could have stayed a few more days, but I didn't see it paying off. It was a real crapshoot. If Powell is still there, he's either out of it; severely injured, or dead, buried under the debris. Their equivalent of our FEMA estimates there are at least 20,000 people still unaccounted for and likely crushed under the rubble. It's a hell of a scene."

"I know you don't ever like to give up. Can you handle this?"

"No choice. And I don't know where we go from here."

Chapter 72

Following a welcomed nap, Rusty enjoyed his first decent meal since arriving at the hospital. A little after eight, there was a knock at the door of his room. He asked the person to come in. Anticipating someone wanting to take some blood or check his vital signs, he was pleasantly surprised to see Angela enter the room. She was in her perfectly starched nurse's uniform, and as usual, was wielding her awesome smile.

"Mr. Smith, I just got to the hospital and wanted to check to see how you are doing. When you were in recovery, they didn't let me come in, because you had not yet seen the surgeon. I only have a few minutes before going on duty. Did the surgery go well? How do you feel?"

"Angela, it's great to see you. Thanks for checking on me. And it's David; at least for the time being. There's much to tell about the operation and what I can expect with the leg from here on. In any case, it looks like I'm going to be here for a few more days, so when you have more time, please come back to visit."

"I will come every day. Actually, I have tomorrow and the next day off, but I will be here anyway. Then we can spend more time together. Are they treating you okay?"

"Pretty good, I guess. They let me have a good nap and the dinner was fine. I've been watching CNN to get all the latest news. It sounds like this section of Hermosillo has managed to survive the quake fairly well. Not so much for the rest of the city. The memory still isn't there. Guess I just have to be patient. But it sure would be nice to know who I am. Are you getting along okay?"

"So far, no problems. My roommate has left for a two-week vacation to visit her parents in Puerto Vallarta. So it's pretty quiet. Anyway, I have to go to work. Can I come by to see you tomorrow morning?"

"Angela, you can visit anytime you like. Seeing your smiling face is the best medicine I can have. I'll be waiting for you to return. By the way, don't you have a boyfriend?"

"There were a few in the past. I guess I am pretty particular. Men that chase me for the obvious reasons end up not being what I'm looking for. Anyway, I am sure you will keep feeling better; see you tomorrow."

She reached for his hand and squeezed it gently, continuing with the spectacular smile. He pulled her down and kissed her on the check. She responded with one on the lips. It was soft, wet and warm. Her touch was magic. After saying goodbye, he watched her walk to the door. She was an amazingly good-looking woman; even from the rear.

Minutes later, a new nurse came on duty to work the night shift. She took Rusty's vital signs, turned out the lights and asked him if wanted anything for pain or a pill to help him sleep. He opted for the painkiller; the leg was throbbing and his head was as well.

All he could think about until falling asleep was Angela; her beauty, her warmth, and the feelings for her that were racing through his senses. At the moment, the past was irrelevant. Other than a little pain, the leg almost didn't matter. At the moment, only Angela was on his mind.

Chapter 73

Day 12

After a fidgety night's sleep, the morning sun made a brief appearance through the large window in Rusty's room. Turning away from it, he realized that there was a patient in the other bed. The older man most likely had been brought in sometime during the early morning hours. He seemed to be sleeping soundly, while being connected to a variety of tubes and electronic equipment.

The sun soon gave way to dark clouds. It began to rain. Breakfast arrived: lukewarm scrambled eggs with bacon, along with juice, toast and coffee. Fairly hungry, Powell worked his way through the food. At a few minutes past seven, the current on-duty nurse appeared, once again rolling in the cart to take Rusty's vital signs. All were normal. There was continuing pain in the leg, but the headache had lessened somewhat.

The nurse told him that his new roommate was scheduled for surgery in less than an hour. He wouldn't return until sometime in the early afternoon. She then pulled the curtain to separate the two bed areas and asked Rusty if he needed something for pain. His IV continued to inject an antibiotic, more or less to stave off any possible infections, which often crop up a day or two following an operation.

"I think I'm okay for now. Thanks. Would it be possible to watch the news? I promise to keep the volume low."

With the nurse's approval he turned on the set, which was already tuned to CNN International. Quickly engaged in the weather and sports reports, there was a short knock on the door and Dr. Ortega appeared. He was wearing a sport coat and slacks, suggesting to Rusty that he was not about to go into surgery, but simply making morning rounds.

"Mr. Smith. Good morning. How is our patient this morning? You're looking much better today."

"Not bad, doctor. The leg hurts, but I guess that's probably normal. I haven't taken any pain medication since last night, so I'm hopeful that's a good sign."

"Well it certainly isn't a bad one. Can you scoot up a bit? Let's have a look at it."

After Rusty shifted his body upward a bit, Ortega moved the blanket and sheet away and began to remove the bandages. That hurt Powell quite a bit. Wincing in pain, he clenched his teeth as the surgeon carefully did the unwrapping, until the leg was totally exposed. Looking at it made Rusty feel like throwing up.

"Looks kind of nasty, doesn't it? The swelling has gone down a bit, but as you would expect it is greatly discolored from being bruised during the operation. I'm going to order an x-ray to see how it's doing inside. Then, this afternoon, we're going to get you on your feet: not for long, but just to provide a little circulation. If the swelling continues to subside, we will put a cast on it: hopefully sometime tomorrow or the following day. It's important that we get it properly supported before you start moving around. I'll have your nurse get you ready for the move to radiology. Any questions?"

"Not offhand. Are you sticking around for a while?"

"That hasn't been decided just yet. They are still quite shorthanded here. Something tells me they will ask me to stay on for several more days. So you won't be rid of me that soon."

"Oh, I didn't mean it that way. Frankly, the longer you're around, the better."

"Very well, then. We'll get fresh bandages on and after the x-rays we will leave you alone for the balance of the day. If I can, I will stop back to check in on you this evening. By then we'll have results of the x-rays and decide where we go from here."

Ortega departed, and a few minutes later, Angela walked in. No longer in uniform, she was wearing white Capri pants, a peach-colored blouse and flats. Her hair was let down; shimmering and long, just below her shoulders. The spectacular smile was still there, on her beautiful face.

Rusty's roommate was taken to surgery. They were alone.

"David; good morning. How are you feeling?"

"Better, I guess. You look great. I really like your hair that way."

"Thanks. I can't wear it down when I'm working. I washed it this morning, brushed it out. Sometimes I feel like cutting it short; especially in the summer. But my mother says it should be long."

"I think she's right. But it would look great either way. So what's your plan for the few days you have off?"

"I need to do some grocery shopping, and clean the apartment. The rest of the time I want to spend with you. Even if I am off-duty I can be your private nurse. Would you like that?"

"Better than anything else I can think of." Rusty held out his arm, beckoning her to come closer to the bed. Without hesitation, she moved next to him and took his hand. "You make me feel so alive, David. I have never felt this way before."

"Me too. At least I don't think this has ever happened to me. I still have no idea who I am or where I used to call home. Please be patient with me. I just don't know what my past might have been, or what my future will be. It's scary. If it wasn't for you, I'd be petrified."

Dropping Rusty's hand, Angela scooted next to him on the bed. The warmth of her body was an elixir, helping to ease the pain in his leg. She stroked his moppy hair and kissed his forehead. "You could use a haircut and a shave. I won't even try to deal with the hair, but I can give you a shave. We do it for patients all the time."

"Maybe tomorrow. Anyway, I expect the nurse to come to get me any time now. Dr. Ortega wants to take more x-rays to see what's happening inside the leg. Before long they're going to put it in a cast, but I'm not looking forward to that at all. In the meantime, you should go do your shopping and housecleaning. Call me on the room phone this afternoon. Maybe you can bring us some lunch. Does that sound okay?"

"Sounds fine to me." Angela bent over and kissed Rusty tenderly on the lips. "I will see you later." She rose from the bed and threw him another kiss as she left the room. A few minutes later an orderly came in, lifted Powell into a wheelchair and escorted him down to radiology. It was 11:15AM

Chapter 74

Richard thought long and hard before giving Lowell Fox a call. It was never easy for him to admit any sort of defeat. The job wasn't over. His missing border patrol agent was nowhere to be found. He finally relented and phoned the FBI Director shortly after noon, Arizona time. It was 3:10 on the east coast.

One of Fox's admin assistants took the call. "He's at the White House, Special Agent Martinez. Would you like me to ask him to phone you later?"

"That would be fine. He can try my cellphone first. I'll be heading to the federal courthouse for a deposition. No problem; it'll be on vibrate. I'll excuse myself and step outside to take the call."

Next, he phoned Dan Bolger to bring him up to date on his extended search. "I checked several hospitals and a few bars on the way back to the border. No dice. Powell is either deceased, or in hiding for some reason. Go figure. How was your trip home?"

"Fun and games. I missed the flight from Guaymas to Mexico City. Luckily my office in Mexico City helped to arrange for a small plane charter. But I didn't get back home until after ten. Sharon had made dinner, but I was too tired to eat it. So that's my story. What's *your* next move?"

"I don't have a clue. Placed a call to Fox a little while ago, but he was over on Pennsylvania Avenue for a meeting with POTUS. I'm not sure what to say to him anyway, but he deserves an update. My guess is he will go easy on us. The reports on Hermosillo are still horrendous. He didn't want us going down there in the first place."

"Copy that. If I have any bright ideas, I'll give you a ring. And say hi to Lowell. With the trouble in Algeria and the Sudan, he can't be having much fun."

"Will do. Say hi to your beautiful bride. I'll be in touch."

He then called Sally and asked her to contact Roland Escobar. They owed him a status report. Richard also suggested she ask Escobar to bring Melinda Powell up to speed as well. "Or you can contact Melinda and do it yourself. Your call."

"I'd like to do it. She trusts us; has asked me to stay in touch with any news. She's not going to like what I tell her, but it is what it is. Have you talked with Fox?"

"He was tied up with the president. I should hear from him by the end of the day. Got to go, Sally: due in court at 2 o'clock. Take care."

Martinez packed his briefcase with the needed files and headed out the door. He grabbed a sandwich at the In-N-Out Burger a few blocks from the office and made his way to federal courthouse shortly thereafter.

CHAPTER 75

ANGELA CAME BACK to see Rusty a few minutes after two. She had a bag of Subway subs, chips, and two Diet Cokes. Powell was just waking from a nap. He looked up as Angela bent over to give him a kiss. "Brought us something to eat. Are you hungry?"

"Starving. They brought me a lunch tray, but it didn't look very good. And I knew you would be coming with something much better. So what's in the bag?"

"A tuna sub and a meatball sub. Your choice. Also, ranch or classic chips?"

"Either way is fine. And if you can help me over to one of the chairs, we can eat like human beings."

Being an experienced nurse, Angela deftly assisted Rusty out of bed and over to one of the chairs. She brought the food over to the sitting area and unwrapped the subs.

"How is the leg? Did they take the x-rays?"

"They did, but I won't get a report until Dr. Ortega gets here. He said he would try to make it back this this afternoon. Hey, this tuna sub tastes great. You are very sweet for bringing it for me. So, did you get your chores done?"

"Did the grocery shopping. The apartment can wait. I will probably get to it tonight or tomorrow morning. Any progress on the memory front?"

"Not really. Every once in a while, my mind seems to go blank. It's just for a few seconds, but it kind of scares me a little. I guess the brain needs to kind of shock itself into bringing me back to reality. Does that make any sense?"

"I know very little about amnesia. Maybe you need to see a

neurologist. They could probably explain what's going on inside your head. In the meantime, try not to worry about it. Time will tell."

"Angela, I'm also afraid that when I do get my memory back, it will affect our relationship. Right now, all I can do is live for the present. And *you* are the one thing that gives me hope for the future. I think I'm in love with you. Does that make any sense?"

"Eat your lunch. Then I will tell you what you mean to me."

"So I have to wait to hear it? Give me a break."

"Eat your lunch."

As they finished the subs, Dr. Ortega walked in. "Mr. Smith, good afternoon. Oh, I am sorry: I didn't mean to barge in. Would you like me to come back a little later?"

"Not necessary, doctor. Please meet Angela. She is a nurse here at the hospital. For some reason, she likes to keep tabs on me." Rusty didn't know Angela's last name.

"Pleased to meet you Angela." He shook her hand and smiled. "So how's the leg."

"I guess you need to tell *me*. It feels about the same. How do the x-rays look?"

"Promising. Fortunately, there is no infection. Everything we did to it is holding up well. But of course, you haven't been walking around as yet. I want to give it another 12 to 18 hours to quiet down before we fit it with a cast. So sometime tomorrow we will very likely get that done. In the meantime, I will ask your duty nurse to help you take a few steps a little later on. She will bring you crutches to do so. How is the pain?"

"Not bad, but as you say, I haven't used it a hell of a lot. Actually, my head hurts more than the leg."

"We will need to keep an eye on that. But do not be afraid to take as much as you need to help the pain. I will see you again tomorrow morning. My plan, unless another surgery gets in the way, is to be there when they get you into the cast. Very nice meeting you Angela. Mr. Smith is very fortunate to have you at his side." Ortega smiled and made his way to the door.

Angela helped Rusty back to bed. "David, or whoever you are; I love you." She kissed him tenderly, and said goodbye.

CHAPTER 76

LOWELL FOX RETURNED Richard's call a few minutes after six, Arizona time; two hours later in the nation's capitol. "So, you're back in Phoenix. Any luck?"

"Not really. We couldn't find Agent Powell anywhere. The good news is his corpse isn't lying in one of their twenty temporary morgues. We checked all the hospitals. No record of him anywhere. Hermosillo looks like Cologne after the Second World War. His body might turn up, once they clean up the mountains of rubble. I also checked a number of places between there and the border. Nothing. Nobody has seen or heard of the guy. Right now I'm trying to figure out the next step. Bennett Frost and Pepe Sanchez might have some ideas."

"Frankly, Richard, I'm just relieved to hear that you made it out of there in one piece. In any case, Powell may just show up one day on his own. Stranger things have happened. You know?"

"Lowell, I feel really badly for his wife, Melinda. Henkel's been looking after her since he disappeared. One way or another, she needs to know the truth. Trouble is, nobody knows what it is. It's what you're paying me to find out. I'm not going to let her down."

"Hey; you're not a miracle worker. You went down there, risked your own neck, to get some answers. And you did it. Stop beating yourself up. We don't promise a happy ending. You know that. You've got a great track record, Richard. But you can't win every time."

"I know that. Anyway, this will remain an open case until we find Rusty Powell, dead or alive. Okay?"

"How was your afternoon at the courthouse?" Fox decided to change the subject.

"At least that went well. We got three really outstanding depositions.

I'll talk with the U.S. Attorney's office here, but we should end up with an indictment. I want to see this scumbag home-grown terrorist go away for life."

"Got to go, Richard. Keep the faith; say hi to Sally Henkel. By the way, she's a candidate for a promotion to our office in Chicago. Assistant Special Agent in Charge. You should get word in a couple of weeks, but I think it's going to happen. Stay tuned on that one. In the meantime, go out tonight and get laid."

"Sage advice; coming straight from my happily married boss. Don't know if I have the energy, but we may give it a try."

CHAPTER 77

SALLY PLACED A call to Roland Escobar. Connecting with his voicemail, she left a message, letting him know that she was available for an update on the case. She then phoned Melinda Powell, who answered on the second ring. "Special Agent Henkel, I've been waiting to hear from you. Any news?"

"Melinda, Richard Martinez just returned from Mexico. He and another agent with the Bureau in Mexico City made a complete sweep across Hermosillo and the area between there and the border. Unfortunately, they found no information that could lead them to Rusty. The good news is that none of the many morgues set up to handle the thousands of earthquake victims had any record of your husband. The same appears to be true of the hospitals they contacted. None of them had any record of someone with his description. So we're back to square one."

"So what's next, Agent Henkel? Where do we go from here?"

"Richard and I are working on it. There's no immediate solution to the puzzle. It's not inconceivable that your husband could pop up on the grid, in which case we go and get him and bring him home. We have two law enforcement contacts in Mexico that are working with us to plan our next move. I know it's getting more and more difficult for you to wait this out. All I can say is: don't give up. We won't either. Any other questions? Can we help you with anything else."

"Not really. Somehow, I know Rusty is still alive. But that doesn't help much. My parents need to return to Missouri. They're leaving tomorrow. After they leave I guess I'll lean on my friends for support. Call me the minute you have any news."

Sally again made it clear that she and Richard wouldn't give up, and said goodbye.

Roland Escobar returned Henkel's call. "What's up Agent Henkel?" You said something about an update. Any news?"

"Roland, I wanted you to know that Richard is back from Mexico after making a thorough search for information on Rusty. He searched mainly in Hermosillo, but Richard also checked out a few other towns between there and the border. In Hermosillo he was joined by another agent from our Mexico City office. Unfortunately, they struck out. Agent Powell is nowhere to be found. We won't give up the search, but it's not looking too good. There are about 20,000 people missing in Hermosillo, most of the them still buried under the rubble. All we can do is keep our contacts busy looking, and hope for the best."

'You're right, Henkel. It isn't looking good at all. We have CBP investigators conducting a very thorough search on this side of the fence as well. But it's been almost two weeks since he disappeared. If he was alive, he certainly would have tried to make contact with us by now."

"No question about it. But my crystal ball tells me that Powell is still alive. Can't put my finger on it; just a gut feeling. And I can assure you that we won't give up. You can take that to the bank."

"Keep me posted, Special Agent Henkel. And if *our* investigators come up with something worthwhile, I'll let you know. Take care."

CHAPTER 78

THE DAY NURSE brought Rusty a pair of crutches. She adjusted them slightly to fit his tall frame. Helping him get out of bed, she held him firmly while he placed the crutches under his arms and began to take a step.

"Easy does it Mr. Smith. I'm going to keep hold of you the entire time. We don't want you to fall. Baby steps. Let's go."

Rusty's arms were shaking, as he positioned himself to take the first few steps. He kept his weight entirely off the left leg. There was substantial pain just bending it slightly to avoid contact with the floor. They walked together toward the door at a slow, deliberate pace. The other patient originally assigned to the same room had been reassigned to another one first thing that morning. So Powell had the room to himself for the time being.

They managed to walk out into the 3rd floor hallway. Rusty was covered in perspiration from the effort. He hadn't walked at all in almost two weeks. It was hard work.

"Easy now, Mr. Smith. That should be enough for today. No sense pushing it. When we get you into the cast we can do a good deal more." The nurse took him back to the room and helped him into bed. It was close to 5PM, and the dinner trays were coming around.

"There is fish on the menu, Mr. Smith." The nurse sponged Rusty down a bit to cool him off. She moved the bed tray toward him as the orderly brought the meal tray into the room. Powell picked at the food, drinking the iced tea and eating the peach cobbler. He was thinking about Angela, and hoping she would get there before he fell asleep.

The nurse left the room for a few minutes, returning with the cart full of vital signs equipment. When he finished the part of the meal he ate, she moved the bed tray aside and checked his blood pressure, heart rate and temperature, all of which were normal. "We are going to take some blood, Mr. Smith, to check for any signs of infection. If the test is negative, according to the doctor's orders, the cast will be put on sometime tomorrow. Is there anything else you need?"

"No thanks. I'm okay. But a little later I would like something to help me sleep."

"Dr. Ortega already has that on your orders. Just let me know when you want to take it. I will see you later."

Angela arrived a few minutes before seven. Rusty had begun to worry that she might not show up. Tonight she was wearing a blue skirt, white blouse and had her hair once again pulled back into a ponytail. The blouse perfectly accentuated the curves of her soft and ample breasts. Rusty was immediately aroused, as she moved closer to the bed. He wanted her to join him under the sheets.

"You look better tonight. The nurse tells me you were up and about a short while ago. Is the leg hurting much?"

"A little. My head still hurts worse. But if you kiss me the pain will go away."

She reached over and kissed him warmly on the lips. "You are perspiring. I will get you a nice cold towel. She went into the bathroom, took one of the face towels and ran it under the cold water. Returning to the bed, she gently folded the towel and placed it on his forehead. "How does that feel; better?"

"It feels wonderful. Thanks. So what did you do this afternoon?"

"I got ambitious; did some laundry and cleaned the apartment. I wasn't very hungry, so I stopped at a little taco stand nearby and had two tacos with rice. The little man who runs the stand makes the best tacos. You will have to try them."

"As soon as I get out of here you can take me for some tacos. Promise?"

"I promise. What would you like to do now? I brought some playing cards with me. Or we can watch TV if want to."

"I want to make love to you. I've wanted to since the first time I saw you in the E.R."

"Not here, David. Besides, your leg is not yet well enough. Maybe when you get the cast on and are able to leave the hospital. Okay?"

"I don't know if I can wait that long. But I'll try. Come here and sit beside me on the bed. Can we just talk for a while? I love the sound of your voice."

Angela came over and sat down. The mere closeness of her sensuous body and the calm demeanor of her personality provided the best pain medicine for the time being. As she bent over to kiss him, the fullness of her breasts and the soft floral scent of her body-wash, further fueled his desire to make love.

"I never want you to leave", Rusty whispered in her ear. "Do you feel the same way?"

"I do, David. I want you more than you know."

CHAPTER 79

DAY 13

RUSTY WAS AWAKENED early in the morning by the sound of thunder. A sizable rainstorm was making its way across northern Mexico. His head still ached, but the leg pain seemed to be less than the day before. He guessed that the reduced swelling was easing the pressure on the muscles and nerves surrounding the bone repairs.

He watched some CNN until breakfast came. The day nurse just coming on duty entered with the vital signs equipment and greeted Powell with a smile. "Good morning, Mr. Smith. My name is Alicia. I will be your nurse for most of the day. How are you feeling?"

"The leg feels a bit better today. The headache seems to be hanging around. Will I be getting the cast today?"

"The orders indicate that this will be the case, but we expect Dr. Ortega to stop in while he is making rounds. I understand that he will be with us for at least one more day. Once he takes a look at the leg he will let you know when the cast can go on. In the meantime, we want you to walk just a bit, just to get the circulation going. Are you ready to do that now?"

"Fine with me. He scooted up as best he could, while Alicia brought him the crutches. "Let's take our time, Mr. Smith. There is no need to rush." She gently helped Rusty out of bed and made sure that the crutches were firmly in place under his arms.

They walked to the door together. Alicia at his side, Powell made his way down the hall. In a little less than a hundred feet, they turned around and made their way back to the room. "Well done, Mr. Smith.

You are doing just fine. Would you like to sit in the chair for a little while?"

Rusty nodded. Alicia took the crutches, as her patient sat himself down in the rather uncomfortable vinyl-covered chair. He was relaxing in it for a few minutes when Angela walked in. Enjoying her second day off, she was in a red and white warm-up suit, finished off with silver New Balance sneakers. Once again her hair was back in the ponytail.

"Well you must be feeling better. I am happy to see you sitting in that chair. Your barber has arrived to give you a shave."

"Are you sure you want to do this? Your nerves may be steady, but I'm not too sure about mine."

Walking over to his chair, Angela bent down and kissed him on the cheek. "Have no fear. You are safe in my hands." She opened her handbag and pulled out a razor. "It's the four-blade type. If you like, you can do it yourself. She then withdrew a small can of shave cream, wetted his face with a damp washcloth, and began to coat his stubbly beard.

"Have at it if you like", Rusty said.

Angela seemed quite at home with the process. "I told you that I am very experienced at this. But please hold still and let me do this right." In less than two minutes the work was done. She used the washcloth again to get rid of the excess shave cream. Then she pulled a small bottle of aftershave from the handbag and patted it on. "There. A first class job. You look like a new man. This time she kissed him on the lips. "You smell wonderful." Followed by another kiss.

Rusty wanted to put his arms around her and give her a giant hug, but his position in the chair would have made it a painful process. Instead, he asked her to give him a hand getting back to bed. "I'm waiting to hear from Dr. Ortega about the cast. Hopefully it will go on today, so I can start thinking about being released."

"And go where?" she asked. "Not only that, but who will take care of you when you get there?"

"I have no idea. Give me a few hours to come up with an answer." He was pulling her leg, but realized that when the hospital cut him loose he would quickly be up a tree without a ladder. He didn't hold out much hope that the social services department would come up with a decent answer.

Angela was prepared for that moment. "I have the solution. You will be coming home with me. Just think; your own private nurse. That's as good as it gets."

Rusty saw it coming, but was completely unprepared to respond. "You can't be serious. You've only known me for a few days. I care for you a great deal, but I can't ask you to do that. What if my memory returns while I'm there and the truth of who I really am confronts us both? I'm afraid for what that might mean. Do you see what I'm saying Angela?"

"Listen David, or whatever your real name is; at the moment you do not have many options, other than some kind of charity institution. You have no money, no memory, and a badly injured leg. My roommate is gone for two weeks. You will have a bedroom to yourself. And while I am at work during the day you can do whatever you like. The apartment is on the ground floor, so when you are stronger you can take walks and get some needed fresh air. If and when you decide to leave, then that will be the end of it. Fair enough?"

Powell was tongue-tied. The scenario she painted was the absolute best he could hope for. Bottom line, he was falling in love with her, so the danger of discovering his true identity made the decision incredibly difficult. "You've got me there. But let's agree on the following: whenever you've had your fill of me, I'm out the door. And if my memory returns, we agree that what is best for you is what we do. Those are my conditions. Agreed?"

"Yes, but we can worry about those things later. Right now, you need me, and I can give you a nurse's care and a woman's love and affection. Not a bad deal, wouldn't you say?"

Rusty was about to answer, when Dr. Ortega walked in. "Good morning, David. And good morning to you miss, as well. How's the leg?"

"Feeling better. It seems to be less swollen as well."

Ortega pulled back the sheet and took a look. "Not bad. You must have had a terrific surgeon. Seems to me that we can get a cast on it today and maybe let you go tomorrow. Sound okay? Importantly though, do you have a place to stay?"

"It looks like I do." He turned to Angela, who was all smiles. "Guess I'm a pretty lucky guy."

"Indeed. So, I will be shipping you down to the 2nd floor get your cast molded on. You will no doubt experience some pain in the process, but it shouldn't take very long. Then, you need to do a fair amount of walking to let the cast settle in. If there is any problem with it, we certainly want to find out before we send you home. I will be by tomorrow morning. If all is well, you will be discharged sometime later in the day. Any questions?"

"Not off-hand, doctor. Thanks. We'll see you tomorrow." Ortega departed. Angela was ecstatic. Tears ran down her cheeks. Rusty held her in his arms and had no desire to let go. He was excited about the immediate future, but scared to death about what might happen down the road. Angela went out and returned a few hours later with a picnic-style lunch.

CHAPTER 80

A FEW MINUTES past four in the afternoon, Powell was wheeled down to the second floor to have his cast made. A medical tech assisted a house intern in the process. The material used to make leg casts was changed a number of years before from plaster to fiberglass, which is stronger and doesn't get soggy when wet. After the med tech slipped on the stockinet, Rusty's lower leg was placed on a cast stand, which held the leg at a 90-degree angle.

After rolled padding was applied, a 4-inch fiberglass bandage was dunked in a bucket of water, which activated the curing process. The leg was then carefully wrapped with the fiberglass. The end of the stockinet was then pulled over the fiberglass wrapping at both ends, preventing the foot from rubbing against it. The cast was smoothed over with water. The entire process took about an hour. It was not an entirely uncomfortable process.

Rusty was wheeled back to his room on the third floor. The second shift nurse, an older woman everyone called Willie, was all smiles as she welcomed him back. "Now, Mr. Smith, you are ready to start some serious moving-around. If you are a good boy, you may have some dinner. And it is possible that tomorrow Dr. Ortega will let you go home."

Powell noticed Willie's nametag, and spoke to her in Spanish. "Thank you Miss Willie. I will do whatever it is you want me to do. What happens next?"

"Next, we take a walk." She grabbed the crutches that were sitting next to one of the chairs, brought them over and helped him position them properly. Now, you can see that your leg is not hanging straight down, but at an angle. So you really do not have to worry about it touching the floor. The main thing is to take it slow and watch where you are going. Okay?"

"You're the captain. Lead the way."

Rusty and Willie took off down the hall. Powell quickly got the hang of it. The fiberglass cast was reasonably light. Within a few minutes, walking was a relatively painless and straightforward process. Visiting the 3rd floor nurses' station, they stopped. to show off the new cast. Rusty had become quite a celebrity, given that the entire hospital staff was now aware of two facts: he had amnesia, and Angela was now his romantic interest. None of the nurses or orderlies let on that they knew these things. But hospitals are like small neighborhoods. Rumors travel with lightning speed.

Chatting awhile, Powell decided that he needed to sit down. Willie walked him back to his room, where he now had a new roommate. It was a teenager that had just come out of surgery to remove a benign tumor from his spine. He was brought up from the recovery room and fell fast asleep. Rusty didn't think he would have much time to befriend the youngster, assuming he would be released sometime the next day.

"Mr. Smith, would you like to sit in a chair or climb into bed?"

"If I sit in the chair for a while, will I be able to get into bed on my own? I may need you here until I can master the move."

"You will be fine. Get into the bed from the left-hand side. That will enable you to negotiate the move using your right leg. Just take your time." Willie watched Powell slowly make his way into the chair.

Rusty sat there and watched CNN for half an hour. Then dinner came. So did Angela, carrying another basket of food. "You are going to love this dinner. My neighbor made a pot roast, and her pot roast is the best. Boiled potatoes and salad to go with it. Banana cream pie for dessert. I baked the pie."

"Guess I won't even bother looking under the hospital dinner lid. Maybe my roommate will want it when he wakes up."

"You're cast is on. Wonderful! How does it feel?"

"Not bad. They say it will itch after a while. But right now, it's okay. You should have been here. I walked up and down the 3rd floor hallway without breaking the other leg. You look especially great tonight."

She was wearing a blue and light green floral print dress, with a pair of high heels. Her hair was down again. Her deep blue eyes shimmered in the light of the setting sun, peeking through the window. Although Angela was tiny: only about 5' 4"; in heels, and weighing only about 110 pounds, she looked like a supermodel. As usual, Rusty couldn't take his eyes off the strikingly beautiful woman.

Reaching into the basket, she pulled out a bottle of pinot noir, along with the pot roast and the sides. "So, can we eat now?" she asked. "I am extremely hungry. You too?"

"Absolutely. Let's do it."

Angela handed the crutches to Rusty and helped him out of the chair. "I spoke to the nurse and she said we could eat in the 3rd floor lounge if we like. How does that sound?"

"That sounds great. Let's go."

Angela put the wine and food back in the basket. The twosome left the room and walked slowly to the lounge, about 150 feet away. She carried the basket and Rusty hobbled along on his own. Once there, Angela pulled a long coffee table close to the large sofa, where they began sipping the wine and enjoying the meal.

Chapter 81

"Richard, it's Bennett. How's it hanging, my friend?"

"Frost, you son of a bitch. Why haven't you found my border patrol agent? What the hell do you guys do all day?"

"Protect the United States of America from all enemies, at least the foreign ones. And what's wrong with the FBI? I heard about the $10 million. So now we're padding the bank accounts of drug cartels. Shameful. And nothing to show for it."

"Are you purposely trying to piss me off? I don't need this. Anyway, why is it that you called?"

"Word on the street in Hermosillo; what's left of it, is that your CBP agent may still be alive. The two guys that were holding him are dead, but there's no sign of Agent Powell. Didn't you find that out when you and Bolger were down there?"

"Where did you get that information?"

"My dear friend; this is the Central Intelligence Agency. You sell us short. We happen to be pretty good at this stuff. What else would you like to know?"

"If what you're telling me is true, and the CIA is so good, then send your undercover people to find the guy. We'll come down, pick him up and take him home."

"Hey dude, you were down there and saw the mess. Give us a little more time. He can't hide for long."

"Why the hell would he hide? That doesn't make any sense. He has a beautiful wife waiting for him at home."

"Amigo, I don't have all the answers yet. Stay tuned. Gotta go. Bye, bye."

Frost then dialed a secure phone belonging to Miguel Castro. The undercover CIA agent was in Hermosillo at Frost's direction, attempting to get the Calimar people to lift the lid on Powell's location. Castro was a master spy. Able to infiltrate the most dangerous organizations in Mexico, he invariably succeeded in getting whatever he went after.

His immediate target was Domingo Fuentes. But to get close to him, Castro worked some mid-managers within the Calimar chain of command.

"Miguel, it's me. Do you have anything for me? Any progress on our missing piece of the puzzle?" Frost was speaking Spanish.

"Nothing hard, yet, but my contacts are gradually getting back to work. It has been very slow. The city is still a pile of rubble. I am hopeful that something will open up for us soon. What I *do* know is that Rico Morales, one of Fuentes' most trusted lieutenants, is dead. And his strong man is also history. I have been told that these guys were assigned to look after our missing person. But that is all I have at the moment."

"Okay. Stay on it. I'd like to show our pals in the FBI that we can beat them at their own game. You get this one done, and I have a much sweeter job for you in a couple of weeks. All for now."

Chapter 82

Day 14

Rusty waited for Dr. Ortega to show up and bless his release. It was 8:15 in the morning, and the breakfast tray arrived, with orange juice, cereal, a bran muffin and tea. Powell was not particularly hungry, owing to the hefty pot roast meal he and Angela enjoyed the night before. He pecked away at the food.

The new on-duty nurse arrived, armed with the vital signs equipment; hopefully for the last time. All signs were normal. An orderly then came in for the breakfast tray. The phone rang. It was Angela. "Good morning, David. I just wanted to see if Dr. Ortega has been there this morning."

"Not yet. I hope he gets here pretty soon. How is my beautiful Angela today?"

"I am fine. Your bedroom is ready for you. I have to work tonight, but can come and get you if you are discharged before eight o'clock. I go on duty at ten."

"I'd better be out of here a lot earlier than that. I will call your cellphone as soon as Dr. Ortega says the word. One more time: are you sure you want to do this?"

"David, you don't have a choice. No money, no memory; where will you go? And yes, I am certain that I want to do this. So please do not bring it up again. You need someone to care for you, at least for a little while. And I am your best option for the time being."

"Okay, I'm sorry Angela. It's just that I don't want to be a burden to you. I care for you very much. But you have a life of your own."

"At the moment, you are my life. Call me when you know what time I can bring you home."

Powell's leg was aching, more so than the day before. He thought that it had something to do with the cast keeping it in a 90-degree angle. The headaches continued as well. He buzzed for the nurse. She answered on the intercom.

"Can I please have something for pain?"

"Certainly, Mr. Smith. I will be right there."

In a few minutes she walked in with the medication in hand. Rusty was taking the pill with some water, when Dr. Ortega appeared.

"Mr. Smith; good morning. How's the leg? Is the cast giving you any problems?"

"It just aches a little, doctor. But I definitely would like to be discharged sometime today."

"Your vital signs are all normal, so I am confident that there is no infection. Let's get you out of bed. I would like to see you walk a bit."

Powell was careful to slowly move the leg off the bed before trying to lift the rest of his body over and into a standing position. He did so with relative ease. The crutches were close by. Ortega handed them over and Rusty was ready to begin the walking test. The two men exited the room and started to move down the hall. Powell walked on his own, appearing to be confident of each step.

"I am impressed", Ortega said, as they traveled almost two hundred feet before stopping to turn around. "Let's go back to the room and talk." There were no problems on the return trip. Rusty was perspiring a bit, but Ortega wasn't concerned.

Getting back to the room and into a chair, Powell took a deep breath. Satisfied that he had passed Ortega's test, he anticipated a positive response. The surgeon looked at Rusty and smiled.

"I guess you are wanting to leave this fine hospital, Mr. Smith, or whatever your name is. Well, I see no reason to keep you any longer. Tomorrow is my last day here. I return home the following morning, so we will say goodbye. From now on you be the patient of Dr. Andrew Sandoval, a very fine orthopedic surgeon. He has been reviewing your chart and would like to see you, here in the hospital, a week from today.

I will leave you now and issue the discharge order at the nurse's station. You will be able to leave the hospital by noon. Be patient with the leg. And I hope your memory will return very soon, so that you can get on with the rest of your life. Good luck."

"Doctor, I can't thank you enough. You have saved my leg and quite possibly my life."

"It was my pleasure. Goodbye."

Ortega departed. Powell sat in the chair for quite a while. He said hi to his teenage roommate. Then he called Angela and let her know he would be discharged by noon. She was delighted and committed to be there no later than 1PM. The shirt and trousers he was found in had been cleaned and pressed. The hospital also provided a pair of white boxer shorts. Angela had brought him a pair of sandals. He put on the clothes and sat waiting to be discharged.

Rusty's emotions were swirling inside. He wiped away a few tears, not really knowing what was going on in his head. In many respects, he feared what the immediate future would bring. Nothing was certain. He had to admit to himself that nothing ever is.

CHAPTER 83

CONSISTENT WITH HOSPITAL rules, Powell was taken by wheelchair to the front entrance, where Angela was waiting in her Honda Civic. It was 12:50, and beginning to rain. An orderly helped Rusty into the front passenger seat, placing the crutches in the rear. A pair of his nurses, Willie and Alicia, stood at the door, smiled and waved goodbye.

Fifteen minutes later, the Honda was parked in a space a short distance away from the front door to Angela's apartment building. She walked to Rusty's side of the car, handed him the crutches and helped him to his feet. "I'm fine, Angela. Just let me do this on my own." The twosome slowly walked into the building and took the elevator to her first floor apartment. It was called the first floor, because it was the lowest floor of apartment units. There were sixteen apartments in all.

Approaching the door, Angela unlocked it and Rusty followed her in. It was relatively small, but neatly decorated, with large windows that normally showered the living room with sunlight. There were two small bedrooms, a reasonably good-sized kitchen and a single, well-equipped bathroom. Powell looked and felt weak and tired. He sat down in a soft, comfortable chair.

Angela picked up on it right away. "David, you should lie down. I will make some coffee. She pointed to her left. "Your bedroom is over there. Can I get you anything else?"

"I'm fine. Just let me sit here for a while. The coffee sounds great."

Angela leaned over and kissed Rusty on his forehead. He looked up and smiled. "Well, here we are." Then the smile quickly disappeared. "A few small details. First, I have no money. And you cannot afford to support me for long. As soon as your roommate returns, then what? So the bottom line is that I will have to go the American Consulate and ask for their assistance. I don't know what that means, but hopefully they will be able to help."

"We shouldn't worry about that for a while. Marisa will not be back for another week. Right now, you need to regain some strength and hopefully clear your head. I have enough groceries for several days. When you feel strong enough we can go out to eat. There are men's toiletries on the shelf in the bathroom. They are yours when you need them. Okay?"

"Okay, for now. Angela, I'm really sorry that I've put you in this position. We have strong feelings for each other, but I can't take advantage of your kindness for long. I have to find out who I am and let the chips fall where they may. If we're to be together down the road, I need to know that the road is clear. You do too."

"I understand. In any case, you need to let me care for you for now. I have faith that all will work out for the best."

Rusty stood without the crutches and reached for Angela. She caught him before he fell. They kissed and held on to each other for some time.

CHAPTER 84

RICHARD WAS ON an elliptical, working out at an nearby health club when his cellphone vibrated in his warm-up pocket. He glanced at caller ID. It was a call from the Border Patrol. Roland Escobar needed to touch base.

"Roland, how are things down at the border?"

"I wanted to run something by you, Special Agent Martinez. Sorry to bother you, but timing may be an issue."

"Please, it's Richard. Let's not be too formal Roland. So, what could be a timing issue that we need to discuss?"

"I believe I mentioned to both you and Sally Henkel, that CBP has an investigator working on the Agent Powell disappearance. His name is Roger Wells, a former Border Patrol Agent, now assigned to DHS headquarters in D.C. I have asked him to make contact with your office, or at a minimum with Henkel here in Tucson. Sally tells me she spoke with him on only one occasion, about a week ago. I assume you haven't heard from Wells as yet. Am I correct?"

"If he's been in contact with Special Agent Henkel, that's good enough for me. Is there something about this we need talk about?"

"Wells would like a meeting with you. He believes he has some information that might assist the FBI in your search for Agent Powell. Obviously, he is powerless to conduct any investigation of his own in Mexico. If you or Henkel, or both of you, can meet with Wells, it might be useful. It's only a timing issue because he plans to head back to Washington in a couple of days. I believe that he would like to turn over to the FBI whatever information he's got. What do you think?"

"Sounds fine to me, Roland. Why don't you ask him to set something up with Sally? I'll be happy to attend if schedules permit. In the meantime, if Wells has a written report, or even some notes on his progress, let's ask him to get us a copy to read over in advance of the meeting. That way, we'll be better prepared to deal with the material right then and there. Make sense?"

"Absolutely, Richard. That being said, I can't say if he will agree to do it. But I'll give it a shot. I spoke with Sally yesterday, and she indicated that your contacts in Mexico have been able to narrow the search."

"Yes and no. If Powell *is* alive, he certainly is making it difficult to find him. The hospitals and morgues in Hermosillo and the towns north of there to the border have no record of him whatsoever. We're hoping that he isn't one of the people buried under the rubble caused by the quake. But quite frankly, Roland; it isn't looking good."

"I agree. Just looking at the damage we've had around Tucson, including some major building collapses in Nogales, it doesn't paint a positive picture for Powell. Okay, I'll talk with Roger Wells and see if we can organize something before he leaves. I will send emails to both you and Sally and we can go from there. It's probably going to have to happen within the next two days."

"Okay, let us know. Thanks for the call." As the call ended, Martinez decided to finish his elliptical workout and take a shower before heading home. He had a dinner date later that evening with an old classmate at UNLV. She was a pretty good professional golfer and had recently gone through a divorce. A tall, trim, gorgeous blonde, she would make a great catch. But Martinez wanted nothing to do with a woman looking for a new husband. A good friend, and potential bedmate, might be another story.

CHAPTER 85

ANGELA COOKED SPAGHETTI and made a Caesar salad for dinner. Rusty was only mildly hungry, but ate all that was served to him out of deference to the cook, who would soon leave for her night shift duty at the hospital. The food was accompanied by an inexpensive bottle of chianti. Dessert was lemon sorbet.

"Are you sure you will be okay here alone, David? I can call in sick tonight; no problem."

"Angela, don't worry about me. I will do the dishes and then watch TV. By then I'm going to be ready to hit the sack. You go on ahead to work. I'll be fine. See you in the morning."

"This "hit the sack"; what does that mean?"

"It means, "go to bed". Thought you would know that expression; sorry."

"I guess my short time in the states was not long enough to hear that expression. And David, please do not do the dishes. They can sit in the sink until morning. That is the way I want it. Okay?"

"Whatever you say, Angela, but I have to do something, and the doctors want me to get around on this leg. And I should be earning my keep. That is the way *I* want it. Okay?"

"Whoever you are, you are a very stubborn man." Powell was standing by the kitchen sink. Angela came over to him and kissed him warmly. They held hands, walking to the living room sofa and sat together listening to music until it was time for her to leave. He walked her to the door and hugged her goodbye. It was 9:20PM.

Rusty was unsure about his options for the immediate future. There was no way he would continue to live off of Angela's affection and concern for his well-being. He thought seriously about going directly to the U.S. Consulate first thing in the morning. Having no proof of his identity, knowledge of where he comes from or how he got to Hermosillo, he had no idea what the Consulate could do for him. Most likely, he thought, they would notify the FBI, in an effort to see if his description matched with someone on a database of missing persons.

Disobeying Angela's instructions, Rusty washed and dried the dishes. He was getting used to standing with the crutches, maintaining his balance, and moving around with relative ease. A gifted athlete, his sense of balance and lower body strength were outstanding. And he was coming to grips with the likelihood that he might be walking with a cane for the foreseeable future.

Angela's TV was cable-based and offered a number of English language channels. Powell watched a local Spanish station for most of the evening. His training in the language provided by the Border Patrol Academy was ample for the job, but functioning in a Mexican environment, where the dialects and speed of speech varied, was a different story. He knew that Angela would be more comfortable in her native language, but she was persistent in wanting to speak English with Powell.

The local station continued to broadcast detailed news and emergency service information throughout its programming. The city was gradually coming back to life, but the infrastructure damage was considerable and the rebuilding process slow. Half the city was still without electricity. And running water was being rationed to ease pressure on the few pumping stations that were operational. The city, under normal conditions, maintained an excellent supply of natural gas for industry and residential use. It was now severely reduced, due to fire and explosion dangers, still widely feared.

Beginning to doze off, Rusty turned off the only TV in the apartment and made his way to the roommate's bedroom. He brushed his teeth and took one of the pills Ortega prescribed for pain. Removing the only pants and shirt he currently could claim as his own, along with a pair of white cotton skivvies provided by the hospital nursing staff, he maneuvered himself into bed. By eleven, he was sound asleep.

Chapter 86

Day 15

SALLY HENKEL DROVE to her small office after driving her daughter to a friend's house and went through a mountain of new emails. One was from Roland Escobar, letting her know that Roger Wells would be giving her a call. Escobar copied-in Martinez, suggesting that Arthur knew something about Wells and the reason for making contact with the Bureau.

While parking in her reserved spot in the underground garage, a cellphone call came in. Sally decided to let it go to voicemail, preferring to return the call once she was settled at her desk. The caller ID indicated a CBP phone number.

"This is Special Agent Henkel returning your call." It was less than five minutes later.

"My name is Roger Wells, special investigator with Customs & Border Protection. Roland Escobar may have given you a heads-up that I would be calling. Is this a good time to talk?"

"No problem, Mr. Wells. What can the FBI do for you sir?"

"I have been assigned to assist in the Rusty Powell disappearance case. It's my understanding that Special Agent-in-charge Martinez and an associate were unsuccessful in their effort to locate Agent Powell during a recent trip to Mexico."

"That's correct. Powell has completely fallen off the grid. He was to be released by some people we believe are connected with a major drug cartel based in Hermosillo. You no doubt know about the devastating earthquake that shook that city. Unfortunately, the quake began just about the time Powell was to be driven to a contact close to the border and released from there. Information we recently got from government sources in Mexico indicates that the men responsible for getting it done were killed, but there is no information regarding Powell. He may be dead. We just do not know."

"Thanks for the recap, Agent Henkel. I've been made aware of most of this information by Roland Escobar. Our sources more or less confirm this assessment. There are a few additional pieces of intelligence that we would like the FBI to have in hand. I was hoping to meet with you in the next day or so to pass the information along. Unfortunately, I've been called back to Washington tomorrow afternoon. How's your schedule look?"

"How much time will you need? I have a court date tomorrow, but can meet with you briefly this afternoon."

"Three o'clock okay with you? Will Mr. Martinez be able to attend?"

"My boss is based in Phoenix. I have no idea what his schedule looks like later today. Let's just you and I plan on meeting in my office at three. I'll certainly brief Martinez on the outcome."

Wells agreed to the one-on-one session. Sally called Meredith at her friend's home and was told that her daughter would be spending the night there. She then buried herself in some legal paperwork in an effort to clear her schedule for the three o'clock meeting.

Henkel was puzzled that Wells could have information that the FBI could have missed. It was worth seeing what they had, whether it was useful or not.

CHAPTER 87

ANGELA ENDED HER shift at 7AM. She stopped at a nearby convenience store and bought a half-dozen donuts to surprise Rusty for breakfast.

Powell was in the process of waking when Angela made it home. She walked to her roommate's bedroom, where she found him slowly lifting his cast-borne leg out of the bed, followed by the rest of his body. "I was trying to be quiet when I came in the front door." She waited until he was completely out of the bed before giving him a hug and kiss.

"You didn't wake me up. It was the morning sun. How was work last night? You must be ready for bed yourself."

"It was busy. We had a number of very bad accident victims brought to the ER just after midnight. A number of them went to surgery right away. I am a little tired, but let's have some breakfast. I brought you a surprise."

She handed Rusty the crutches and walked with him to the kitchen. The box of donuts was on the table. Powell smiled as he peeked into the box and saw the treats. "Awesome. You must be trying to fatten me up."

"Not really David. You look fine to me." She filled the coffee maker, turned it on, and put some plates and napkins on the table. They each had two donuts and two cups of coffee. Angela then went into her bedroom, took off her uniform and wrapped herself in a robe.

Returning to the kitchen, she cleaned off the table and handed Rusty the morning paper. "I need a shower", she said. "Why not go into the living room, relax and see if there is any good news? After I get cleaned up we can go out and buy you some other clothes to wear."

"Angela, I do not need any new clothes. If you can wash what I have that would be just fine. I really do not want you to spend any more money on me. Okay?"

"No; I want to do it. Stop worrying about my money. I make a good salary and can afford to buy you something inexpensive to wear. Any way, your plain, worn out clothes look terrible. So not another word about it. I *will* wash those when you have new things to wear. Understood? And by the way, if you would like a shower as well, I will help you get in and out. See you in a few minutes."

Powell was tongue-tied. It was obvious that Angela had made up her mind he was getting new clothes to wear. She left the kitchen and as she suggested, Rusty ambled into the living room and leafed through the morning news.

Less than ten minutes later, Angela returned from the shower in her bathrobe, her wet hair draped across her neck, and smelling like a rose. She sat next to Rusty, leaned over and kissed him on the cheek. As she leaned toward him, her bare, sweet-smelling breasts were visible under the robe. Powell was losing whatever was left of his self-control.

"You are the most beautiful woman I have ever seen. He reached toward her and kissed her on the lips. She threw her arms around him and gravity opened the robe. All she had on was a pair of black panties. He could feel Angela's pulse quicken as he gently touched a breast and softly kissed it at the same time.

She rose, took one of Rusty's hands and led him to her bedroom. She supported his upper body as he hopped along, without the crutches, to her bed. Angela removed the robe, as they crawled under the sheet and began caressing each other in a flood of passion. Separating briefly from their embrace, she reiterated something she had told him once before. "David, I have never made love with anyone. Please be gentle with me. I love you very much."

Rusty clumsily rolled over on top of Angela, gingerly maneuvering his cast-laden leg into position. Their kisses were filled with emotion. The beauty and warmth of her perfectly formed anatomy was enough to make him feel like he wanted to explode. He removed her panties. She was surprisingly supple and wet as he passionately entered her, making every effort to delay his explosion of joy and bring her to a spectacular climax. They both came at once. They were soaked with perspiration and locked in each other's arms.

CHAPTER 88

HENKEL PHONED MARTINEZ, who, seeing her number on caller ID, answered on the second ring. "Sally, hey, what's up?"

"Just wanted to let you know that this guy Roger Wells, from CBP Washington, gave me a call and wants to meet. He claims that he has some information on Powell that we might need. I agreed to meet with him here at 3PM today. There's no need for you to drive down, but it's up to you."

"Your call; my afternoon is open. I don't think you need me, but I certainly can be there if you like. What does this guy Wells sound like. You think he might have something we don't know about?"

"Don't know, but he seems to be okay. Escobar thinks he's worth talking with. Bottom line, you don't need to come down. Take the afternoon off. Play some golf. I'll handle it."

"It's too hot to play golf. Maybe when October rolls around. But let me know how the meeting nets out. I'll be here. If you need me on speakerphone, just dial me in. Otherwise, it's all yours."

She then called Roland Escobar. Getting his voicemail, she left a message, inviting him to the meeting, if he wanted to attend.

A little before three, Wells arrived at the office. With curly blonde hair, light blue eyes and a medium build, he carried himself confidently and displayed a pleasant demeanor. "Special Agent Henkel, good to meet you. Thanks for agreeing to meet on such short notice."

"No problem. Can I get you something to drink; water, coffee, cola?"

"No thanks. I'm fine. How much time do you have?"

"I wouldn't worry about that. Why don't we just get into the subject at hand? By the way, I asked Roland Escobar to join us. Not sure if he makes it, but we don't need to wait. Let's hear what you've got."

"Very well. You can certainly record this if you like. Our interest is in providing the Bureau with information you might not have, so that we can all close the file on Randall Powell."

"Sounds good, Mr. Wells. So, what you tell us that you think might help the case?"

"A CBP contact in Nogales, Mexico informed us of the plan concocted by Calimar cartel strongmen to release Agent Powell and bring him to the border. That contact has also recently told us that it is very possible Powell is still alive and recovering from surgery that was performed at a hospital in Hermosillo several days ago."

"Mr. Wells; that may be a possible, but not very likely scenario. Richard Martinez, and another FBI agent, were in Hermosillo a few days ago and either physically visited or called every hospital facility of any size in that city. No one with Powell's name or description was treated medically up to that time. So your contact may be misinformed."

"Maybe, Agent Henkel, but have you and your fellow investigators considered the possibility that Powell either did not use his name, had his appearance altered by the accident, or didn't know who he was while a patient in one of those facilities?

"Are you suggesting that Powell could be suffering from amnesia, or was hiding his identity from people providing the treatment?" The hospitals that were visited indicated there were no American patients on their admission lists."

"I don't have an answer to your question. CBP authorities simply wanted to provide this to you for further consideration. If Powell was seriously injured by a fall or some other accident during the earthquake, it's certainly possible that he may have a brain concussion or more serious head damage that's affected his memory or appearance. Our Nogales contacts seemed fairly certain that there is some merit to the assumption. That's all I can say."

Henkel acknowledged to herself that there might be something to it. She thanked Roger Wells, asked for some ways he could be reached if needed, and ended the meeting. Wells thanked Sally for her time, provided the contact information and left the office.

CHAPTER 89

AFTER CLEANING UP and dressing, Rusty and Angela went for a walk. Powell was getting stronger. His arms, muscular to begin with, were recovering from two weeks of virtually no exercise. This was making it easier to deal with the crutches and lessen the walking effort. They moved slowly, making their way to a small men's clothing store not far from the apartment.

Inside the store, Angela chose a pair of tan trousers and a blue striped, short-sleeve cotton shirt. She also grabbed a package of boxer shorts, asking Rusty his sizes along the way. The sales clerk bagged the merchandise, as Angela pulled a credit card from her purse. Powell noticed the receipt. The total was only 600 pesos, or about forty-eight dollars. Nevertheless, he felt lousy that without a dime in his possession he was totally dependent on Angela to pay the bills.

She was all smiles as they left the store. "Now you will look halfway decent. We could actually be seen in public." They approached a nearby park, where Angela often went to read and enjoy the shade of the trees that lined the walking paths. "If you like, we can just sit here and talk for a while. She led him to a wooden bench, taking the crutches as he bent to sit down."

They stayed there for nearly an hour. Rusty was silent for much of the time, as Angela talked about her job, her parents and her time in America. Her hair was once again pulled back into a ponytail. It glistened in the sunlight that peeked through the trees. A cheerful-looking yellow print sundress completed her late summer wardrobe. Powell spent much of the time just enjoying the beauty of the young woman lighting up his day.

On the way back to the apartment, they stopped for fajitas at one of Angela's favorite lunch cafes. They sat outside at a table in the shade. There was a pleasant summer breeze rustling through the trees. Rusty inhaled the chicken fajitas. Angela chose the shrimp version. Both drank Dos Equis with lime. They held hands most of the time.

As they finished their lunch, Powell put a more serious expression on his face. I'm keeping a record of every peso you are spending on me Angela. I don't know when, but sooner or later I'm going to pay you back. And there's no way you can talk me out of it."

"If you insist", she said. But in the meantime, you have to let me enjoy what I am doing. It really *is* fun. Can you understand that?"

"I guess so. But it doesn't change the fact that I have to take advantage of your kindness to get through the day. I can't let that go on. It just isn't right."

"Okay, enough of this subject. What would you like to do this afternoon? I have the night shift, so there is plenty of time to enjoy the day."

"But you haven't slept a wink. I say we go back to the apartment. You need to have a nice long nap. After that, we'll see."

Angela was tired. Their time in bed together didn't provide any rest. She smiled, and nodded, as they made their way back to her flat. She fell into a deep sleep as soon as her head hit the pillow. Rusty turned to a phone directory on a table in the living room. Flipping the pages, he eventually landed on the number he was looking for: the office of the U.S. Consulate General.

CHAPTER 90

SALLY CALLED THE Bureau office in Phoenix. It was 3:30PM. Richard was on the phone with a U.S. Attorney. His admin assistant suggested that she put Henkel on hold. "He shouldn't be more than another five minutes, Agent Henkel. I'll put a sticky note under his nose that you are on the other line. Oh, wait, he's hanging up now. Just a second."

Martinez saw the admin's signal that it was Sally. "Hi, it's me. What's up Sally? How was your meeting with the CBP guy? Learn anything new?"

"I'm not sure Richard. His name is Roger Wells. Seems like a pretty solid citizen. He pretty much knew what we had on the case. What his contacts were telling him did make a little sense. Bottom line, the word they have is that Powell may have been to one of the Hermosillo hospitals, but was either in such bad shape that they couldn't identify him, or that he may have lost his memory. What I can't figure, though, is why he wouldn't have had some ID on him at the time."

"Sally, it may well be that the drug boys who grabbed him took off his uniform and got rid of his identification, and most likely everything else on him at the time. And he was probably either wounded during the encounter in the desert, or later when they had them under wraps down there. Who the hell knows? I kind of suspected something along these lines, but there just weren't any clues to go on."

"Do you want me to do anything with this, boss? I can call Pepe Sanchez and see if he can do some more snooping around."

"I don't think so. I'm counting on Frost and his cartel implants to dig something up. In the meantime, who knows: Agent Powell may wake up, remember who he is, and find his way home. I know you'd like to give Melinda some hope right now, but there just isn't enough to go on."

Sally had another call coming in. It was her daughter. "Gotta go, Richard; Meredith's on the other line. See you tomorrow afternoon." Martinez had a regularly scheduled Wednesday afternoon meeting of all the Phoenix Division agents.

"Take care, young lady. See you then."

Meredith needed a ride home. The regular carpool mom for the week couldn't make it to the school. "Tracy's mom can't pick us up. Band practice is over. Can you come after us?"

"Certainly. I should be there in about twenty minutes. Is Tracy's mom okay?"

"I think so. She might have car problems. Not sure."

As Sally was packing up her briefcase for the next day's trip to Phoenix, the office phone rang. It was Roger Wells.

"Agent Henkel, it's Roger. I'm getting ready to leave Tucson and head back to D.C. Have you had an opportunity to discuss our conversation with Mr. Martinez"

"I did, Roger. He really appreciates your input. It does provide another avenue for us to pursue. We don't see any need for additional follow-up. But thanks for checking back in. Have a good trip back east."

Wells sized up the meaning of Sally's comment. "No problem. Good luck. I hope you find Agent Powell. CBP is ready to help in any way. Bye for now."

Henkel headed for the door.

CHAPTER 91

MIGUEL CASTRO, BENNETT Frost's informer in the state of Sonora, and with close ties to many Calimar insiders, had more information to pass along. Once again, he contacted Frost with his secure cellphone, getting through to him on the second ring. "Señor Frost, this is follow-up to our last conversation regarding the possible whereabouts of the American Border Patrol agent."

"Let's have it Miguel. Is this something I can take to the bank?"

"Well, it is something. You can decide if it is worth cashing in. The two lieutenants in the Calimar crew were found dead near the strong man's apartment on the Paseo de la Cascada. It is believed that one of the dead men was going to deliver the agent to a bank in Nogales. He was found in an SUV sitting in a sinkhole next to what was once the residence. It is now a pile of rubble."

"It's just a guess, but one would be led to believe that the agent was injured and taken to a hospital for treatment. Apparently there were bloodstains in the front and back seats. I am getting this information from a contact on the federal police force. So that's it. If your friends in the FBI have not checked the hospitals in Hermosillo, they should do so. So that is it. For now."

"Sounds like it may be worth checking out. Thanks amigo. Stay in touch."

****

Frost immediately dialed Martinez's cellphone number. Getting voicemail, as he expected, he left a cryptic message. It was one that Richard knew and would likely respond to as soon as he got it.

It was close to 6PM when he checked emails and connected with Frost. "Bennett, I was going to call you in the morning, but you saved me the dime. How are things in Langley?"

"Beats the hell out of me. Did you forget, or what? I'm sitting in a dingy little office in Mexico City. Anyway, my man who hangs around the Calimar people had some additional pieces of info to pass along. You may have figured this out yourself, but it might confirm a few of your assumptions.

Bottom line, it does look like your border patrol guy was injured in a vehicle found sitting in a sinkhole caused by the quake. The scuttlebutt is that he was probably taken to one of the hospitals down there. Which one, nobody knows. You should have run across him when you checked them out. But obviously you didn't. My suggestion is to call those hospitals again. He may not have had any ID on him when they brought him in. But I still think it's worth another try."

"We visited most of the main facilities, except two or three of them, all of which I had called the day before. No dice. But in deference to you and your sage advice, we'll try them again. Thanks Bennett. I'll keep you posted. Bye."

Martinez immediately placed a call to Dan Bolger in Mexico City. He picked up on the first ring, seeing "FBI Phoenix" on caller ID. "Richard, is that you?"

"It is. I need a favor. You kept the list of hospitals we checked. Do you still have it?"

"I do. What's up?"

"Either send it to me in an email, or if you can, it would be great if you could call those places again. There's a good chance that Powell might show up, possibly as a John Doe, in one of them."

"What makes you think so now? I'm not sure I understand."

"I don't know, Dan. I can't give you the specifics on my intel source, but it's a real possibility. Anyway, either you call or I'll do it. It's your call."

"No problem Richard. I'll get it done and let you know what I find out. Is tomorrow okay?"

"Tomorrow's great. Thanks Dan. Talk with you soon."

Martinez left his office and drove to one of his Phoenix agent's home. He was invited over for a barbecue dinner and a swim. The evening temperature continued to hover in the high 90's, fairly normal for late August in southern Arizona.

CHAPTER 92

ANGELA WOKE AT 6:15. Rusty had fallen asleep as well. She found him on the sofa in the living room. Bending down, she kissed him on the forehead. Somewhat startled, he jumped a bit, but then smiled as he looked up and saw Angela's wonderful smile. "How are you feeling David? You must be getting hungry."

"I feel pretty good. Did you get a good sleep?"

"Yes, wonderful. I have the night shift again tonight, but if you feel like it, we can go out and eat. I know a very good Chinese restaurant close by. Do you like Chinese food?"

"I do; at least I think so. Weird, isn't it? But sure, let's go for it. Do we have enough time?"

"We can walk there, even slowly and be there in ten minutes. I will put on my uniform, so we won't have to rush to get back. As long as I leave for the hospital by nine or so, we should be okay."

"Sounds great." Rusty eased himself to a sitting position. Angela helped him off the sofa and handed him the crutches. She went to get dressed and Powell headed for the bathroom to wash up and brush his hair. His new shirt and trousers were a great fit. He looked and felt as good as he could remember.

They left the apartment a few minutes before seven.

There was a pleasant late summer breeze in the air, as Rusty and Angela made their way to the China Restaurant, a well-known oriental eatery that was spared any significant earthquake damage. At this hour, the China began to fill up. The couple arrived and was seated at a table facing the window with a view of the sidewalk and the people passing by.

A tiny, cheerful waitress arrived with menus. Rusty ordered two glasses of chardonnay. "That's my limit", Angela said. This is a work night. "Please bring us two glasses of water as well."

The traditional Chinese menu was extensive. They ordered a family-style dinner, which was about twice as much food as the couple could handle. They finished what they could, ordered hot tea, and Angela asked for a box to take the balance of the food home. Once again, Rusty was frustrated that Angela had to pay the check. It was one more brick added to the burden of being unable to fend for himself.

They walked home at a slightly quicker pace than when they left for the restaurant. Rusty was getting better at getting around on the crutches. Angela still had some time before she had to leave for the hospital. The twosome arrived at the apartment, got comfortable on the living room sofa and watched the local news. The city was recovering, but slowly. Electrical power was now restored in 50% of the city. Quake victims were still being discovered under the millions of tons of rubble.

A few minutes after nine, Angela departed. Her Honda needed gas, but she had to go past several service stations, still closed because of structural damage. The one station on the way to the hospital had a line of cars waiting for fuel. Deciding there wasn't enough time to wait, she left the station and headed for work. Arriving at the hospital, Angela took several minutes tying to find a place to park. The closest space was far from the emergency entrance. Walking to the ER, she noted three emergency vehicles lined up to deliver patients. It was a sure sign that it was going to be a busy night.

CHAPTER 93

DAY 16

DAN BOLGER BEGAN calling Hermosillo hospitals a few minutes before ten in the morning. There were twelve facilities on the list. He asked the very same questions on each call, but the answer was invariably the same. *"We have no American's on the admission roles, and there is no one here without some form of identification."*

Except for one. Bolger was connected with the patient services department. The clerk on duty scrolled through the admissions database. "Sir, what name were you asking about?"

"I don't have a name. The individual we are looking for is an American. We believe he may have been brought to your emergency department several days ago. His name is Randall Powell, but he may not have had any identification on him at the time."

The clerk continued scrolling down the list of admissions over the past ten days. "Sir, I do not see a name even close to the one you mentioned. There was an unnamed patient brought in with multiple injuries and hospitalized after surgery on a fractured lower leg. For identification purposes, it appears that he received the name of David Smith. There is no mention of his nationality in the record."

Bolger thought to himself that this was their man. "Is David Smith still a patient there?"

"No sir. He was discharged two days ago. We have no record of a home address. Would you like me to check with the surgical patient floor to see if they have any information on his discharge destination?"

"Yes, please. Can you do that while I wait? If not, I can give you my cellphone number for a callback."

"Sir, let me see if I can reach someone who can help you. I will be able to transfer you to their line." The clerk put Bolger on hold.

Three minutes later, another voice came on. "This is head floor nurse Gonzales. I understand you are looking for David Smith."

"Yes ma'am. Can you tell me if Mr. Smith is an American?"

"I believe so. Unfortunately, I was not working on the days that he was a patient on this floor. But if you can hold, there is another nurse who might be able to help you."

"Yes, I can hold. Thank you."

In less than a minute, a new voice came on the line. "This is Alicia speaking. You are asking about David Smith?"

"Yes, I am, Alicia. What can you tell me? Do you know where I might find him now?"

"All I know is that when he was discharged, he was picked up by one of our nurses, Angela Contreras, and driven away. I do not know if she took him to her home, or to somewhere else."

"Can you give me her address or phone number?"

"I am sorry sir. We are not permitted to give out that information."

"Alicia, I am a United States law enforcement officer with the Federal Bureau of Investigation. This David Smith may well be a missing U.S. Border Patrol agent. Is there someone at the hospital who can help me out?"

Alicia handed the phone back to nurse Gonzales. "Please hold, sir. I will try to connect you with the hospital administrator."

This time the hold was much longer. Bolger was preparing to hang up and see if he could find Angela Contreras another way. Fortunately, someone came on the line before he disconnected. "I am the assistant to Arturo Lantos, the administrator of Hospital San Jose. He is not in the office this morning. I understand you would like some information on a discharged patient."

"Actually, what I would like is the address or phone number of one of your nurses; Angela Contreras. I am a U.S. federal law enforcement officer. The location of the patient is what I am trying to find out. Apparently he was discharged in nurse Contreras' care."

"Sir, I believe you can appreciate the importance of protecting our patients and valuable employees. If you are able to meet me here in the hospital to provide some physical identification, we should be able to comply with your request."

"Ma'am, I am calling you from my office in Mexico City. It is not possible for me to get there anytime soon. I was hoping that you would understand. Our mission is to help Mr. Smith and return him safely to the United States."

Bolger struck out. His next best option was to find Angela's address and phone number from the Hermosillo white pages directory. Getting hold of it from Mexico City meant that he would have to access it online. Unfortunately, the address and phone number were listed under the name of Angela's roommate. Nothing showed up under her name. Bolger placed a call to Martinez. Seeing Bolger' number, Richard picked up right away.

"Richard, good news and bad news. Here's the deal. I think we found Agent Powell. It isn't a sure thing, but the San Jose Hospital had a patient they named David Smith. He came in without any identification and had surgery on his leg. They told me he was discharged the other day, and one of the nurses, a woman named Angela Contreras, picked him up and drove away. Unfortunately, they wouldn't give me the nurse's contact information: hospital policy. So I tried to find her in the online Hermosillo white pages. More bad news: she isn't listed anywhere."

"Maybe not, but if she has a cellphone, we may be able to find her that way. Let me work on it. You said "Angela Contreras"?" Martinez spelled out both names to confirm. "Let's see what we can do. I'll keep you posted. And thanks for getting us this far. Sounds like David Smith is our man."

CHAPTER 94

ANGELA ARRIVED BACK at the apartment and went right to bed. The ER was a madhouse the entire night. She was involved in four crash cart cases; all four were cardiac arrests. A generally healthy, fit young woman, the stress of emergency room wore her down this time, nonetheless. Rusty didn't hear her come in: a few minutes after eight. She peaked into his bedroom, but had no intention of waking him up.

About half an hour later, Powell awoke. He hobbled into the kitchen and started the coffee brewing. Angela's door was closed. It was obvious she was in there asleep. Having written down the address and phone number of the U.S. Consulate, Rusty was determined to make contact and enlist its aid in getting him back home, wherever that might be. It was a scary scenario: a real name, home and the people who must be franticly wanting to learn his fate.

There was no way that he would simply walk out on Angela without saying goodbye. But just saying goodbye and leaving her life was going to be unbelievably difficult. He was growing more and more in love with her, which was making the decision to go increasingly more difficult. He feared that this would turn into a very long and painful day. Pouring himself a cup of coffee, he gulped down orange juice, ate one of the leftover donuts and went into the living room to watch the news.

The U.S. President was dispatching the Secretary of State on her way to Indonesia. That country's president was requesting substantial foreign aid to combat the growing violence caused by al Qaida militants. They had just slaughtered hundreds of women and children in Jakarta's main square and threatened more. The war on terror now threatened the world's most populous Muslim country.

Separately, with the States still suffering a weak economy and growing inflation, the flood of illegal Hispanics across the border was trickling to a manageable level. Customs and Border Protection was in the process of enforcing new laws, consistent with America's dramatic changes in its immigration policy. Somehow, the term "border protection" struck a chord with Powell. He wasn't sure why, so it let it go.

Locally, in Hermosillo, curfews in a number of sections of the city were being lifted. Looting decreased and law enforcement, in general, was returning to normal. The oppressive heat was easing a bit. Rain was forecasted for the next several days, not unusual for late August in northern Mexico. With that, Rusty turned off the TV and again looked in on Angela, who remained fast asleep.

Was now the time to contact the Consulate and start the ball rolling? He argued back and forth with himself. Once he opened that can of worms, there would be no turning back. The future would have to play itself out; the past would have to be laid before him. That was the scary part.

No; let's give it another day, he decided. What's one more day? Plus, it would at least give him a little more time to bring Angela around to accept it. Rusty settled his thoughts back down and waited for her to awaken. He thought it would be fun to take her on a little picnic. There was a small park close by. The rain wasn't due to arrive until the next day. With that in mind, he went into the kitchen, made some chicken sandwiches and packed them in a basket with some grapes and a bottle of white wine.

Angela slept until two-thirty. Rusty heard her go into the bathroom. She came out in a pink bra and panties. Before she could get her robe on, Powell met her in the hall and pulled her close, giving her a passionate kiss. "Good afternoon, beautiful lady. Guess what?"

"What are we talking about?" I am not a good guesser."

"We're going on a picnic! Sound like fun?"

"Sounds like a wonderful idea. But you have to let me put some clothes on first."

"If you insist. But I like you just the way you are right now."

"Maybe so, but I do not intend to make a scene where we are going. By the way, where *are* we going?

"To the little park we passed on the way to the restaurant. We can walk there. I need the exercise. Okay?"

"Okay. I will go and make us some sandwiches and something to drink."

"Already taken care of. You just make yourself decent. We can go whenever you like."

Angela dressed quickly, in yellow shorts and a black tee top. Leather sandals completed the picture. She kept her hair up in the ponytail. Rusty wore his newly purchased wardrobe. There wasn't much of a choice. Angela brought along a blue blanket. In less than ten minutes, they were out the door.

A gentle breeze was blowing from west to east, as they ambled along the street leading to the park. A cool front carrying the breeze was ushering in the rain, expected the following day. It was less than a ten-minute walk. Rusty and his crutches made it with ease.

There was a handful of people in the park, mostly sunning and reading something or other. Angela pointed to a spot near the water fountain and a bench. She spread out the blanket and set the basket down. Rusty set the crutches down and maneuvered himself into a sitting position.

"I am starved", Angela admitted. My last bit of food was a donut in the ER. It was one of the nurses' birthday."

Powell smiled, as he began to unwrap the sandwiches. "My last food was also a donut. Let's eat."

The cork to the wine had been pulled and stuck back in at the apartment. There were two plastic cups in the basket. Rusty poured the wine. Bon appétit!" He gave Angela a tiny kiss on the lips. They downed the sandwiches in short order, finished off the grapes and enjoyed the wine. Not far away, a teenage boy was playing the guitar. It was a lovely Latin tune, and it capped off a wonderful afternoon in the park.

Rusty hesitated to bring up the subject of going to the Consulate. He had no intention to rain on Angela's parade. It could wait.

CHAPTER 95

MARTINEZ BEGAN THE search for Angela Contreras that afternoon. The FBI had access to all cellphone numbers in the U.S. and a large chunk of them in Canada and Mexico. His search source at Bureau Headquarters searched the proprietary database and got back to him within the hour.

"Special Agent Martinez, it's Wally Branch. I have some information for you, but unfortunately, not very good. Our search brought up several thousand records showing Contreras last names in the Mexico database. Oddly enough, there is not a single Angela among them. There are Angelicas, Angies and Angelinas, but no Angelas. Of the Angelicas, there were ten found in the Hermosillo area, and five Angelinas. That's it. What do you want me to do next?"

Martinez quickly ascertained that someone else very likely purchased the cellphone Angela Contreras used. Possibly a relative, such as a parent or sibling bought the phone and may even be billed for it. Or it was a prepaid phone given to her as a gift. In any case, this appeared to be a blind alley. What they needed was the actual cellphone number, so that they could call and trace it. Even that, however, might not deliver Angela, or help find Powell. And getting the number would not be a simple task.

Richard thought long and hard about going back down to Hermosillo, using his FBI leverage, and getting to Contreras one way or another. He was running out of other options: this could well be his last hope of finding Powell and closing the case.

Before ending his call with Wally Branch he made one request. "Wally, cmail me the information on the Contreras names you mentioned that showed up in the Hermosillo area. Chances are they're not going to be helpful, but I'll take them anyway." There was, of course, the remote possibility that one of those individuals was Angela's relative, or that Angela was their shortened name.

Branch agreed to do it. Martinez thanked him for his quick response, gave him his secure email address and poured a cup of coffee to clear his head. Time seemed to be running out. If Powell was alive, but suffering from memory loss, he could be virtually impossible to find. Not being able to contact the one person that apparently knows who and where he might be was, at the moment, his only hope.

As soon as he received the names and numbers, and using his very best northern Mexico Spanish dialect, Martinez called each one. The only promising one was to an Angelina, who had a cousin named Angela, living at present in Monterrey. Coincidentally, that was where the relevant Angela was born and raised, but it clearly was not the right woman. It was one more blind alley. The alleys were becoming few and far between.

It was now pretty clear to Martinez. If he wanted to find Powell he would need to go back, locate Angela through the hospital, and track Rusty down. He suddenly realized that San Jose was one of the two remaining hospitals he and Bolger decided not to visit before heading home. It might have been possible to find Powell then and bring him home. As a highly respected and experienced lawman, Richard Martinez just didn't make those kinds of mistakes. But he did, and now he had to make it right.

Chapter 96

Angela had one more night shift on the current rotation. After that, she switched to mornings for the next five days, and then had three days off.

After the picnic and the wine, sandwiches and fruit, she and Rusty decided on having gazpacho and Italian bread for dinner. They had spent a leisurely afternoon walking through a flower market and listening to music back at the apartment. Powell was quickly coming to the conclusion that if he didn't get to the Consulate soon, he would run into difficulties with the Mexican government, having no identity but needing to get some sort of job to earn his keep.

Finishing the delicious homemade gazpacho, Rusty made up his mind. Tomorrow morning, as soon as Angela returned from work, he would sit her down and with much difficulty and consternation, let her know that he was going to the American Consulate that afternoon. He would face the consequences, and she would have to as well. This evening, however, until Angela had to leave for the hospital, he wanted to make love, even if it was for the last time.

Rusty helped her clean up the kitchen. They watched TV from the living room sofa for less than an hour. It was almost eight o'clock. Angela had already taken a shower and washed her hair. Now in her bathrobe, she had an hour or so before getting dressed and preparing to go. Powell snuggled up to her and kissed her on the cheek. She turned to face him and looked as though she wanted to cry.

Rusty was concerned. "What's wrong? Is it something I've done? Are you feeling okay?"

"I am afraid, David; very afraid. I can see it in your eyes. The time is coming very soon for you to leave me in search of who you are and where you belong. I want you to be happy. If that means leaving to find your other life, then so be it. But I love you. It will be the end of something that has been very good. My life has been changed forever. Do you understand?"

"More than you know. I too am afraid. We've only known each other for a few days, but leaving you will be like falling back into that hole. You've given yourself to me and nothing can ever take that away from us. The future scares the hell out of me. Especially if I have to face it without you."

They hugged each other and held on. "I want you David", she said, with tears in her eyes. She handed Rusty the crutches and they made their way to her room. Once in bed, they held each tightly, thinking perhaps that it was their final intimate moment together. It was a magical experience. Angela removed her robe, helped Rusty to undress and made love with every bone in her body. When she came, Powell's loins exploded with joy. No matter when or where his memory would eventually return, this particular night would never be forgotten.

Soaked and utterly drained of a myriad of emotions, Angela needed to shower again before putting on her uniform and heading to do her job. She gently kissed Rusty, letting him stay in her bed for the time being. He watched her leave for the bathroom, her naked body, perfectly formed, moving with beauty and grace. He reveled in the thought of what he had just experienced, while she got herself ready to go.

CHAPTER 97

RICHARD HAD AN idea. He made a call to the General Garcia Airport in Hermosillo. The news was positive. The airport was now open and flights to and from Phoenix were operating on a modest schedule. Damage at Garcia, located on the west side of the city, was extensive. All air traffic ceased for almost a week. The tarmac had been badly torn up by the quake, but large crews of workers managed to open a runway that could handle medium-sized aircraft. The terminal building itself was still in need of major repairs, but a sufficient number of gates and passenger facilities were functioning fairly well.

Rather than make the drive again, he booked a seat on an Aeromexico flight at 10:15AM the next morning, returning on the same airline at 9:20AM the following day. Aeromexico indicated that taxis were operating out of the airport on a regular basis.

His next call was to the U.S. Consulate. Philip Boyce, the Head of Mission, was in Washington and was due to return sometime later in the day. His executive assistant volunteered to help Richard with anything he needed while in Hermosillo.

Martinez planned to be there for only one day. "Thanks for wanting to help. The reason for my call was to say hi to the Consul General and as a courtesy, let him know that I would be in town. If, by chance, I run into any unforeseen challenges, I will let you know."

After ending that brief conversation, Sally Henkel called in. "You rang, fearless leader?" Martinez had called her earlier to discuss where the Powell case was and how it altered his plans. He knew full well that she would go ballistic over his decision to go back to Hermosillo.

"Sally, there is every reason to believe that Rusty is not only alive, but is recovering from surgery with the help of a nurse. We even have her name. That's the good news. Unfortunately, the woman has no phone that she owns, and the hospital where she works won't give us anything on her unless we show up in person and prove we're the cops."

Henkel's reaction, even over the phone, was palpable. There was a moment of absolute silence; then the response. "So you're going back down there. What's wrong with Agent Bolger? It's in *his* territory. Let him go get Agent Powell and bring him home."

"Sally, it's not that simple. This is *our* case. And it's very possible that Rusty has a memory problem; maybe full-fledged amnesia. That's probably the reason nobody's heard diddlysquat from him. We have the continuity here in the States. And besides; I kind of like Hermosillo. The place is a total disaster, but the people are amazing. They keep on going, and they are very proud."

"I want to go with you. Powell is actually my charge. Okay, you're the boss, but the Border Patrol thinks I'm the lead dog on this assignment."

Martinez was afraid this was coming. Fact was, she was right. A very capable FBI agent, she was totally able to take care of herself in the field. "You know something: you're absolutely right. Here's the deal. I'm booked on an Aeromexico flight tomorrow morning to Hermosillo. Their airport is partially back in business. If you can arrange for Meredith to have some cover, you're on."

"Not a problem. I'll call her best friend's mom. If it's only for a few days, it'll be fine. Give me the flight information. I'll get booked and confirm it to via email. Okay?"

"I don't expect to be gone for more than a day; my return flight is at 9:20 the following day. If we have to stay down there another day or two, I can go it alone."

"Forget that. I'm with you all the way. Meredith will be fine. She's fifteen next week and acts like she's twenty-two. Let's get down there and bring Rusty back."

Martinez gave her the flight information. He was having second thoughts about the decision to take her along, but it was too late. Henkel was going. That was it.

Henkel drove up to Phoenix early the next morning to travel with her boss. There was no direct flight from Tucson.

CHAPTER 98

DAY 17

ANGELA GOT BACK to the apartment a few minutes after eight. It was a dark, damp morning, with a light drizzle and heavy sky, promising that at least a significant portion of the day would be less than pleasant. Changing into her bathrobe, she tiptoed into the kitchen and saw the coffee maker doing its thing.

Rusty was in the other bedroom, having taken a cool shower, and was getting dressed. He could hear Angela handling some dishes. She was making French toast, and getting a skillet ready to grill some bacon. Powell said to himself that this would likely be the last morning he would spend with her. Before the morning came to a close he would make his case with Angela and later make his way to the U.S. Consulate. He couldn't imagine a scenario that wouldn't mean the end to their relationship.

"Smells great", Rusty said, as he and the crutches arrived in the kitchen. He walked up behind Angela, who was grilling the toast, lifted her ponytail and kissed her on the back of her neck. "What's on your agenda for the day?"

She turned and kissed Powell on the lips. "Get some sleep, at least for a few hours. Then, I don't know. It isn't a very nice day, so I might read, or write some emails to my sister and mom. My sister has a six-month old daughter. We Skype each other from time to time. She has her hands full. Her husband works nights, so they rarely have any time together, and when they do, the baby is awake. Anyway, what about you?"

The opening was there. Rusty had put this off long enough. "You're probably not going to like this, but I think it's time that I make an effort to find out who I am. Neither one of us might like the answer, but sooner or later we have to know."

"David, I knew that this was coming. It would be selfish of me to try and keep us together without us knowing who you are. So what are you going to do?"

"Since I'm fairly certain that I'm an American, my first stop is the U.S. Consulate. I have no idea what will happen then. They may already know about me and can direct me to where I need to go. If not, they'll probably contact the FBI. Then, who knows? In any case, I have to do something. I was hoping that the insomnia would go away by now. It may *never* go away. But at least the people that may be looking for me will then know I'm alive. Maybe they'll be able to help me get back to my former life. Does that make any sense?"

"Of course it does. But I do not want you roaming around the streets of Hermosillo, trying to find the Consulate. I will take you there. That way, we will be taking the next step together. So let me nap for a few hours after we finish breakfast. Then we can go."

"You're the best, Angela. Staying as David Smith, sharing my future with you, would be just fine." They sat at the kitchen table. Rusty took her hand, and held it until she suggested the food might get cold. Once they made their way through the French toast and bacon, Angela want to her room. It was nearly 10AM when she fell sound asleep.

Rusty had already looked up the phone number and address of the U.S. Consulate. Rather than try to explain his dilemma over the phone, he decided to physically be there and take his chances. Wanting to make sure that someone would be available to help, he called. The woman answering the phone indicated that the Consul General would arrive there later in the day. Either of two of his senior aides would be available if needed. Powell hesitated to make an appointment for a specific time.

At one-thirty, Angela walked into the living room. She was wearing a white cotton skirt, navy tank top and sandals. Rusty had fallen asleep watching TV. A gentle kiss on the forehead woke him up.

"I am ready to go, David. We need to get this thing behind us. Okay?"

"You don't have to go, Angela. I can get myself there in one piece. It's not a problem."

"You are not going to talk me out of it. We are wasting time."

Chapter 99

Martinez and Henkel landed at the General Garcia Airport at 11:55AM. Richard had booked a Budget rental car. Their first stop was the Mexico National Police office, not far from the airport. It was a wise move. Martinez was concerned that the people at Hospital San Jose might not release Angela Contreras' address and cellphone number without Mexican authorities present.

The police officer assigned to work with the two Bureau agents was a woman. Helena Benitez, a sergeant on the force, was not unattractive, but as tough as nails. She would not be a passenger in the rental car, and insisted that the three of them travel in an official National Police Force SUV. A native of the city, Benitez knew exactly where they were going. Richard, however, insisted that they stop for lunch on the way. Here again, the sergeant was most helpful. She took them to her favorite hamburger place. Martinez had to admit that they were fabulous burgers. Although a reluctant meat eater, Henkel had to agree.

The rain showers increased to a full-fledged downpour, as the threesome pulled into the parking lot at Hospital San Jose. It was 1:25PM. Martinez opted to head straight for the Administrative Office, where they were coolly greeted by an armed security guard. Sergeant Benitez, in street clothes, flashed her ID. The guard backed off and emitted a nervous smile, as the hospital administrator entered the room. "Ladies and gentlemen, how can I be of assistance?"

Martinez displayed his credentials and in a flawless northern Mexican dialect, took the floor. "Sir, my name is Richard Martinez of the American FBI. This is Special Agent Henkel, and we are joined by Sergeant Benitez of your National Police Force. I have only one or two questions to ask, and we will be on our way."

"Mr. Martinez, what is it that you need to know? We will do our best to provide it.

"You employ a nurse on your staff: I believe she is assigned to the E.R. Her name is Angela Contreras."

"Yes, Angela is well known here at San Jose. She is an outstanding young nurse and a wonderful employee. Why, may I ask, are you looking for Miss Contreras?"

"We believe that she is looking after one of your former patients; a man who underwent surgery here, and who very well may be suffering from some form of amnesia. Your admissions department provided him with a name. Apparently, at the time he was brought in to the E.R. he did not know his real one. The name they gave him is David Smith. If it turns out that he is who we believe he is, Mr. Smith is actually a United States Border Patrol Agent, who was injured on duty and brought to Hermosillo against his will."

"My Lord! So you are here to obtain information such as Miss Contreras' phone number and address. Is this correct?"

"Yes it is. The young woman's home address is not listed in her name. Neither is the cellphone she uses. I contacted your hospital the other day to get this information, but not surprisingly, the person we spoke with would not provide it. She was obviously following hospital rules. So here we are."

"I am truly sorry, Mr. Martinez, that you had to travel from the States to get this information. We might have provided it to the Federal Police without you present, but we will certainly provide it to you now. The administrator asked his assistant to search their computer file for Contreras's contact information. It was printed out and handed to Martinez. At 1:55, they were back in the SUV and on their way to her apartment.

Sally thought that her boss was masterful in handling the situation. "Not bad, Martinez. See what a couple of tin badges can accomplish?"

"Wouldn't have been possible without Sergeant Benitez and the Mexican National Police. Many thanks for giving us a hand."

"Not a problem, Mr. Martinez. I have asked my office to return your rental car to the airport. I will take you there whenever your work in Hermosillo is finished."

"That is very kind of you, Sergeant. Let's hope that our Border Patrol Agent is in fact the man they are calling David Smith. We should know soon enough."

CHAPTER 100

THE RAIN WAS subsiding as Rusty and Angela arrived at the Consulate at 1:50PM. The receptionist, speaking Spanish, greeted them as they approached the large front desk in the lobby. "Welcome to the United States Mission. What can we do for you?"

Rusty, responding in English, took the lead. "This is a very strange situation to explain, so please bear with me. I believe I am an American, but because of an accident caused by the earthquake, my memory is gone, at least for the present. I have no idea where I live, or how I got to Hermosillo. But my guess is that there are people in the States who have been looking for me for quite a while. If I could speak with your Consul General, or one of his aides, they may be able to help solve my problem."

"Sir, the Consul General is in a meeting, and will be for some time. I will, however, see if one of his aides can see you now. Please take a seat and we will see what can be done."

Rusty and Angela sat waiting in the lobby, fidgety and apprehensive. Five minutes later, the receptionist smiled and signaled them to return to the desk. "One of our aides, Jeffrey Lang, will see you now." She rose from her seat and motioned for them to follow her down the hall. In one of the private offices, a young man came from behind his desk and walked to the office door.

"How do you do? My name is Jeffrey Lang. I am special assistant to Consul General Philip Boyce. Our receptionist provided a very quick recap of what you shared with her about your problem. It would be helpful if you could fill in some of the blanks."

Rusty first introduced Angela. She extended her hand and displayed one of her magical smiles, as Lang asked them both to have a seat.

Powell took his time explaining the dilemma. Lang was taking copious notes on his MacBook. Angela waited patiently, but opted to stay in the background for the time being.

Stopping to catch his breath, Rusty waited for Lang to respond. "So, you have been living with Miss Contreras as David Smith? Did I get that right?"

"Essentially, yes. Miss Contreras was one of my nurses at Hospital San Jose. She was kind enough to invite me to stay in her apartment until I could sort things out. Her roommate returns in a few days, so my stay with her needs to come to an end. And I need to find out who I am and where I belong."

Lang read over his notes, and scribbled something on a sheet of paper. Rusty and Angela squirmed a bit in the rather uncomfortable vinyl chairs. Carefully choosing his words, Lang re-started the conversation. It was obvious that he was finding it difficult to come forward with a recommendation. But he gave it a try.

"Mr. Smith, or whatever your real name might be; sorry for the way that came out. As I see it, your best bet is to make contact with the FBI. They have access to a national database of missing persons. Given that you have no idea what your name is, it will really put them to the test, but frankly, I can't think of another way to go. I'll be happy to take your case to Consul General Boyce. He should be out of his meeting within the next hour or so. Would it be possible for you to wait? There is a vacant office two doors down. Instead of waiting in the lobby, you are welcome to wait there."

Angela chimed in without hesitation. "We will definitely wait. The office would be appreciated. Thank you for offering it."

"Happy to do it. If you will follow me?" Lang ushered them out of his office and into another one close by. "Would you care for some coffee or a soft drink?" They both thanked him but declined. Lang excused himself and went out to the lobby to let the receptionist know they were in the vacant office, waiting to see Boyce.

****

Angela had turned off her cellphone when they arrived at the Consulate. Martinez decided not leave a voicemail message, and requested that Sergeant Benitez take them directly to her apartment. It was a relatively short drive from the hospital. Benitez parked and the threesome walked to the apartment entrance and rang the bell for Angela's unit. There was no answer. Reluctantly, Richard made a request of the sergeant.

"I hate to do this, but can you let us into Miss Contreras's apartment? We need to get whatever information we can find in there that may tell us where she or David Smith might be.

"Mr. Martinez, I cannot do this without a court order. There is no indication that any crime has been committed, or that anyone is in immediate danger. I hope you can understand my position."

Richard wasn't about to argue. "I do understand. We'll play by your rules." He decided to go ahead and call Contreras's cellphone once again; this time, if she didn't answer, he was going to leave a message. He pushed the Call button on his iPhone, and the number was re-dialed. Still no answer. He left the message in Spanish. "Miss Contreras, this is Special Agent Richard Martinez of the American FBI. When you access this message, I would appreciate a callback as soon as possible. We are trying to locate a missing U.S. law enforcement officer, and we believe that you may be able to help us. Many thanks."

Martinez had one more option up his sleeve. Henkel was all ears. "Okay, what now? There doesn't seem to be anything more we can do until Contreras returns your call. That could be quite a while."

"I'm thinking that a good place to park ourselves is the U.S. Consulate. Philip Boyce is a good guy. He may be able to help. Do you know where that is, Sergeant Benitez?"

She nodded. "We can be there in ten minutes."

CHAPTER 101

IT WAS CLOSE to three o'clock when Boyce ended the meeting in his office. Lang, as promised, explained the situation and requested that he meet with Rusty and Angela. Boyce agreed. "Okay Jeff, ask them to come in. I've got maybe twenty minutes. Then I have to leave for Mexico City."

Lang ushered the duo into the Consul General's office. He introduced them and was asked to join in the conversation. Rusty took the lead. After a five-minute explanation of his dilemma, Boyce responded. "As I believe Mr. Lang suggested, it makes sense for you to contact the FBI. Fact of the matter is: it appears that they may have been looking for you for several days. The head of the Phoenix office was here just the other day.

Angela looked at Rusty, who had an anxious expression on his face.

Boyce continued. "I will be happy to contact this agent for you. His name is Richard Martinez, and I happen to have his cellphone number in my contact list. Or you can call him on your own. Your decision."

Rusty responded without hesitation. "If you would call him, I would appreciate it, sir."

"My pleasure. Boyce went to his PC and pulled up Richard's number. He dialed it straight away. After the second ring, Martinez answered. Boyce's name and number did not appear on caller ID.

"Richard Martinez here. Who's calling?"

"Richard, it's Philip Boyce. "I believe there is a gentleman sitting across me in the office who just might be your missing Border Patrol Agent. How would you like to proceed from here?"

"You're kidding, right Philip? You won't believe this, but I'm here in

275

Hermosillo again, looking for Powell. We got some leads and I've been following them up. In fact, Special Agent Henkel and I, along with a Federal Police Officer, are on the way to the Consulate. Go figure."

Boyce had the call on speakerphone. Rusty looked over at Angela, and appeared to be holding on to his seat for dear life. Her emotions were off the chart. The end of the mystery was a few minutes away.

Boyce was ecstatic that the Consulate was going to help the FBI close its case. "Well then, I guess we'll just relax and wait for you to get here. See you soon." He then offered Rusty and Angela a cup of coffee. They happily agreed. Both of them were literally on fire emotionally and welcomed the beverage.

Lang went to the lobby, alerted the receptionist and returned to Boyce's office. Five minutes later, Martinez, Henkel and Benitez walked through the front door and approached the reception desk. "You must be Mr. Martinez. Consul General Boyce is waiting for you in his office. She punched an intercom button and let Boyce know that they had arrived. "Maria, please escort them back to my office."

She did so at once. Walking in the door, Martinez quickly scanned the room and immediately recognized Powell from photos in the file. Rusty and Angela both stood. Henkel and Benitez followed Richard in. Boyce got up and went to shake the hands of his newly arrived guests, and introduced Jeffrey Lang. "Good to see you again, Richard. Well, I must say, you couldn't ask for better timing. This is unreal."

Martinez introduced Henkel and Benitez, then turned and addressed Rusty and Angela straight away. "Mr. Smith, I presume. And Miss Contreras. Pleased to meet you both." Dispensing with his title, he went on. "My name is Richard Martinez. I've been waiting for this moment for quite some time."

Rusty was dumbfounded. "Mr. Boyce, you said something about a Border Patrol Agent." Turning to face Martinez he asked: Is that what I am? And what's my name?"

"You are Agent Randall Powell, known as Rusty to just about everybody. It appears that you were kidnapped while on patrol in the Sonoran Desert, near Nogales. I'm sorry to say that your partner on that patrol, Agent Gary Childers, was shot and killed. We believe that members of the Calimar drug cartel were responsible. Does this ring any bells?

Rusty wasn't able to speak. He hesitated, looked at Angela, then turned to Martinez to try and respond. "Not a thing, sir. I'm sorry." He hesitated again. Richard helped him out.

"I see you've been hurt." Martinez noticed the crutches propped up against Rusty's chair. The cast was still on, and would be for another six weeks.

"The doctors told me that I had been shot in the leg. They operated on it, put it back together, but I'll probably have to walk with a cane from now on. And Mr. Martinez, this young lady has been my savior. No telling where I would be right now, if she hadn't taken me under her wing."

Richard looked more intently at Angela and smiled. "Miss Contreras, it seems to me that the United States Government owes you a debt of gratitude. You are not only a beautiful young lady, but a very special and kind one as well."

"Mr. Martinez, I have fallen in love with this man, whether he's David Smith, Randall Powell, or the man in the moon. I assure you; I do not care."

Rusty then took the initiative to get right to the heart of the matter. "So, if I am Randall Powell, where to we go from here? Do I have a family; wife, kids? Will I still have the Border Patrol job when I get back to the States?"

"Some of these questions, and I'm sure there are many more, will be answered in due time. Right now, we need to get you home. And at home, you do have a wife. Her name is Melinda. We need to let her know you are alive and we are bringing you back to her. Miss Contreras, I am sorry to be so direct about this, but Rusty needs to know."

Angela was losing emotional control, but made a stab at a response. "I guess I have known all along that David; I'm sorry, Rusty, would be leaving to go back to something. And I feared that there was someone waiting for him to return. I will have to live with that. I have no choice."

Powell's head was spinning. "But I can't remember anyone I knew before waking up in a car at the bottom of a big hole in the street. If my memory returns down the road, that's one thing. If it doesn't, then what?"

"That's going to be up to you", Richard said. "Once you get home, hopefully things will start to fall into place. If they don't, then you'll just have to go on with your life from there."

Boyce needed to leave for the airport. "Ladies and gentlemen, you'll have to excuse me. I need to catch a plane. Mr. Lang can assist you from here. Mr. Powell, I wish you much luck as you sort everything out. Miss Contreras, all the best to you." He rose, went over and shook hands with everyone and departed.

Martinez spoke. "Rusty, and Angela, we're going to leave you alone for a few minutes. Then, Rusty, we need to speak with you alone about getting you back to the States. Is that okay?"

"I guess so. Thanks."

The law enforcement trio exited, along with Jeffrey Lang. The room was now dead quiet. After a brief silence, Angela was the first to speak. "You have to go. I have said many times that I knew this day would come. It is here, so you need to go." Tears began rolling down her cheeks. Rusty was struggling to find the right words.

"I will go. But I refuse to say goodbye. You are now a part of my life. No matter what happens, that's not going to change. Even if my memory comes back, you will always be in my thoughts. I can never repay you for what you've done for me. Right now, I can't find any other words to say. Somehow, things will work out for both of us, together or not."

It was Angela's turn. "I have told you I love you. That too will never change. But for the time being, you need to go back to your home and be with your wife. I will miss you."

They held on to each other for quite a while. "We need to go", Rusty said, as he ended the embrace and wiped Angela's tears. They left Boyce's office and headed to the lobby, where the three law enforcement officers were waiting, along with Jeffrey Lang.

Martinez pulled Powell to one side for a brief conversation.

"Rusty, do you have anything at Miss Contreras's apartment that we need to get before we head out of Mexico? I have called Aeromexico and they have put us a flight to Phoenix at 6:20 this evening. So we have a little time."

"Mr. Martinez, I have nothing anywhere in Mexico that can't be left behind. Any time you'd like us to leave is fine with me."

Richard asked Sergeant Benitez to drive them to the airport. As they were leaving the Consulate, Angela walked by, on her way to the parking lot. Rusty went to her, wrapped his arms around her and kissed her for what he believed would be the last time. It was a brief embrace. Angela reluctantly pulled away and ran to her car. Powell watched her until she was out of sight.

PART VI

Heading Home

CHAPTER 102

BENITEZ DROPPED RICHARD, Sally and Rusty at the airport. Although proper protocol required that the Mexican authorities handle Powell's return to the border, an exception was made in this case.

Their flight left in an hour. They grabbed sandwiches and coffee to tide them over, as they waited to be called for departure. Aeromexico 812 took off twenty minutes late. Henkel and Powell sat together for the one hour and twenty minute flight. Martinez was in an aisle seat directly behind them. He was busy making notes on his iPad, to be incorporated into his final report.

Rusty bombarded Sally with questions. His greatest immediate concern was seeing his wife, whom he did not remember. The second most important issue was his job as a Border Patrol Agent. It seemed obvious that it was no longer in the cards. Even though he didn't as yet remember doing it, being hobbled with the bad leg and having to rely on a cane to walk closed the book on that position. There was no telling what DHS might propose as a job for him that didn't have the physical demands of an agent in the field.

Richard booked rooms for Rusty and Sally at the Radisson Hotel, near the Sky Harbor Airport. His plan was to drive Powell to Tucson sometime in the morning. Sally had left her car at the airport and was on her own. Before leaving the hotel Martinez was going to phone Melinda and prepare her for her husband's homecoming. He anticipated arriving at their West Tucson home around noon. Martinez also sent an email to Roland Escobar, asking him to expect his call at 9AM. The note merely mentioned that Powell was found and was on his way home.

It was a hot, and unusually humid night in Phoenix. Heavy rain earlier in the day left a good bit of moisture in the late August air. The flight landed at 8:27. There was a Wal-Mart a few miles from the airport. Richard took Rusty to buy a change of clothes and some toiletries to get him through the next couple of days. Sally went directly to the Radisson, checked into a room and almost immediately fell asleep.

Checking Powell into the hotel, Martinez invited him to the bar for a beer. Half an hour later, having finished the Amstel Light, Rusty was mentally exhausted and excused himself. After taking a shower he watched one inning of a baseball game on TV before drifting off.

Martinez got back to his condo around ten o'clock. He emptied his overnight bag, which he ended up not needing for the trip to Hermosillo. Fingering through the mail, there was nothing of great urgency, so he threw it on his desk and headed to the bedroom. Just as he was pulling on some sleep shorts and a t-shirt, his cellphone rang.

It was Roland Escobar. "Hello Richard; sorry to bother you at this hour. I got your email and couldn't wait until morning. It's great news! How is Powell doing?"

"Roland, he seems fine, except for two things. His left leg was shattered by a bullet out on the patrol. He's going to need a cane to get around for the foreseeable future. And he apparently has insomnia; didn't know who he was until we told him, so he's got some distance to travel before he's ready to restart his life. I wanted to take more time to go through this with you, and frankly, I'm a little tuckered out. Can I still phone you tomorrow morning?"

"No problem. I'll be traveling to Nogales around the time you want to call, but you can get me on the cellphone. And again, I apologize for calling you so late."

"It's okay Roland. If I were you I'd probably have done the same. I know this case has been a rough one for the Border Patrol. Looks like we're in the home stretch. Talk with you tomorrow."

Richard jotted down a note to himself to place a call to Lowell Fox in the morning. His boss needed to get the good news. The $10 million wasn't wasted after all.

CHAPTER 103

DAY 18

RICHARD CALLED POWELL'S room at the hotel. He was already awake and putting on his new clothes. "It's Martinez. How's Rusty Powell doing this morning?

"Guess I have to get used to that name. For the last few weeks I've been David Smith."

"You'll get the hang of it. Don't be impatient. Just let it all happen. Anyway, you ready to take a trip back in time? We can leave for Tucson anytime you feel up to it."

"I'm a little scared. But let's do it. You can come by for me anytime you like. I'm in the process of getting dressed. This new Wal-Mart wardrobe will work just fine."

"You must look like a million dollars. Ten million, actually."

"Rusty was puzzled at that remark. "What's ten million all about?"

"Don't worry about it. I'll tell you later. See you in about twenty minutes."

Henkel was already in the hotel restaurant, grabbing some breakfast before taking off for home. Powell walked in, saw Sally, and joined her for a sweet roll and a cup of coffee. They chatted for a bit. Then Henkel said goodbye and departed. Rusty obviously had no luggage; only a small sack with some toiletries and the clothes Angela bought for him. He decided to wait for Martinez in the lobby.

A few minutes after nine, Richard arrived in his pickup. Rusty saw him pull up to the hotel entrance and walked out to climb into the vehicle. It wasn't easy. While he had mastered the use of the crutches, the high clearance of the F-150 made it a challenge. Martinez offered no assistance, guessing that Rusty wouldn't want it. They headed to the highway for the trip to Tucson and Powell's former life.

On the way, Richard placed the call to Melinda, counting on her being at home. She answered on the second ring. "Melinda, it's Richard Martinez. I'm on the way to see you, if that's okay. Sitting next to me is a guy named Randall Powell. Ring any bells?"

Melinda was speechless. Richard waited a few seconds, and repeated the news. "Melinda, are you still there?"

"Are you serious? Rusty's okay? When did you find him?" Her mind was racing with emotions. "I can't believe it. My God; where has he been?"

"It's a long story. We'll tell you all about it when we get there. Rusty is fine. He's been injured and will need some time to recuperate. I wanted to give *you* some time to get ready. Are you okay?"

"Not really. But I'm going to make myself beautiful."

"You already are. See you in a couple of hours."

Richard's next call was to Lowell Fox. It was almost lunch hour in D.C., but Fox rarely had lunch, and was having some coffee at his desk, when his assistant buzzed to let him know that Martinez was on the line.

"Lowell, it's Richard. Am I interrupting anything?"

"Not really. What's up?"

"We got our CBP agent back! Rusty Powell is back in the U.S., safe and sound. We're on the way to Tucson. I'm taking him directly home to see his wife. Powell's a little banged up, but doing fine. His biggest problem may take a while to solve. It looks like a knock on the head has screwed up his memory. Just wanted you to know. The little gift to the cartel probably saved Rusty's life."

"Fantastic! Give my best to everyone down there. This is great news. I see the President in about an hour, and he'll be delighted. Tell Agent Powell we're behind him all the way. Whatever he needs to fully recuperate, he'll get it."

"Thanks Lowell. We'll keep you posted." Martinez ended the call and placed another one: this time to Roland Escobar. Leaving a voicemail message, Richard asked Escobar to return the call whenever he could.

Powell was fidgety and clearly apprehensive about the next few hours and days. On I-10 there wasn't much scenery to look at, pretty much all the way to Tucson.

At 12:05, the F-150 turned into the driveway of Rusty's home. Melinda, watching through the dining room window for the past fifteen minutes, ran out the front door to welcome her husband back. She wore white Capri pants and a yellow tank top that flattered her long, slender frame. Her hair was cut short and glistened in the sunlight. Powell opened the car door, stood without the crutches and waited for his wife to fall into his arms. A few seconds later, they were locked in a passionate embrace. Rusty was seeing this woman, his love since college, like it was the first time. Eighteen days ago, she was the only woman in his life. No longer true, Powell has serious feelings of guilt, but was not going to show them to this beautiful woman. At least not yet.

Melinda's eyes were now trained on the cast with the healing left leg inside. "Rusty, you're hurt! What happened to your leg?"

"I don't really know. The doctors told me that it had happened several days before they found me. It was a gunshot wound. They guessed it might have been torn up when the kidnappers took me away. I will probably have to walk with a cane from now on."

"But you're alive! That's what counts Rusty. Let's go inside." Powell grabbed the crutches. Melinda wanted to help him go up the front steps. He waved her off. "I need to do this myself." Martinez followed the couple inside.

Something looked familiar to Rusty about the place. But he didn't know what it was. His head was beginning to ache. It hadn't done that for some time. Melinda walked with the two men into the living room. "I've made us some lunch. Nothing special: a salad and cold potato soup. Give me a few minutes and I'll get it on the table. Then we can talk; the rest of the day and then some. Be right back."

Richard looked at Rusty, as they sat down and waited for Melinda to return. "What are you thinking? Does anything look familiar?"

Powell leaned the crutches up against an arm of the chair. "I don't know. It's weird. It's like I've been here before, but I don't feel like I'm home. Make sense?"

"I wouldn't expect too much to make sense for a while. As I've said before, Rusty, you need to give it time. I'm going to stay here in Tucson for a day or two. When you feel like it, you and I will go down to Nogales and visit the Border Station. Maybe that will help. In the meantime, get to know your wife again. After lunch, I'm going to get out of here. Sally and I need to do some work together. I'll give you a call this evening to see how you're doing. Okay?"

"I guess so. It's kind of scary, but Melinda seems great. She is one terrific-looking woman."

"No kidding, dude. You are one lucky guy. And by the way, I was told that she's four months pregnant. You're going to be a daddy."

Melinda came to get them. They walked to the kitchen and sat down for the light, but tasty meal. Martinez wanted Rusty to open up about the insomnia, but it didn't happen. A plate of chocolate chip cookies was devoured in short order. Richard decided that it was time to leave. Before heading out the front door, he whispered in Powell's ear. "Rusty, you need to tell her about the memory problem. She needs to know."

Rusty nodded, acknowledging that Martinez was right. He wanted to thank him for everything, but had a difficult time finding the words. "I don't know what to say." Tears were dripping on his shirt.

Melinda walked Martinez to his pickup. "Richard, we owe you more than I can say. If it wasn't for you, Rusty would be lost to us forever." As he opened the pickup door, Melinda gave him a hug and kissed him on the cheek.

"Be patient with him Melinda", he said as he climbed behind the wheel. "He's going to need all the TLC you can give him. Full stop. I hope to see you some day soon. Take care."

CHAPTER 104

MARTINEZ DROVE OFF. He placed a call to Henkel, who wanted to meet with her boss privately before he headed back to Phoenix. "Sally, I just left Rusty's home. Let me know when and where you want to meet. I'll be around for the next day or two. Before I leave I want to take Powell to the Nogales Border Station. He needs to get a first-hand look at where he worked, and meet some of the people. No telling: it could jar his memory loose. When we get that done, I can go home." He left that voicemail message and headed to the Tucson Bureau office.

Sally returned the call in short order. "So how did it go, Richard? What happened when he saw his wife?"

"I'll tell you when we meet. I'm headed to your office. Where are you now?"

"Just leaving the house. I had to bring Meredith home from school. She was running a fever and the school nurse said she should go home and get in bed. I'll meet you at the office in half an hour."

"Hey, if you need to stay home with her, no problem. We can get together tomorrow morning. Meredith is more important right now."

"She'll be fine. I gave her some Motrin for the fever. Hopefully, she'll sleep it off. If not, I can take her to a walk-in clinic later on. In the meantime, we can do our thing. See you at the office."

Martinez didn't have time to respond. Sally ended the call.

****

They met at the office around 3:30. Richard had some news for Sally, having nothing to do with Rusty Powell. Sitting in the small conference room, they both sipped their ice coffees that Martinez picked up at a nearby Starbucks. He knew she liked them.

Sally took the lead. "So, tell me how it went down with Rusty and Melinda."

"It actually went down pretty well. I was waiting for Powell to open up about the amnesia, but he didn't seem too anxious to do it while I was there. Maybe now that I'm gone, he'll let it out. She obviously needs to know, and like right away. For the most part though, it seemed that Rusty accepted the fact that he was back home. Nothing was familiar to him, but that's really not surprising. That bang to the head must have been a doozy. He said that the x-rays didn't show any major brain damage, but from what I have read, it could take weeks, maybe months, before his memory comes back."

The two agents talked about a few other pending cases on the Tucson docket. Then Richard gave Sally some news that just came across his desk from Bureau Headquarters Personnel.

"So, Special Agent Henkel, guess what? You will be rid of me soon. Or I'm getting rid of you. Take your pick. Anyway, you'll need to go out and buy yourself a winter wardrobe. Assuming you accept the position, you are going to Chicago to be an Assistant Agent-in-Charge. And they want you by October 1. Comments?"

Henkel had a feeling that a new assignment was in the works. But this was a big deal. The third biggest Bureau office in the country; a major move. "I don't know what to say, Richard. That's only a few weeks away. I need to consider what this will mean for Meredith. She's a good kid, and an excellent student, but a move to Chicago: that's a whole different ballgame."

"You're going to get a call from Paul Castle, the agent in charge of the Chicago office. Talk with him about it. He's a really good guy. Size up the job and make a decision, one way or the other. But if you really want to climb the Bureau ladder, this is a terrific next step. And that's about all I'm going to say about it. Okay?"

"Okay. I'll wait for Castle's call. What else?"

"That's about it. If you want to go down to Nogales with us, let me know. Rusty and Melinda need some time alone. I'm thinking sometime tomorrow, maybe early afternoon, we can take him down there. After that, I'll head back to Phoenix."

"Richard, I'm not trying to duck out of it, but why don't you take Powell down there without me as third wheel. You're the guy that found him and got him home."

"Hey, you were in on it all the way. But you don't need to go. Take care of Meredith and I'll look after Agent Powell."

CHAPTER 105

RUSTY THOUGHT ABOUT the baby. It would complicate everything. He thought about Angela. His head was spinning, as Melinda finished in the kitchen and joined him in the family room, sitting next to him on the sofa. It was nearly a month since they were in bed together. It was easy to see that she longed for his touch and wanted to love him while she could, considering that before long it would be difficult to have sex, at least until after the baby was born.

"Honey, do you want to talk about what happened? If it's too soon right now, that's fine. When you're ready.   Cindy and Scott are leaving for San Diego next week. The garage sale was a huge success. We worked our tails off, but it was worth it. If you feel up to it, we should ask them over for a goodbye dinner."

Powell had no idea who Cindy and Scott were. And it wouldn't work to try and fake it for long. He saw his opening, and began to talk. "Melinda, I need to share something with you that won't be easy. All I ask is that you try to understand."

She didn't know what to make of his comment, but wanted to make it as easy for him as she could. "Sweetheart, you can tell me anything. It's always been that way with us, and it always will."

Rusty began by describing how we was discovered in the back of the Xterra, in the bottom of the sinkhole. "You obviously know about the quake. Hermosillo was literally torn apart. It was a really bad scene. Anyway, they took me to the hospital. I don't know how it happened, but the leg was torn up pretty bad. The surgeon that patched it up said that it was a mess, torn up by a rifle of some type. And my head was bleeding when they found me. It was a severe concussion. That's what I need to tell you about. When they brought me to the hospital and the nurses and doctors started asking me questions, I couldn't answer them. Melinda, I don't know how to tell you this. I have amnesia. My memory only goes as far back as the moment I regained consciousness in the back seat of that SUV."

"My God! You're telling me that you didn't know who you were?"

"If I wasn't sitting here, knowing that my name is Randall Powell and yours is Melinda Powell, and that I am, or was a Border Patrol Agent, I wouldn't have a clue. There was no ID on me when I was found. No wallet, no cash, no credit cards; nothing. At the hospital they gave me a name for their records: David Smith. So that's the only name I knew. I can't describe how that feels. A fully-grown man without a past. I don't even know how old I am." Rusty began to cry.

Melinda was losing control herself. She put her arms around her husband and began to weep as well. "It's okay, Rusty. We'll get through this. You're alive. The hell is over. We can start again from here." They held each other for several minutes, without uttering a single word.

Powell knew that the rest of the story would have to be told. He just wasn't able to tell it yet. He didn't even know how. But until he did, it would be impossible to live with it for very long.

For now, Melinda resigned herself to the fact that Rusty, hopefully limited to the short term, had no past. She decided to ask a logical question, afraid of what the answer would be. "Will the memory loss be permanent?"

"The doctors really don't know. Usually, people regain some or all of their memory, but it could take quite a bit of time. The brain scans they did were basically negative, except for some swelling, which is normal with a concussion. So all we can do is hope."

"And pray", she added. "We need to pray." The phone rang. It was Melinda's mother. She finally let go of her husband to answer it, leaving the room.

"How are you Melinda? Any news on Rusty?"

"Mom, he's home! A little beat up, but home. He just got here today, so I'm just now finding out what he's gone through over the past three weeks. At least some of it anyway."

They spoke for a few more minutes, but it was obvious that Melinda was anxious to get back to Rusty and the rest of the story. "Mom, I'll call you in a couple of days. Right now, I need to have some time alone with my husband. Love you. Say hi to dad."

She returned to the family room. Rusty was sound asleep.

CHAPTER 106

ANGELA HAD THE day off. Not able to sleep very well the night before, she spent the day cleaning the apartment, changing the linens on her roommate's bed and doing her own laundry as well. She couldn't get Rusty out of her mind. The fact that he was back in Tucson, and would likely regain his memory before long, weighed heavily on Angela's mind. She feared that he would forget her completely, as well as the love they briefly shared.

Facing the FBI at the Consulate was the most difficult reality she had ever experienced. Knowing in an instant that Rusty would be taken from her, and being helpless to stop it from happening, was awful. But she knew that it had to be, and that she had to get on with her life.

Angela's roommate called that afternoon and told her that she would be coming home a few days early. That meant tomorrow. Angela looked forward to her return. They had similar careers, and had most other things in common. She was a tall, slender beauty, pursued by a host of admiring men. She would no doubt help Angela get things back on an even keel.

After finishing her housework, Angela phoned another good friend, also a nurse at Hospital San Jose, and suggested they meet for dinner. Married, with two children, she had no problem leaving the kids with her husband and having a night out. The friend agreed. A few minutes after seven, they met at a popular restaurant halfway between their homes. Angela needed a good friend to help her start the healing process. They ended up talking mostly about Rusty, who, as David Smith, became a much talked-about celebrity at San Jose. Further depressing Angela, they eventually changed the subject. Indulging in tiramisu for dessert, they washed them down with espressos and called it a night.

****

Melinda cooked one of Rusty's favorites for dinner: pot roast. Out of the oven by seven, she served it with mashed potatoes and a salad. They enjoyed a bottle of pinot noir and followed the meal with a pay-per-view movie on their satellite-delivered TV. Both were emotionally wasted and decided to get to bed. Melinda undressed and slipped into a flimsy satin teddy. Although beginning to show the baby, her figure was still intact. Beginning to produce milk, her breasts were getting larger and the cleavage above the negligee was getting Rusty aroused. As they climbed into their king sized bed, he leaned over and kissed her, softly at first, but then with increased passion. She turned onto her side, facing her husband, which accentuated the fullness of her bosom even more.

Rusty's mind wandered off to his time in bed with Angela. It bothered him a lot. Instead of continuing the kissing and petting with his wife, he got up and sat on the edge of the bed.

"Honey, what's wrong?" Angela said. "Are you okay?"

Fibbing somewhat, Rusty fell back on a believable excuse. "The leg is bothering me. It's throbbing and itches a lot. Think I'll indulge in one of my heavy-duty pain pills. I'm sorry, Mel." It was the first time he used her nickname since coming home. "It's not going to be easy to make love with this stupid cast on."

"I understand, Rusty. Just lying here next to you is wonderful. Frankly, I was worried that it wouldn't happen again."

Powell turned around, bent down and kissed her again. Lying back down, he stared intently at Melinda's marvelous face. "You are *so* beautiful. I wish I could start remembering the times we've had together. I obviously had great taste in women when I chose you."

"Rusty, give it time. You're going to be fine. It'll happen soon. You'll remember everything. Right now, let's just live for today." Rusty wanted the day to end. He turned out the light. Melinda fell asleep in short order. Powell had too much swimming around in his head. It was nearly 1AM before he finally drifted off.

CHAPTER 107

DAY 19

MELINDA OPENED HER eyes, looking for her husband. It was a few minutes before seven. He was already up, in the kitchen, having a glass of orange juice, when she found him. "Did you sleep okay last night? I didn't hear you get out of bed."

"I slept okay; didn't want to wake you this early, so I tried to be quiet. How about you?"

"I was up a few times, but managed to go back to sleep. Can I make you some breakfast?"

"I'm just going to have a bowl of corn flakes. Maybe some coffee. But thanks."

"Think I'll do the same." She went to the cupboard, pulled out the box of cereal, and took the milk out of the fridge.

Melinda made coffee. They sat on the barstools by the kitchen-island and finished breakfast without saying a word. Rusty leafed through the morning paper. On page three of the first section, a headline and sub-head immediately caught his eye.

Kidnapped Border Patrol Agent Found Alive in Mexico

FBI Agents Bring Randall Powell Home After Disappearing For a Month

He went on to read the entire article. The bulk of it was true. There were a few erroneous points, which Rusty wrote off to sloppy reporting. No mention was made of the $10 million ransom payment. The names Martinez and Henkel were not identified.

Powell took the paper, opened it to the article, and handed it to his wife. "Your husband is famous. No telling how they got the information. I doubt that the FBI told them much of anything."

Melinda read the article; then read it again. "It doesn't say a word about the kidnappers, or the ransom money. That's a little strange. I thought the media liked to print that kind of stuff."

"They usually do."

"Randy, shouldn't you see a doctor about the amnesia? Maybe there's something you can do about it. I won't mention it again, if you don't want me to. I just want you to get well."

Powell remembered what Dr. Ortega had said about it. "I think we just have to let it work itself out. It's only been a few weeks. The surgeon said it could take months."

"But you've said that the headaches are still there. Maybe a neurologist can prescribe something that can help. Taking Motrin or Advil doesn't seem to do the job."

"Let's give it another week or two. If things don't improve by then, I'll see a doctor. Okay?"

"Fine with me. It's your head." As Melinda was about to say something else, the phone rang. It was Martinez. Rusty answered. "Hello; Rusty Powell speaking."

"Rusty, it's Richard Martinez. I hope I haven't gotten you guys out of bed."

"No, we've been up for a while. Just finished breakfast and the morning paper. Did you see the article in the Daily Star"

"I did. Looked okay to me. You'll probably get lots of phone calls if you have a listed number.. Even if it isn't: people will find a way to get it. Take my advice: if you have caller ID, and you don't recognize the name or number, don't answer. Anyway, I'd like to drive you down to the Nogales Border Station. You up for it?"

"Think so. Guess I need to know if I'm going to have a job. When do you want to go?"

"As soon as you're ready. Just say the word and I'll come by and pick you up." Richard was hopeful that seeing the station, the people, the activity, might jar his memory loose. It was worth a try.

"How about this afternoon? Say around two o'clock?"

"See you then." Martinez had hoped they might go earlier, but he didn't want to push Powell too hard.

Rusty wanted the balance of the morning to be invested in getting to know his wife a lot better. He had a sea of questions he wanted to ask. Questions only she could answer. He was still reluctant to share anything more of what happened in Hermosillo.

After cleaning up the kitchen, Rusty took a shower and dressed for the day. Melinda did the same. It was a pleasant morning, with a slight breeze coming out of the north. They decided to sit on their patio. Rusty cranked open the table umbrella, and Melinda brought out a pitcher of iced tea. Powell's smartphone was confiscated and destroyed by Rico Morales. He needed to buy a new one. His laptop hadn't been opened since he left home almost twenty days ago. He booted it up and opened his Google Account page. The number of emails was mind-boggling. He deleted all but the last two days worth. "You don't realize how much utter crap you get", he said, as he cleaned up the mailbox."

"No kidding honey. I can't image the amount of garbage you collected."

While outside on the patio, a number of phone calls came through their landline. Most came up on caller ID as unidentified, or a name either one of them knew. They were left unanswered. Melinda got a few meaningful calls and decided to take them inside.

Rusty made a concerted effort to conjure up a mental picture of the Nogales Border Station. He went to YouTube for some footage, and found plenty, but nothing that jarred his fractured memory banks. He would have to wait to experience it firsthand.

CHAPTER 108

MARTINEZ ARRIVED AT the Powell's home a few minutes before two. Rusty was ready. Melinda was somewhat concerned that her husband might have a difficult time dealing with a visit to the Border Station.

"Honey, are you sure you're ready for this? Maybe you should get a few more days of rest before going down there."

"I'll be okay. And it makes sense to make the trip with Special Agent Martinez. He still thinks my case won't be closed until he gets me back to the Station. And even then, he's not going to be satisfied his job is done unless my memory comes back. I don't see that as his responsibility, but he is really a special guy. Let's keep in mind: he went looking for me twice, and to a place that was a major disaster area. I owe him a lot."

"*We* owe him a lot. And the Border Patrol does too. So, you go on. Be careful and don't expect much. You are still not yourself." She gave him a kiss at the door, as he took the crutches and made his way to Richard's pickup truck. Once Rusty was seated and his bent leg situated as comfortably as possible, they took off for Nogales.

It was a drive of about an hour and twenty minutes. The afternoon was sunny and hot. There was virtually no traffic on I-19, until they reached the town of Nogales, where they were slowed by heavy truck traffic, most of which was headed to the border and into Mexico. Rusty seemed fairly relaxed, but was rather quiet. Richard didn't attempt to force a conversation.

Nearing the Border Station, Martinez used his Bluetooth connection to dial Roland Escobar, who was waiting for them at the Station office. With him was Carroll Page, the senior agent that was on duty the day of Powell's abduction in the desert. Richard had arranged for Page to be present when they arrived. Martinez was given a dashboard pass to display. Pulling into a parking space next to the Station office entrance, he was met by a Border Patrol Officer, who checked Richard's FBI credentials and allowed them to enter the building, which was an elevated structure that ran across the actual border crossing facility.

Once inside, Richard and Rusty walked down the hall to the office of the station head. Powell noticed the two men waiting there. "Agent Page, good to see you again!"

Richard was flabbergasted. Powell recognized Carroll Page.

Martinez pointed to Page. "Rusty, you know who this is!"

Powell displayed a somewhat disoriented expression on his face. "Guess I did. How did that happen?" He walked over to Page and shook his hand.

"Rusty, it's great to see you. Welcome home.", Page said, as Escobar came over and shook Powell's hand.

"How are you feeling, Agent Powell? Escobar asked, We've missed you. Good to have you back." Rusty hadn't met Escobar before. But he smiled and extended a hand to Roland as well.

Powell was feeling weak in the knees. He ambled over to a chair, propped the crutches on the side of it and began to sit down. "If you guys don't mind, I'm a little shaky right now. I'll just sit here for a few minutes before we do anything else."

Martinez responded. "No problem, Agent Powell. You take your time. There's no hurry anyway. So what's it feel like to be back in your old stomping grounds?"

"Pretty cool. Agent Page, you were in charge the day Childers and I went on patrol."

"That I was. Sounds to me like the old memory's on its way back. We heard from Roland that you were found in Hermosillo. Hell, you are one lucky individual. The last reports we heard estimate the dead from the quake at 40,000, and they're still finding more bodies under the rubble. When we figured out that you were kidnapped, we didn't think we'd ever see you again. The cartels usually don't let anybody go alive."

"Rusty's proven a lot of people wrong", Richard said. "We understand that the surgeon who patched up his leg originally didn't think he'd be able to save it. Well, it's still attached. Looks like the good Lord was on his side."

"No shit", Page said. "So what happens next, Rusty? Ready to get back to work?"

Powell knew full well he couldn't return to regular patrol duty. "Beats the hell out of me. Guess it depends on what the CBP thinks I'm any good for." He looked over at Escobar, who needed to be careful with his response.

"Rusty, all I can say right now is, get yourself some rest. You've got sick leave and vacation to use. When the dust clears, we'll see. Bottom line, though; the Border Patrol needs all kinds of trained, experienced people. We can talk all about this a little later on."

"Rusty, would you like to walk around and see what the Station's up to these days?"

"That sounds great, Richard." He turned to Escobar. "You guys lead the way."

The four men exited the building and made their way around the crossing. Several Agents recognized Powell and came over to say hello. Rusty moved slowly, still reeling from the fact that his memory was coming back. Not everything was coming through clearly, but identifying Page at first sight was a major breakthrough.

Within half an hour, Rusty suggested that he'd like to come back another day. This fit ideally with Martinez's plan, as he wanted to head back to Phoenix that evening.

"No problem, Rusty", Richard said. "We can head back to Tucson right now." They began to walk over to the Ford-150, when Powell, dropped his crutches, collapsed and started to fall straight down. Martinez caught him before he hit the ground. Escobar helped Richard support Rusty as they brought him to a nearby bench and laid him down. "Carroll, get some water. It looks like Rusty just passed out from the pain medication and too much excitement." Powell was already starting to come around.

Page ran into the building and came back in seconds with a bottle of water. Rusty was now sitting up, shaking it off and looking like he was fine. He took a few swigs of water and handed the bottle back to Page. "Sorry guys", he said. "Guess it's been a little too much good news for one day. I'm fine."

"Let's go", Richard said, with the emphasis on "go". Powell smiled and waived to Page and Escobar, as he and Martinez got into the pickup. A few minutes before five, they were on I-19 and on the way home.

CHAPTER 109

ANGELA'S ROOMMATE CAME home. Poor, rainy weather on the coast convinced her to shorten her vacation and get back to Hermosillo. Contreras had talked with her earlier and mentioned that her temporary "guest" had left the apartment, freeing up her roommate's bedroom.

Sitting in a nearby restaurant, having dinner together, Angela confessed that she was in love with the temporary guest, an American, who returned to his wife, but was suffering from insomnia. "I know he loves me too. But what will happen when his memory returns? And how does he feel about his wife, now that their lives have changed? My head is spinning. I don't know what to do."

"If you love him, go to America, and find him. Get a job there. You are a nurse. Hospitals need good nurses. You are a great one."

"That is crazy! He is married. What would I do? See him in secret? And when he remembers everything in his past; then what?"

"You said you love him. And he loves you. What other reasons do you need? Go to him. You can get another Green Card. You told me he lives in Tucson. You lived there before. There are some really good hospitals in the city. Any one of them would be crazy not to hire you Angela. Life is too short."

"You sound like you want to get rid of me. Do you have a new boyfriend of your own?"

"No, I do not. But I can afford to keep the apartment. And if things do not work out for you in Tucson, your room will probably be waiting for you when you return. What do you have to lose?"

Angela didn't answer. The two young women sat quietly finishing their meal. Contreras was on night shift duty, so they went directly back to the apartment. She changed into her uniform and watched some TV before leaving for San Jose Hospital, in time for the 11PM shift change.

Looking after her E.R. patients throughout the night, Angela couldn't get Rusty out of her mind. Her roommate's encouragement to go after him was ringing in her ears. Around 3AM, an American was brought into the E.R. with heat exhaustion. A young American firefighter from Yuma, he was in Hermosillo temporarily to help rescue quake survivors. He was nothing like Powell. But being there reminded Angela that going to Arizona to start a new life was not as crazy as it sounded just a few hours ago. On her break, she went to the Homeland Security website and pulled up a Form I-140. It was the application for a permanent U.S. work visa. As a registered nurse, she qualified for relatively quick acceptance.

CHAPTER 110

IT WAS ALMOST 6:30 by the time Martinez and Powell drove into Rusty's driveway and parked the pickup. Rusty struggled with the crutches, finally managing to extricate himself from the vehicle. Melinda was waiting on the front steps, as the two men approached.

There was a wide grin on Powell's face. He kissed his wife and the three of them went inside. Martinez wasn't staying much longer. "Got to go, sports fans. You two look like you need to be alone. Rusty, I'll give you a call in a few days to see how things are going. I'm heading back to Phoenix from here. My fun is over; now it's back to work."

"Richard, I don't know what to say."

"No need to say anything. You take care of yourself and this beautiful lady and I'll be happy. Take care."

Melinda put her two cents in, as the tears came. "We'll never be able to forget what you've done for us." She went up on her toes and kissed Martinez on the cheek. "Never. You will always be in our thoughts."

"This is getting kind of mushy. I'd better get out of here. You guys be good." Richard took his leave.

Melinda hadn't planned on dinner, not knowing when they'd get home. "Let's order in some pizza. Sound okay?"

"Sounds fine. I've got some good news to tell you. Let's have a beer."

Not waiting for an answer, Rusty went to the fridge and pulled out two Coors Lights. He popped them open and poured them into a couple of mugs. Melinda called and ordered the pizza. They moved to the family room. Powell plopped down on the sofa. Melinda followed.

"So what's this good news all about?"

"Hold on to your hat, but when we walked into the Border Station offices, I recognized Carroll Page. He was the senior agent on duty the morning Gary and I went out on patrol."

"Honey, that's fantastic! You must have felt like a big weight was lifted off your shoulders. What about other things? Is everything coming back?"

Rusty was hesitant with his answer. In fact, Page was and still is the only person he remembers from before he woke up in the back of the Xterra. "I wish it was. It just happened; like a light busting through a doorway. There was just something in my head that triggered the recall. Carroll's name just popped out; then I remembered him from before. Talk about weird."

Melinda didn't know what to say. It wasn't exactly the best news she could have hoped for. They sat there for a moment; then she responded. "Rusty, that's really great. It's got to be a sign that everything will come back to you and probably real soon."

"I hope you're right. It sure was a lightening bolt when I saw Page standing there. In fact, it really threw me for a loop. A few minutes later, Martinez had to pick me up off the floor."

"You mean you passed out?"

"Just for a few seconds. I don't know what caused it, but I've felt fine ever since."

"Rusty, that's a little scary. You definitely need to see a neurologist, and soon."

The pizza arrived about thirty-five minutes later. They polished it off in short order. Melinda then told Rusty she was going to take a bath. While she ran the water in the Jacuzzi tub, Rusty looked through the mail. Among the catalogs and credit card solicitations, there was a letter from his parents. Melinda had called them as soon as she knew that Rusty was safely home. His mother created an enclosed Welcome Home greeting card on the computer. He phoned and thanked them right then and there. His dad was reasonably sure that they would be coming to visit before the end of September.

Rusty's CBP paychecks continued to be deposited, as scheduled, directly into his checking account. The headquarters in Washington, wanting to do the right thing, requested a complete billing statement from Hospital San Jose, to cover the care they provided to the American they named David Smith. That included the relatively expensive surgery to save Powell's shattered leg. The manager of the hospital's billing department, totally blown away by the U.S. Government's offer, mailed them a statement a few days later. It was for 600 thousand pesos, or about 50 thousand dollars. His treatment would likely have cost double that amount in a U.S. Hospital.

Before going to bed, Melinda convinced her husband that he needed to have the leg checked out. It would be several weeks before the cast was scheduled for removal, but it made sense to get an orthopedist to take over Rusty's care. She also reiterated her wish that he see a neurologist to look after the evolving insomnia condition.

CHAPTER 111

DAY 20

THE NEXT MORNING, after breakfast, Powell followed through on his wife's requests. Calling their family physician, Rusty explained his physical travails. Naturally, the internist wanted to examine him in his office first, before recommending that any specialists be consulted. Rusty made an appointment to see him at 2PM the following day.

His next call was to the CBP Sector Office in Tucson. He wanted to speak with the personnel officer, specifically to discuss his next assignment, which he was hoping would be somewhere in the Tucson-Nogales corridor. At that moment, however, there was a transfer taking place in the personnel position, with the newly assigned officer on the way from her previous assignment in El Paso, Texas. The individual Rusty talked with suggested that he call back sometime the following week.

Sally Henkel called Powell to wish him well. Martinez had briefed her on what had taken place at the Nogales Border Station. "Rusty, you should see a neurologist about the passing-out incident in Nogales. That's not the kind of thing to fool around with."

"I'm seeing our family doctor tomorrow. He wants to examine me before he recommends a specialist. The same goes for the leg."

"Okay; that makes me feel a little better. Please keep in touch. And you should know that our investigation into the kidnapping continues. We've been told that the men who abducted you were killed in the earthquake. We're almost certain that there's someone higher up in the cartel's chain of command we can go after. I'll let you know if we make any progress. In the meantime, get well. And say hi to Melinda. You guys both deserve some good luck from here on. Bye for now."

"Nice of you to call, Special Agent Henkel. You take care."

Rusty looked in the bedroom closet for something different to wear. Two Border Patrol uniforms hung neatly on the rack. Not much of a clothes horse, he owned a couple of suits, three sport coats, and lots of khakis and jeans. Nothing appealed to him at that moment. He went to his chest of drawers and pulled out a pair of shorts and a t-shirt. Nike running shoes completed the outfit.

Rusty and Melinda planned a shopping trip in the afternoon. The Tucson Mall was quite a distance from West Tucson, but it was the largest shopping complex in the city. There were a few good restaurants there as well, so they decided to head there for lunch. They chose the Brio Tuscan Grill, since Rusty was craving Italian food. After lunch, they looked for some clothes for his somewhat slimmer physique. Powell had lost about twenty pounds while suffering through his Mexican travails. Angela tried to help him gain some of it back, but she didn't have enough time.

Rusty was tiring from the walk around the mall. He was fairly comfortable walking short distances on the crutches, but there was too much ground to cover on this trip. They stopped at a Starbucks for some iced coffee; then headed home a little after 3PM. Melinda did the driving. She was extremely capable behind the wheel. Tucson traffic was beginning to thicken. They took their time, getting to the house about twenty-five minutes later.

Rusty continue to struggle with his memory. He could recall only a few things from the past. Melinda used photos and videos to help the process. Their wedding album, school photos, and videos taken at family events helped, but much of it failed to break through. It was like he was seeing most of it for the first time.   Powell looked quite a bit like his father, so Rusty could easily pick him out in the family shots. With his mother usually standing next to his dad, spotting her was a no-brainer as well.

An hour or so before starting dinner, Roland Escobar called to see how Rusty was getting along. "Just wanted to check on you", he said.

"All the folks here keep asking me how you're doing. I usually say that you just got home and are trying to settle back in. Then I tell them that you need some time to get healthy before making any decisions about going back to work."

Powell was somewhat surprised that Escobar would even mention a possible future with the Border Patrol. A field job was obviously out of the question, but there were many positions that didn't require the physical side of U.S. border protection. Rusty was smart enough to learn almost any job within the Homeland Security organization. And he was well-liked by those who could influence the direction his career might take.

"Sir, I appreciate the call. Feel free to tell anybody who asks that I'm doing really well. I don't think it'll take very long for me to want to get back to work. Hopefully there's a spot somewhere in CBP where I can play a role."

"As we've said, Rusty, let's get you feeling a little stronger before worrying about that. You've been through hell and back. Nobody expects you to punch a time clock just yet. In the meantime, is there anything that you or Melinda need? If something comes up, just let me know."

"Thanks for asking. We're okay. And we really appreciate the calls. You guys have been great to Melinda while I was away. It meant a lot to her. Say hi to everybody back at the border."

As they were ending the call, another one came in. A familiar voice from the recent past gave Rusty the chills. It was Dr. Ortega. "This is your leg surgeon checking on the former David Smith. How are you doing?"

Powell was blown away. "Dr. Ortega, how did you know how to find me?"

"It really was quite easy. Your generous government not only paid all of the hospital bills at San Jose, but somehow they managed to track me down and pay me for my services as well. The FBI apparently made all this happen. The hospital administrator mentioned the name Richard Martinez. Do you know this man?"

"Doctor, you sure as hell saved my left leg, but Special Agent Martinez saved my life."

Powell and Ortega talked for a while. The surgeon wanted to know how the leg was coming along. "One reason for my call was to provide you with the name of an excellent orthopedics man in Tucson. His name is Scott Belden. He practices at the Tucson Medical Center's Orthopedic Institute. I believe they just opened a new facility at TMC. We did our residencies together at U.T. Austin. I know you will like him a lot. If you give me your email address, I will send you his contact information."

"That sounds great, doctor. I really appreciate the call." Rusty gave him the email address, thanked him again, and said goodbye.

CHAPTER 112

MARTINEZ PLANNED A Phoenix Division farewell party for Henkel. Sally finalized the decision to accept the position of Assistant Special Agent In Charge in the Chicago Bureau office. September 15th would be her last day in Tucson. Personal recognition was antithetical to her operating style. But she had great affection for Richard and his team. So she agreed to let the party happen.

Richard chose the private room of a popular Phoenix club-style restaurant for the event. September 10th was the date. The Division's entire team of agents and support people would be joined by Sally's daughter and a handful of her closest Tucson friends.

When last in Washington for a Bureau meeting, FBI Director Fox told Martinez that he wanted him to accept a position at D.C. headquarters, supervising a new group of highly trained and experienced agents on the subject of cyber-crime, a rapidly increasing problem around the world. Reluctant to change assignments before the end of the year, Richard agreed to give it serious thought and let Fox know if he would accept the job. He wasn't ready to decide.

CHAPTER 113

THREE WEEKS LATER

RUSTY WAS ANXIOUS to get the cast removed. He had visited Dr. Belden a few days after seeing his own internist, who agreed with Dr. Ortega's recommendation. At that time, Belden advised Powell to wait a few more weeks before taking off the cast. It was time. Melinda called to make the appointment. Luckily, Belden had a cancellation the next day. Melinda took the 3:30 time slot.

Rusty had also visited a neurologist for a consultation on the memory loss problem. The decision was to wait another month, at which time a brain scan would be taken to assess it's overall condition. The neurologist was confident that Powell's memory would continue to improve.

Dr. Belden's office was located in a physicians office building adjacent to the Tucson Medical Center. Rusty and Melinda arrived there for the 3:30 appointment, and were told that Belden was called to emergency surgery and was scheduled to return by 5PM. They decided to head over to a nearby Starbucks to relax and enjoy a cappuccino.

They returned to the office a few minutes before five. Belden had already returned and was seeing a patient with an earlier appointment. At 5:15, a nurse called for Powell, who was ushered into a large treatment room. Melinda joined him. Belden joined them a few minutes later.

"Mr. and Mrs. Powell; good to see you again. So, Rusty, let's get it off and take a look."

Rusty removed his khakis and lied down on the treatment table. The cast had several autographs on it, mostly from friends and neighbors. But getting off would be a blessing. Belden's nurse returned with a medical saw that Belden deftly used to slice it down the side and remove it with zero difficulties.

The leg was slightly discolored, otherwise appearing to be in good shape. But looks are often deceiving. Belden worked his hands around the leg, feeling the calf area with careful attention to the section of the fibula where the major work was done. When finished with his digital examination, Belden made his comments.

"Rusty, overall, the bones seem to be healing nicely. I would, however, liked to take a few more pictures to make sure that all the hardware is continuing to settle in. We'll do an MRI this time. It'll give us the best picture. We can go from there. Okay?"

"If you think it's necessary, then it should be done. When can we do it?"

"How about right now? If you have the time, the sooner the better. The nurse will call to see if we can get you on one of the two MRI's next door while you're here."

Rusty nodded and Belden left the treatment room to write the order for the test. In a few minutes, the nurse returned with the good news. "Mr. and Mrs. Powell, you can head right over to the imaging department at TMC. The folks at the reception desk can direct you there. Dr. Belden will call you with the results. Good luck."

The Powells left the office building and walked over to the main TMC building, where the volunteer receptionist directed them to the imaging center on the 2nd floor.

There they checked in with another receptionist. She indicated that the wait would be less than fifteen minutes. A technician came for them in less than five. The MRI procedure took close to half an hour. Rusty found it painful to keep the leg straight and still for that amount of time. When it was over, he was helped off of the table and handed his crutches. "Hopefully you won't be needing these much longer", the technician said. "Good luck with the leg."

Walking back to their car, Melinda noted a somewhat somber expression on her husband's face. "What's wrong honey? You don't look very happy with getting rid of the cast."

"I'm cool, but why did Belden want more pictures? He took some the first time I saw him. He must have some concerns."

"Rusty, that doesn't sound like you! I'm not surprised he wants to make sure that everything is healing okay. You need to think positive about it. Let's wait and see what he says about the MRI before we draw any conclusions."

"No problem. Let's go home. Powell found it much easier to get into the car without the cast. The leg was stiff, but he didn't have any pain. They returned home shortly after seven-thirty. Rusty decided to take a shower and scrub the leg that was closed up for almost two months. Melinda cooked some pasta. After eating, and enjoying a couple of glasses of wine, they hit the sack.

Powell was restless in bed. Straightening the leg was somewhat painful. The stiffness seemed to be wearing off, but the aching had Rusty concerned. He got out of bed and went to the bathroom to take some Advil. When he returned, Melinda faked being asleep. She could tell that her husband was going to have a restless night. Normally, not being able to sleep he would get out of bed and move to another room to watch TV or read. This time, he just lied there, eventually dozing off.

Belden's office called around 10AM the next morning. Rusty answered the phone. "Mr. Powell, Dr. Belden would like to see you this afternoon. Can you make it by 2:30?"

This didn't sound very good at all. "I guess so. Can you tell me anything about the MRI results?"

"I believe that Dr. Belden would rather do that, sir. We'll see you at 2:30."

****

Powell decided to go it alone. Melinda argued, but Rusty won out. "I'll be fine. I can handle the break and gas pedals okay. Truth is, I'm tired of having to rely on people to get me anywhere. I'll be okay."

Losing the argument, Melinda watched her husband leave the house, get into the driver's seat, start the engine, and head down the driveway. She would be on pins and needles until he returned. Rusty typically didn't like talking on the phone, so she didn't expect a status report until he walked back in the front door.

Belden invited Powell into his office, purposely not using a treatment room to deliver the news. "Rusty, here's the bottom line. The hardware Dr. Ortega planted in the tibia is not performing as it should. That's the sum total of the bad news. The good news is that we can easily fix the problem. I believe you can have it done as an outpatient, going home a few hours after it's done, without an overnight stay. There's an eighty-percent chance that this will be the case. Once we get in there to do the repair, we'll know for sure. Your wife will need to be with you in any case. Incidentally, this is not an unusual situation. With major bone surgery like yours, we often have to go back in and tighten things up. But I'm confident that the repair should last you a very long time, most likely as long as you do." Belden could easily tell that Rusty was not taking the news very well. "You okay with this, Rusty? I want you to be confident that it'll turn out well. I won't make any promises, but there's a 50-50 chance that you might not need the cane beyond a few months after the procedure."

That perked Powell up a bit. "Okay, that sounds promising, but I won't count any chickens just yet. When do you want to get it done?"

"See the receptionist on your way out. Hopefully we can schedule it for one day next week."

Rusty stood, grabbed his cane, shook Belden's hand, and headed for home. All the way there, he rehearsed the lines he would need to bring his wife up to date. All in all, the news wasn't that bad. But he was certain that the idea of more surgery would not be welcome news.

Melinda was in the kitchen, when Powell walked in. She was chopping vegetables for a dinner salad. Rusty came up behind her and planted a kiss on her long, slender neck. "That's the way you used to do it", she said, turning around and looking up at his grinning face.

"Seems like I vaguely remember doing that before. Hey, let's have a glass of wine. It's about that time of day." Rusty walked over to the wine fridge and started to make a selection. "What's for dinner, Mel?"

"We're having salmon, which you will need to throw on the grill, and a salad."

Powell reached for a bottle of Sauvignon Blanc.

She stopped chopping as Rusty began to open the wine. "So, are you going to tell me why the doctor wanted to see you, or do I have to guess?"

"I'll tell you, if you promise not to over-react. It's not that bad."

Melinda simply smirked and stared at her husband. She now anticipated that the news wasn't good. "Okay, let's have it. I'll be fine. As long as you don't tell me that the leg has to come off."

"The hardware needs to be tightened. Dr. Ortega did a masterful job under the circumstances. He saved the leg. It was very swollen and disfigured when he cut me open. Fact of the matter is I was shot while we were on patrol. So it was shattered and sat that way for quite a while. Now that it's back down to its normal size, some of the metal is not as secure as it needs to be. So Dr. Belden will go in and tighten everything up. And that's it. He said I would be as good as new."

Melinda was visibly relieved. "When will this tightening happen?"

"Don't know yet. We should get a call from his office with a date; hopefully within the next couple of weeks."

"So you'll be back on crutches, I assume?"

"We didn't talk about that. But I would think so. I've mastered those babies though. Shouldn't be a problem."

"Go sit down and cool it. I'll tell you when it's time to light the grill."

Chapter 114

Two Weeks Later

Melinda drove her husband to the Tucson Medical Center's Orthopedic & Surgical Tower. She dropped Rusty off at the entrance and parked in the visitors lot. It was 6:30 in the morning. The leg repair was scheduled for 8AM.

The Tower had opened in the summer of 2013, and was state of the art. The operating suites were equipped with the latest in surgical technology. The Southwest's finest orthopedic surgeons were instrumental in providing the medical community's input for its creation. Powell was blown away by the place, and hadn't yet gotten past the lobby.

Melinda joined him as they were ushered into the registration area and immediately seated with an administrator that plugged Rusty into that day's patient database. The Powell couple then sat and waited until Rusty was called for surgical prep. About twenty minutes after seven, a nurse came in and called Powell's name. Melinda stood with him and they hugged before Rusty was escorted out of the waiting room and into a curtained-off section of the prep area.

"I love you very much", Melinda said. "See you a little later."

A different nurse started an IV. Powell was then introduced to the anesthesiologist who briefed him on the medications that would be administered to put him to sleep and keep him under during the surgery. She was a young, slender woman with a very soft disposition, putting Rusty immediately at ease. "Dr. Belden is the best", she said, as she injected a sedative into Powell's IV tube. "You're in exceptionally good hands. You probably won't see him until you're in recovery. Good luck, Mr. Powell."

Rusty was wheeled into the operating room at 8:10. The surgery lasted nearly three hours. At 11:08, he was taken to recovery, not yet completely awake. A nurses' aid went to get Melinda and bring her to her husband's side. The recovery room was buzzing with activity. It was a busy morning at the new Tower.

A few minutes after being wheeled in, Rusty was ostensibly conscious. He opened his eyes, but didn't think he was awake. Standing by the bed, in her nurse's uniform, smiling at him, was Angela Contreras. Powell thought he was still asleep. Seconds later, Melinda walked in. "How's he doing?" looking straight into the big blue eyes of the beautiful young nurse.

"The doctor will be here shortly", Angela said. She turned to face Rusty. "Can I get you anything, Mr. Powell?" Rusty continued to believe it was a drug-induced dream. He looked at his unsuspecting wife and then at Angela. He was unable to speak. His two different worlds had collided: all at once.

THE END

ACKNOWLEDGEMENTS

KERRY, AN OFFICIAL with Customs & Border Protection, was extremely helpful in providing a real-world perspective on the daily life of a United States Border Patrol Agent.

Her backgrounding on the nature of an agent's job, based on her own experience, was immensely helpful in enabling me to bring the story of these courageous people to life.

****

The Federal Bureau of Investigation's Public Affairs Office in Washington, including one of their senior agents with hands-on experience in the Tucson/Nogales area, provided valuable assistance with respect to background information on the Bureau and its domestic and international network of people fighting drug-related crime.

****

My wife Betty served as an in-house editor and critic, as she had on my three previous novels. She inspired me to keep plugging away at this work and was instrumental in bringing credibility and believable character interest to the story line. An avid reader, she lends a vitally important perspective to my creative writing endeavors.